The Firsts

Xabi Molia

THE FIRSTS:
A History of French Superheroes

Translated by Alexander Hertich

DALKEY ARCHIVE PRESS
Dallas / Dublin

Originally published in French as *Les Premiers: Une histoire des super-héros français* by Seuil

Copyright © 2017 by Xabi Molia

Translation © 2023 by Alexander Hertich

Paperback: 978-1-628974-62-1

Ebook: 978-1-628974-89-8

Library of Congress Cataloging-in-Publication Data: Available

Interior design by Anuj Mathur
Cover design by Kayla E.

Dalkey Archive Press
www.dalkeyarchive.com
Dallas/Dublin

Printed on permanent/durable acid-free paper.

to the young man

"Man is least himself when he talks in his own person. Give him a mask and he will tell you the truth."

—Oscar Wilde

PART ONE

I

His mind was a blank the first time he took flight.

At first, the way he would tell the story was that he was hurrying down the street, despite the muddy snow and the icy spots on the sidewalks. A young woman would be expecting him soon in front of the Gare du Nord train station. He smiled. He was anxious and happy.

Up near Rue Greneta, a crush of people had formed alongside a patch of ice, and he was forced to slow down. Glancing at his watch, he realized he was going to be late when the idea it'd be faster if he were flying came to mind. This was accompanied by a strong tingling in the soles of his feet, immediately replaced by a warm feeling on his cheeks. And then he felt like he should, why not, try to lift off from the ground. The next moment . . .

"Wait," people would interrupt sometimes, "where did this urge to try come from?"

Jean-Baptiste would shrug his shoulders. In any case, no one, not an angel, not some voice inside his head had suggested it. He'd felt the desire, no, the need to. That's all.

The next moment his right foot was standing some twenty centimeters in the air in front of him. Then his left foot followed. He was levitating. A wondrous feeling of euphoria made his heart race.

This was untrue. As he was to admit later to Thérèse Lambert, he had absolutely no clue how he got up there. He had, for a couple dozen seconds, lost consciousness. But, assuming people expected a clear and detailed accounting from him, and also fearing that people had their suspicions—of what lie, he didn't know—he concluded it would be more prudent to provide a lucid recollection of his train of thought and the feelings surrounding it before and then during the first manifestation of his capabilities.

To reporters, he recounted that fear had seized him when he found himself, soon after taking off, twenty or so meters farther down the street above the intersection of Boulevard de Sébastopol and Rue de Réumur. It was 4:17 P.M. on January 19, and light snowflakes were floating above the streets of Paris. A young woman in a pale raincoat, having followed him with her eyes, had just fainted. A bus had slammed on its brakes right in the middle of the intersection. Behind it, in a long line of backed-up cars, drivers were starting to get angry, completely unaware of the marvel taking place before them. But crowds were already gathering on the sidewalks. Telephones were pointed at him.

It wasn't terror that gripped him, Jean-Baptiste Fontane would add, but rather a kind of surprise, tinged with apprehension, as he saw himself floating, almost motionless, his feet slowly dangling in the air seven or eight meters above the crowd, the kind of surprise you feel when you realize you've surmounted some obstacle you thought impossible to overcome, or when you've made a witty remark without forethought: then, he would note, it's like the feat compelled you to do it again, to never again step down from the pedestal onto which you've just hoisted yourself.

"You mean you were already afraid of what would happen

to you?" he was reportedly asked several months later during his umpteenth interview.

"Yes, no question," he supposedly answered.

With his amenable personality, Jean-Baptiste Fontane had taken on the habit of fulfilling the role others had envisaged for him—that this mantle might be ill-deserved had not bothered him for a long while. He was a slim thirty-five-year-old man, neither handsome nor ugly, with a gentle look and an overly long nose. He worked behind the counter at the French National Library where he scanned the bar codes of volumes that had been borrowed and then returned, provided information to patrons, and, more rarely, got up to quash unduly boisterous conversations. Occasionally he regretted his inability to set himself apart with quick wit or charming jocularity. Clever remarks came to mind, but he never found the right moment to slip them into conversation.

The rare times he had done something outrageous so that people might take an interest in him, when he was younger, such as donning a wine-red fedora, or disclosing to a colleague that he had, one fine day, eaten a fish raw right from his aquarium, or even inviting a teaching assistant for a drink right out of the blue, he was only met with furrowed brows and misunderstandings.

From these embarrassing moments he concluded that his repertoire was wrong. He'd never be the type of person whose opinion was sought, whose absence was regretted. He thus resigned himself to play the role of a character that didn't shine, a secondary character. And he must have noticed, as the years progressed, that this role did not displease him. It even had its advantages. Since no one ever came to see him, he didn't need to clean his apartment. His clothes became outdated without his needing to worry, and he could pay no heed to conversations, which he now sprinkled with pat responses and vague smiles. Perhaps some kind of laziness or true lack of character justified this attitude. Instead, I believe that it evinced some quiet fatalism, the kind of abnegation through which one's life becomes simpler.

Moreover, in the hours and days that followed his first flight, he did nothing to refute the portrait being disseminated in the press and on social media. His story seemed both amazing and simple: Joe Average had transformed into a superhero. He was not offended to read or hear the accounts of coworkers, neighbors, and friends who rattled off the typical (but hurtful): "He's a very normal guy." "He's really very ordinary." "I never would've thought him capable of that." He would just smile politely every time a reporter would ask him if his life before 1/19 hadn't been a bit dull. Except for an award in a scale-model building contest, which had earned him a mention in the local paper (the young man had built a 1/87 model of the Bayeux Cathedral and was now planning, according to the article, on recreating the entire neighborhood that surrounded it), his mother's death in a car accident when Jean-Baptiste was twelve was the only notable incident in an otherwise mundane existence, which was so humdrum it bordered on exaggeration: childhood in a subprefecture where his father worked as an accountant, average grades, typical interests (evenings in front of the television, bike rides, several unremarkable years on a soccer team), no enduring impression burned into the memories of the teachers or classmates he'd been close to, no rebellion, no tragic love story, no through line. Several magazines tried to ascribe his self-effacing behavior to suspicious anti-social tendencies, a mystery begging illumination, but the most commonly held belief, one which still prevails today, is that an insignificant librarian, a nobody, had one day suddenly appeared over the skies of Paris.

Above the traffic jam, as crowds thickened on corners, as several passersby went to help the young woman who had fainted, and as the complete standstill of traffic unleashed the honking of cars, several ideas went through his mind. He confirmed that he had first thought of the young woman who might be waiting for him in front of the Gare du Nord where they had agreed to meet after several weeks of timorous messages on an online dating site. He thought of calling to let her know he would be late, and his hand went to the pocket of his coat. But, overcome by a sense of propriety, he halted this movement, perceiving in the throng beneath his feet that all eyes were glued on him. Suddenly, as he began to fathom the many meters between himself and the ground, an unsteadiness came over him. It dawned on him that he was going to crash if this miracle came to an end. So, with this in mind, he started to flap his arms, steadily and fully, and was relieved to notice that his body gained several meters in altitude. His body obeyed him.

A dozen or so cell phones filmed this first aerial movement, which inspired the sculptor commissioned to immortalize Jean-Baptiste Fontane in front of the city hall in Bayeux, the city in Normandy where he was born. The bronze statue, which stands proudly front and center on the Place de la Liberté is faithful in part to the recorded images. The artist scrupulously reproduced the oversized cut of his coat, the tight knot of his scarf, and the unflattering profile of Jean-Baptiste Fontane, whose nose, like a windbreak, points up to the heavens. It's unquestionably the librarian's spindly profile, but, with arms forward and fingers spread, transformed through colossal dimensions and a triumphant pose. Below the knee, his legs disappear into the bronze block, virtually unhewn, as if this national hero were emerging from the ground through superhuman effort. Carved with a knife or written in Sharpie, innumerable inscriptions vowing eternal love cover the plinth. Oddly, Jean-Baptiste Fontane's taut neck and clenched jaw, accentuated by his tightly pursed lips, bestow a look of suffering to his face, which no image from that day, however, portrays.

Continuing to gain elevation, Jean-Baptiste presently noticed the snow-covered mosaic of the roofs of Paris, and through the leaden skies of winter, the grey clump of office towers of Tolbiac and La Défense on the horizon. The cry of a police siren grew nearer and nearer. Later, half-jokingly, he would admit to worrying that he'd broken some municipal ordinance—surely flying over Paris was illegal. According to Thérèse Lambert, it was in fact the siren that had pulled him from his trance and made him realize he was floating in the sky. He remembered nothing before this moment.

Now he was approximately forty meters above the ground. His heart was pounding out of his chest. He was trembling.

In the crowd someone began to clap. Not really knowing what to do, Jean-Baptiste attempted a small wave with his hand. Scattered here and there, others joined in.

The siren's wail ceased as the police car stopped. The doors closed with a muffled thump. For several instants, a hush fell over everything. Even the agitation of the car horns had diminished, and the pedestrians, silent, some solemn and already pensive, seemed to be waiting for the next act. Jean-Baptiste feared he would be asked to give a speech. He cleared his throat, but felt too overwrought to speak.

At that moment, he made out the ring of a telephone, which cut through this serene environment in which the sounds of the city seemed to collide, canceling each other out. The man who'd just answered asked the person on the line to repeat what he'd said. Other phones rang. To find out the spreading news, a few turned their eyes away from Jean-Baptiste Fontane. Murmurs from the crowd swelled. People cried out. For in Marseille, at that exact same moment, Gregory Marville had also just taken off.

II

WHEN JEAN-BAPTISTE set his feet back on the ground he stated his name, address, and birthdate to the officers. They didn't know if they should keep a respectful distance or protect him from the curious onlookers who were circling around asking him for photos and plying him with questions. Finally, his inoffensive appearance persuaded the officers to escort him to their car, taking him to a nearby police station.

Less than an hour later, a co-worker from the National Library recognized him from the images of his first flight, which blew up on social media around the world. At about the same time his name was first cited on radio.

For his part in Marseille, Gregory, feeling a similar urge, had taken off from Boulevard Garibaldi, flown over several city blocks, and landed in Stalingrad Square, which was empty due to the strong rains that were sweeping through the city. As luck would have it, a young journalist interning at *La Provence* was coming out of a building where she was renting a studio apartment for the month. When she saw a flying man descend and gently land in the Square, Cecile Strohe thought of extraterrestrials.

"I was scared for my life," she would later recount. "When you witness something like that, with no preparation, it's shocking, it's really intense . . . It attacks you. There's no other way of saying it. Like an entire part of you collapses." Gathering her courage, she walked up to the man to ask some questions. He proved to be completely willing to answer. Strohe recorded Gregory's impressions on her cell phone. He came across as cordial, even nice. Encouraged, she asked him to repeat what he had just said, but this time she would make a video.

In the shaky frame of the telephone's camera, Gregory Marville's square face, the determined look of his nearly transparent eyes, the calm manner in which he states he'll have to think about what just happened to him and that he's going to reach out to the authorities, contrast starkly with Jean-Baptiste Fontane's distraught look in the images people saw of him the same day.

This filmed interview is much better known today than the first recording of Marville's voice, which Strohe had made several minutes earlier. He says the same things, but the halting delivery allows his anxiety to filter through. For example, when the journalist asks him what he plans to do and he states, "I need to think about all that," there's a short, embarrassed laugh immediately afterward, as if the answer now seems ridiculous to him, as if he were beginning to perceive the distance between the words he's saying and the transformation he's undergoing. His delivery slows down. His mind seems troubled. He's not yet the Captain.

On February 5, a spokesperson for the French government announced there were seven. That evening an individual had reported to the police station in Aubervilliers, informing them of his abilities. The team of scientists appointed by the authorities authenticated him the following morning.

His temporoparietal area was also overactive. Like the others he was very strong, fast, and could fly. Moreover, he had the ability to make himself invisible. People called him Number Seven, and this nickname stuck. Officially, at least, there were no other reported cases.

The extreme reactions that accompanied the sudden appearance of Jean-Baptiste and Gregory had incited the five others to exercise great discretion. Saïd affirmed, "So there we are watchin' TV. We see the throngs in the streets of Paris, Berlin, Rio, Seoul, the completely hysterical special correspondents, and in the studio the self-proclaimed experts who don't know a thing, a bishop talking about archangels, another talking about Lucifer who fell from Heaven . . . People in the streets are talking about it more and more, and right away stuff gets mixed up. It feels like people are going nuts, what with Fontane's and Marville's faces everywhere, people even having 'em tattooed on their arms, and the story of what are supposed to be Jean-Baptiste's shoes selling on eBay for some stupid crazy amount. So, let me tell you, even if you're totally stoked about your powers, the last thing you want to do is stand on your balcony and wave at the crowd."

As a precaution, the authenticated cases were whisked away to a military base whose location did not remain secret very long. It was an ancient fort at the tip of a peninsula in Normandy. The curious flocked there by the thousands, and a primitive camp was set up. People started giving speeches, announcing the advent of other miracles, and the birth of a new human race. Patrols had to be doubled, and even a few canisters of tear gas had to be shot. Nerves were on edge. They were on edge everywhere. Even the stock markets were in a panic.

Except for the first two, no one knew the names and faces of these supermen. Their intentions were not clear. On the other hand, the law forbade their internment. They weren't guilty of anything, they weren't suspects in some plot. What could the authorities do? People wanted to know the next part of the story, and, with fake news stories proliferating, the wait was exasperating. In Germany, a magician almost got himself lynched after he used tricks to make his neighbors think he was Number Eight.

Finally, the government issued a press release. The seven were in good health. They were cooperating. In addition to a range of superpowers they all shared—the ability to fly, physical strength, endurance and dexterity increased tenfold—each one possessed a unique ability. A woman had developed an infallible memory, another speed that defied imagination. Gregory Marville had phenomenal auditory acuity. Jean-Baptiste Fontane discovered he was able to metamorphose. Number Seven could make himself invisible. There was also talk of a man who could read others' thoughts and another who could see the future.

But there were too many gaps in the published statements, the saga's plot too thin. Furthermore, the soothing tone of government officials gave off the irritating whiff of state secrets. The gatherings became protests. People demanded to see the seven.

On February 15th, during a visit with their families, they appeared as part of a television news story, but filmed from a distance and wearing masks, except for Jean-Baptiste and Gregory, whose faces were already known to the public. To avoid potential criticism, the Prime Minister reminded people of the shock that the discovery of their abilities had on these men and women. Obviously, what happened to them was wonderful in many respects, but their entire existences had been turned upside down in the blink of an eye. By using masks and voice modulators, some of them were just trying to protect their privacy. This anonymity, he added, would also be a tactical advantage.

It could now be unveiled: they were going to use their talents for the benefit of all. It was their decision. Jean-Baptiste confirmed this in a prerecorded message at the end of the report, his now steady voice erasing the uncertainty that characterized him when the public discovered him in the images of 1/19. Contracts with the State would soon be signed, a new era inaugurated. In the streets, jubilation, liturgies, and an infinite amount of wide-eyed speculation about these prodigies drowned out the murmurs of those who, inclined to imagine the worst, prophesied future tragedies.

Although initially they went nearly unnoticed, starting January 21st one could find not only in France, but also abroad, gatherings of *skeptics*, as the public came to call all those who joined this spontaneous movement of defiance, even hostility. Many of them said they disapproved of the jingoistic fervor that had bubbled up in the country as the strictly Gallic nature of the event became clear.

Opponents suggested the skeptics' motives were based on jealousy, the unbearable feeling that there existed a chosen caste of which they would never be a part. With some, a feeling of failure set in. During the following months, several suicide victims left behind notes mentioning the French superheroes' discouraging perfection. Although he was exhilarated at first by the events, one of my coworkers fell into a depression that led to his being committed by his wife. I believe it's possible that post-heroic stress also fed the feelings of rejection that were observed.

The seven were hardly worried about this for the time

being. At the base where they were quartered, they were discovering their powers, which were increasing.

The first few weeks Gregory could hear any sound within approximately a 100-meter radius. Over time, this capacity increased to the point that he could hear eight times farther. It was established that his audible frequency spectrum spread from 5 to 50,000 megahertz. As for his ability to amplify a target sound while tuning out interfering noise, this developed to the point that he could soon distinguish the stridulation of worker ants exploring the patio outside his house in Marseille and the heartbeat of a visiting soccer player at a match in Parc des Princes stadium.

While this power of hypersensitive hearing seemed insignificant in comparison to the Prophet's divination skills or Mickaël's capacity to read minds, the tests established that, when comparing their common abilities, Gregory was first in nearly all. He could jump the highest. He had the greatest endurance. His punches could kill. The authorities had no interest in revealing such capabilities, but there were leaks. During this time, in Marseille and everywhere he'd been, those who knew him told reporters he was a warmhearted, hard-working, upstanding guy.

An advisor must have suggested that he, rather than someone else, appear on the nightly news. He accepted.

Although not his decision, Gregory didn't fear living his celebrity unmasked. He didn't like secrets. And it should also be mentioned that his uncovered face proffered him an advantage. He possessed the easy, masculine good looks of a model featured in a cologne or car ad. The available photos, which spanned from his childhood to age 35, showed an honest smile and healthy, bronzed skin that made him appear to have advanced through the years like some being from Olympus, untouched by weariness or melancholy. To this vibrancy, subtle crow's feet around his translucent eyes and wisps of gray adorning his temples added the charm of an English gentleman.

On February 25 on the set of the nightly news, he very calmly responded to innocuous questions. What did it feel like the first time he flew? Were his friends and family proud of him? What seemed the most extraordinary to him, flying or hearing everything? Finally, he assured everyone that he was proud to serve France, his beaming face belying the careful tone he'd just used. However, even though the line had been prepared, I think he was being sincere.

When, after a first series of medical tests and psychological interviews, he met with ministry advisors and officers—now he needed to think about what he planned to do with these powers, they'd basically told him—he proved completely willing to exceed their hopes and expectations.

His mother had hastily married an affable and respected doctor, but she soon discovered that he lacked ambition despite his prestigious ancestry, which in her romantic young woman's mind should have compelled him to have a strong sense of purpose. She raised her children to love their family name and scorn the husband and father who sullied, with his tiny village office, a glorious family history established over two centuries ago when Navy lieutenant Guillaume Bruny de Marville pulled the family lineage from anonymity, winning renown during sea skirmishes against the English in Hudson Bay and later accompanying Lapérouse on his famous expedition which was lost in the Santa Cruz Islands.

His descendants, among which were two generals, an explorer, and a resistance fighter who died at Dora, successfully showcased the panache mixed with quiet reserve which marked, according to Gregory's mother, the Marville greatness.

She claimed that Gregory started speaking at one and reading on his own at two. Starting in preschool, on every weekend and during school vacations, she gave him a series of special cognitive exercises, which she pulled from English textbooks for gifted children.

While she was secretly disappointed to recognize that he was nothing more than a good student among others in middle school, industrious but no genius, she turned her bitterness on the education system. Corrupted by state socialism, it leveled everything to the lowest common denominator. And the teachers, she told her children, will always grade doctors' sons more severely than workers'.

This continued. Neither high school nor law studies showed Gregory to be the future great man his mother expected. So she suspected him of laziness and lack of goodwill. He was betraying his destiny. He was deliberately thwarting her. He was ruining his life.

According to various accounts, Gregory wasn't worried about this fall from grace. While growing up he came to see his mother as childish, revengeful, and puffed up with pride. Both he and his brother had sworn to each other not to be like her.

Gregory advanced down his chosen path. Having entered the magistracy, he took a position as assistant prosecutor for the court of Douai, married, had a child, and then joined the organized crime unit in Marseille, a difficult but coveted assignment. Even if this would never fulfill the imperial dreams of the woman he now saw only on Assumption and Christmas, Gregory stated that he was happy.

And yet, when a heart attack took his mother, remorse overcame him and he cried profusely. Back in Marseille after the funeral, he eyed a vice-prosecutor position, which he had a good chance of getting during the next inter-transfer period. But that wouldn't be enough. In his mind, his mother's face remained displeased, a look he knew too well. Did he need to consider a lucrative career change, something like a corporate lawyer? Should he take the exams necessary to advance onto more prestigious levels of the government? Venture off into some completely new field, even though he didn't know where to look? According to his wife, he lacked the drive, and fear gave him terrible stomachaches. He was looking for what would ultimately make him a Marville.

III

"Something That's Just for Us"

X. M.: How did you feel the first few days?
VIRGINIE MATHIEU-BRUN: I believe there was some apprehension because you realize pretty quick what's gonna happen to you, the media exposure, the responsibility, but big picture I was pretty happy.

Why happy?
The day before, there you were with your extra kilos, tired of being who you are—nothing more, nothing better. Suddenly you discover you can fly, you can run incredibly fast, and your body's as light as when you were ten. And you're stronger, too, you got more endurance, more *everything*. It was just nuts. I remember there was an old basketball hoop behind the building we were staying in and I was having fun taking three pointers. Except now it went in just about every time. I'd played some ball in middle school. I knew the moves and how hard it is. But now I'd look, shoot, and swish—basket, basket, basket. How do you think someone would feel? For a couple weeks I felt like I was tripping, like I'd smoked too much. Plus, we were all the same age, we were in the same boat. We shared the same story.

But at the beginning there wasn't a story yet. . .
Sure there was. Well, we felt that we were, how would I say it, that all of us were uprooted together and sent far away, far, far away together. And that we all had a common story ahead of us. It's like after a bus or a train accident, you know, between the survivors. We were bound from the very beginning by something that's just for us, that we could only share between ourselves. Plus, on a more concrete level, at the center where they'd taken us, when there weren't medical tests or interviews, we had a fair amount of time with nothing to do. We talked for hours. Only Thérèse stayed in her corner, sulking because . . .
It was complicated for Thérèse from the jump. She'd already published two novels and was working on a third, I think, but obviously with 1/19 that wasn't really possible anymore. But Thérèse is super organized, the type of girl who has trouble with speed bumps or a change of plans. Plus I think, on a deeper level, her powers terrified her. To suddenly be able to remember everything—the history of your entire life coming up and smacking you in the face, that's gotta be a little uncomfortable.

What were the first days on the military base like?
Okay, now Saint-Vaast wasn't really a military base. It used to be a summer camp that got money from the Ministry of Defense. I never really understood how we ended up there. It seems—I read it afterward in several magazines—there were these people there who worked on what in the American military they call "unlikely threats"—flying saucers, ghosts, that kind of stuff. To tell you the truth, if they were there, I never ran into them.

So we're housed in these rather rudimentary buildings, each of us in our own room with two twin beds. There's not even a lock on the door. Like I told you, it used to be a summer camp. At first they're mainly trying to understand. "They" were primarily guys from the Defense Ministry, and I think there were also some people from State. They went over our life story. There were lots of questions about any meds we might have taken, diets, trips abroad, potential childhood traumas. From what I recall these interviews were rather laborious, but always courteous. No kind of intimidation or threats, as some people said here and there.

Number Seven says that.
Just so you know, Saïd didn't get there until after everyone else, so he's not the best person to explain how it was. What's more, Saïd's truths, I'd be careful if I were you. No, everyone wanted to cooperate. It might have been harder psychologically for the people doing the interviewing than it was for us. 'Cause like I said, with our new abilities, we were totally stoked. At the same time for them the world was also changing, but they didn't have any control over what was happening to them. And they must have been feeling pressure from every direction to know what had happened, figure out what the plan was, make sure things didn't get out of control . . . Remember, back then nobody knew a thing. People were even wondering if it was some kind of epidemic . . . I totally remember a report from London where they'd isolated so-called "persons of interest." Quite a few people would've liked us to be contagious. [*She smiles.*]

Did you watch TV?
Not too much. They installed them in our rooms around the third or fourth day. Mickaël had asked. But I didn't turn it on much, and I think it was the same for the others, too. It wasn't

like what we were experiencing. It was like some Hollywood movie.

What did the large rallies inspire in you?
Same thing. It was all far away and totally unconnected to what we were experiencing. For me, my parents were left wing, you might even say far left wing. Politics didn't really interest me much, but I still had a conscience , or values, I don't know what to call it. Patriotism, for example, was always something that bothered me. Even at a soccer game, *La Marseillaise* with your hand on your heart, flags waving in the stands, I found that sketchy. After the Vichy regime, the far right's election successes, you know what I mean? . . . So then these rallies—at Trocadéro, or the "French is Beautiful" movement—I wasn't totally comfortable with all that. Later when we were received at the Senate and you saw all the old farts lining up for a photo with us, it kind of made you wanna puke. On the other hand, the skeptics made me angry. Actually, one time on TV, I saw their "Take Off Your Mask" signs and that really bugged me. I would have liked there to be some kindness. But, then again, kindness isn't really a French thing.

What bugged you?
That they accused us of being fakes, that kind of stuff. We'd never asked anything from anyone. Plus for us it was so obviously true it seemed ridiculous, these people talking about microjets hidden in our clothes, demanding that we strip naked and give them a demo . . .

But the skeptics, rather than being non-believers, were really people who were worried about your power and what the State would do with it.

Yeah, you're right, in part. And I can get that, too. If I was in their place, I wouldn't have been demonstrating in the streets, that wasn't my thing, but I would've been concerned, too. And in fact, the second round of interviews were about that, about our intentions, what we wanted to do. It was obvious that some of the people we were talking with were freaked out. They were definitely afraid we'd go out of control, and they didn't know the extent of our capabilities. We didn't either . . . We were learning a bit more every day back then. The most annoying was that we couldn't explore everything 'cause of the place they'd chosen to isolate us. All around the peninsula there were boats loaded with reporters from dawn to dusk and even at night with infrared cameras. You couldn't fly around, for one thing. For me, it was an itch I couldn't scratch. There was only one thing I wanted to do, experience that again and the feeling it gave me. Plus, with my speed, I really felt I had my own thing, and I wanted to see what my limits were, how far I could run, for example. But at Saint-Vaast, obviously, the grounds were too small.

Did you have instructors?
Only after we'd signed contracts with the Government, around February 15th. Then we started a conditioning and hand-to-hand combat training program. One of our instructors kept saying that we had potential but no technique at all. And that we really had to work. After a couple days, we still didn't have any technique, but with our abilities, we could whoop him anyway. [*She laughs.*]

How did you deal with the fact that you were isolated from your loved ones?
I'm sure each of us would give you a different answer. With

me, you know what my situation was. By the way, I would have preferred you hadn't gone and talked to my ex-husband. That really . . . when I found out I was tempted to cancel our interview.

I'm not planning on using what he told me in the book directly. I just wanted to meet as many people as possible to get different points of view.

So, he must have told you I was hysterical and frigid. Did that give you a different point of view? [*She pauses about ten seconds, something she will repeat several times during our interview. During these moments her face becomes expressionless, like she's sleeping with her eyes open. The rest of the time with the way she clenches or rather wrings her hands, which you can tell are itching to flutter about, the efforts she makes to not speak too quickly and the self-control her appearance presents—from sitting upright in her chair to her hair pulled back tightly or her white blouse buttoned all the way to the collar—everything indicates this is an ordeal for her.*] Your private life, yeah, that was hard for everyone. That's one of the first things they talked to us about at Saint-Vaast. They'd left us our phones, and the second day Marc-Antoine Rochelle, who was the Director of Communications at the very beginning, had us meet in the dining hall to brief us on how our status had changed, on the fact that everything we would say or write would be interpreted, deformed, blown out of proportion. Some friends must have talked to the media, I suppose. Again, they didn't threaten us with anything. They just told us that we needed to be careful—for our own interest. That we needed to learn to manage our image. Right away there were specific training modules on that, too. And later people criticized us a fair amount for this. They made fun of us, saying that we were too media savvy . . .

But seriously, what did you want us to do? Would it have been *purer* if we acted like nothing had happened and went out in front of reporters with zero prep? Anyway, no, it wasn't easy to talk with spouses or children. We'd talk to them every day on the phone, but you had to watch yourself, even with them. And then they organized a visit day for us in mid-February.

February 15th.
Right. And our families came to see us. Only Julien came for me. I hadn't wanted my parents or my daughter to come, because it was obvious, even if I hadn't specifically formulated it myself, that the two of us needed to take care of—it was over between us. And he must've immediately understood that when he saw me. There was the official version later, the one he told to the press and put in his book and that he surely trotted out again for you when you interviewed him: that my powers made me lose my mind, that I wasn't interested in my daughter anymore. On top of that, just after Saint-Vaast, add in my crappy relationship with a soccer player and the story of my nose [*Virginie decided to have plastic surgery on her nose in April, approximately three months after the events of 1/19*], and case closed—I was the team slut. You always gotta have one, right? Now if you want my side, it's totally different. With Julien, we met really young, in high school. At thirty-five we were already an old couple with an old couple's life. He talked about our sex life, about how I never found pleasure . . . but do you know many women who still find pleasure after seventeen years with the same man? We had problems conceiving. That lasted close to three years, and when our daughter was finally born, instead of being relieved, being overjoyed, we were both ill-at-ease. The three of us didn't click. And I thought that distinctly the first time I saw us—Julien, Emma, and me—in

the same photo. It was like we were photoshopped together. We were playing mommy and daddy, but it wasn't us. It wasn't something we knew how to do together.

Do you think you would have stayed with him if you hadn't acquired your powers?
I really have no idea, to tell you the truth. Often I tell myself, yes, I would've stayed, that I was too attached to the image of us as a couple, to the promises we'd made each other at seventeen. I didn't feel capable of betraying that. Plus, as soon as a child's involved, right away it's so complicated to leave. It requires so much energy. To find the strength it really has to be unbearable day in day out. I was just, I dunno, tired. Burned out. But sometimes I tell myself I would've left anyway. That it was destined from the beginning. Well, at least since we got married. 'Cause the day we got married, I clearly remember fighting to not admit to myself that things weren't up to expectations— it wasn't what I had expected it to be, I mean. Everything was blah—the half-cold food, the dressed-up guests. Now his mother, you would've said she was the queen of the party. She was laughing, flitting from table to table, totally at ease, whereas normally she was this sort of gloomy woman who never made a peep. I felt like I was going to be like her, and that thrilled her. After the wedding I started putting on some weight, and since she was already a big woman, you know, I really believed my fears were coming true. [*She laughs.*]

You decided to wear a mask. How did that happen?
It happened immediately, well, just after the incident in the bathroom. [*According to her account, Virginie's abilities appeared at home on January 23rd as she was getting ready in the bathroom while listening to the news on the radio. Just after she'd finished*

applying her makeup, she put away the cosmetics she'd used without thinking, just like every morning and noticed she'd done so with exceptional celerity. Doubting herself, she did the same thing two more times. Each time her speed increased. In the living room of their apartment, which her husband had just left, she tried to "do the superhero thing," in other words, levitate. She did.] Gregory and Jean-Baptiste had already shown themselves, and you could see the crazy reactions that caused. I told myself I had to avoid that at all costs if I wanted my daughter to have a normal life with a normal mother.

At that moment were you imagining living a double life?
In any case, I thought we'd find a way to keep up appearances. In the motorcade that took me to Saint-Vaast, I remember I was still looking at websites on my phone for information about part-time jobs, the legal framework, requesting a leave of absence . . . I imagined I'd keep my job at Crédit Lyonnais bank part-time. Rochelle and others made me understand that wouldn't be possible, but they were also for wearing a mask in public for operational reasons—so the targets of our missions couldn't recognize us. Next, they drew up some options, I only knew I wanted something blue 'cause that's my favorite color. One day they showed up with a fusane one, and I wore it.

Now the name, on the other hand, I could never make up my mind. They really pushed me to call myself "Vivacity." I don't know why they wanted something English sounding. Maybe they were already thinking about international markets . . . But I wasn't a fan. They also suggested "Blue," and I agreed 'cause there wasn't anything better, and then eventually Julien told the press who I was, photos came out, and from then on people called me by my first name. It's probably better that way.

Even after your identity was made public, you still kept the mask on.

Yes. And many times I've tried to explain why, but I have to believe that everyone thought it seemed stupid because no one paid any attention to what I said. Officially, I was on family leave and in divorce proceedings. No one was surprised not to see me around as much, even my closest friends. So that could've gone on—I don't know how long, but it could have continued, that's for sure. When Julien decided to throw me to the lions in the media, posting photos of me online, Rochelle told me we had to deny it and say that Virginie Mathieu-Brun wasn't one of the seven, but I refused. 'Cause it would end up being confirmed. The reporters would easily find the information, and then they'd criticize me for lying.

I left my house without my mask on to see what would happen. It was a Friday at the end of May, one of the first days of really nice weather after one of the nastiest springs we'd ever had in France. There were lots of people outside at cafés. A lot of them recognized me. The baker asked if he could get a photo with me. Two or three people came up and said what we were doing was awesome. Anyway, I can't say it turned out bad. But I missed my mask all the same. I'd changed a lot since the end of January. I realized the person I was before was gone and I felt ready to accept my celebrity and all the day-to-day complications it would create for my daughter and me. I was ready, so long as I wore the mask.

So that people couldn't see all of you? To preserve your privacy?
Because the woman I'd become wore a mask. That's all.

IV

On March 29th, a mere two months after their powers were revealed, it was announced that three of them had infiltrated a middle school in Créteil where some jihadists had dug in and were threatening to kill twenty-five hostages. Saïd, invisible, had slipped behind the one guarding the classroom and neutralized him. One of his accomplices wanted to detonate his bomb in the middle of the teenagers but Virginie, quicker on the draw, blocked his movement and broke his arm. The final terrorist had retreated to the kitchen, where Jean-Baptiste, appearing in the guise of his brother who had died in Syria, walked up to him, embraced him, and overpowered him. During the entire operation not one shot was fired.

Initially, extreme precaution was used in determining the situations where the superheroes would be deployed. To avoid controversy, the reasons had to be pure: they would thwart the plans of terrorist groups, they would hunt down serial killers and human traffickers, they would rescue the innocent from the middle of disasters. Every one of their operations would be glorious, miraculous. They wouldn't be sullied.

The temporary mental counselling facilities that had welcomed the mystics, the terrified, the shocked, all those for whom the world had become too unrecognizable after 1/19, slowly emptied. People got used to it.

The superheroes established their headquarters in a building near the Place de la République. Here they trained, received orders, and wrote reports. For its part, the press tried, albeit unsuccessfully, to identify those superheroes leading double lives. There were still four: Miss Memory, The Prophet, Lynxman, and Number Seven. I remember that at the time it was fun to gaze at your neighbor or the bus driver and wonder if maybe they possessed superpowers.

Occasionally the seven would appear on television. They spoke very little and always with great care. Teams started to form around them. They needed communication advisors; publicists; assistants for scheduling, responding to requests, maintaining their Facebook pages and Twitter accounts; lawyers for partnership deals; as well as bodyguards who would keep fans and nutjobs at a safe distance. Resumés in hand, job candidates, frequently young, would wait in front of headquarters.

On the night of April 19th when Gregory emerged from a dilapidated house in Rambouillet and appeared in front of the cameras, his popularity reached its peak. In his arms he held little Leina who had been held captive by a man the press had dubbed "The Ogre," an elusive predator who had been suspected of several child abductions in the nearby forest.

At first people wanted to call Gregory Mr. Marvelous, but then "The Captain" caught on, even though nobody knew exactly why. The heartfelt affection that surrounded him was most certainly a direct result of his exploits—or, according to those who remember his daughter's birth that July, the deftness of his messaging, which was orchestrated like a prince's. However, in order to understand his popularity, I contend that we must also remember France's situation at the time of 1/19. After a century of military defeats, renunciations, and half-admitted divisions and collective mistakes, the French, so frequently ridiculed for the confidence they held in their own greatness, had since had considerable difficulty in persuading themselves of this selfsame greatness. A few major sports victories and the lofty words of its leaders had managed to disguise the state of things at the turn of the millennium, but the economic crisis at the end of the 2000s and the terrorist attacks on the country had brought the situation under a harsh light. Now the cracks were starting to show. Economic conditions were poor. The influence of the former empire was limited to a few impoverished protectorates. It must be stated that besides the jihadists, no one gave a damn about France. This assessment elicited horrified reactions, which, as they trailed off, left nothing behind but self-loathing, doleful weariness, and exhaustion. Just as experts and intellectuals were now hammering home the idea that it was all over, that all was lost— with the same conviction they had used before to exaggerate the aura of their country— the superheroes burst forth from the humiliated masses. Endowed with a pedigree, a handsome face, and an actor's voice, Gregory Marville presented, more so than the others, a staggering refutation to these declarations. France would not founder. France would maintain its place in the world. The country's households, now confident in the future, spent money. The tourism sector announced a record year, especially in the cities where the seven had grown up. It made no sense, but stock in Crédit Lyonnais, the bank where Virginie had worked, continued to rise, as did in fact most of the French stock market. And when The Captain was greeted with thundering applause when visiting a hospital or being received at a city hall, it seems to me that it was their own eternal preeminence, it was they themselves, that the French, were celebrating, through him.

It was always more complicated for Jean-Baptiste Fontane. Regardless of how much the papers reported on the seven's exploits, the public couldn't seriously associate him with the others.

The weightlifting sessions had remade his body in quite a spectacular way, but the thin, bony face and worried eyes of a librarian remained, juxtaposed with his now sculpted physique. Obvious capillary grafts added an unnatural aspect to this incomplete transformation, incurring ridicule. Internet parody videos proliferated. They made fun of his body-builder physique and PR mistakes—for a month he too had decided to wear a costume and mask, then changed his mind when faced with the taunts and jeers. Not only did his chosen appearance, a reptilian get-up that looked like it was right out of some old Martian movie, not flatter him, but the decision itself didn't make any sense. Since his identity had been known from the first day, why did he now want to conceal it? His advisors had thought that such an outfit would help him better assume his duties. *Clothes make the man*, as they used to say.

As for his power to shapeshift, the most common reaction was repulsion. He felt it, too, according to those closest to him. Virginie was enraptured by her speed, as was Number Seven with his invisibility. Jean-Baptiste never showed the slightest jubilation at the idea of being able to increase or decrease his height by 20 centimeters or so, become basically as fat or thin as he wanted, change the length, texture and color of his hair, the pigmentation of his skin, his fingerprints, the shape of his eyes, the quantity of his wrinkles, and even the sound of his voice. He was, it seems, a good actor and possessed a remarkable

sangfroid when the time came to infiltrate a house under surveillance, a troubled neighborhood, or an enemy embassy. But
he didn't like it, and neither did the public. If he could take
on the appearance of nearly anyone, then logically a veil of
uncertainty shrouded everyone's social circle. Over the course
of several months, bewildered plaintiffs came to police stations
accusing Jean-Baptiste Fontane of identity theft. One claimed
his work colleague had developed inexplicable mood swings.
Another noticed that his father was gambling huge sums of
money with his credit card. A third noted that his wife no
longer smelled the same. All had come to believe that the
superhero had replaced them. What if we put an ankle monitor on him? With geolocation we'd know what was going on.
The government opposed this, but promised to impose strict
guidelines on the use of powers.[1] Jean-Baptiste, on the other
hand, was hurt by these allegations, which he continued to
deny long after the accusers had been derided.

In spite of these aggravations, he, just like the others, took
full advantage of the status his new position provided. To
the €9,000.00 he received monthly from the State, was also
added revenue from the sports drink, insurance company, and
e-reader to which he licensed his name and likeness. Like the
others, he had entrusted his business affairs to an agent, an
Italian who had previously worked with elite soccer players.
With the signed contracts, Jean-Baptiste was finally able to

---

[1] The superheroes were contractually obligated, starting at the end of April, to use their
powers only within the context of their service, the authorization of which being subject
to the issuance of a mission order from the hands of the state prosecutor of the Republic
him- or herself. Although these measures were condemned by civil rights defenders—as the
capabilities of the seven were consubstantial, they explained, they should be able to exercise
them as freely as any other attributes that are inalienable from their being—they still remain
in effect today. To enforce this, a series of new offences or aggravating circumstances were
even created: starting in May it was illegal, except in situations where special dispensation had
been previously obtained (for example those of the superheroes exercising their functions),
to fly outdoors, make oneself invisible, change one's appearance, read others' thoughts, etc.

move out of the one-bedroom place he had been renting near Père-Lachaise Cemetery to a large apartment near the Opera with creaky parquet floors, just like at rich peoples' places, which he never tired of hearing.

His schedule was determined only at the last minute based on the missions he was assigned and the paparazzi milling beneath his windows. As he had agreed not to use his powers of metamorphosis outside of work, he used other strategies to elude the photographers. His hosts would exfiltrate him through hidden exits. He would wear dark glasses and a ski cap out of season. The services of a body double were even solicited, just after his affair with a married woman had been revealed.

One might imagine that he had no free time, but missions were few and far between during the first several months. Plus, he'd been able to limit his formal engagements, his interactions with the press, all that gossip column fodder for which he said he had no flair. He frequently stayed home alone in his new apartment.

As a consequence, he was able to devote himself to an old dream that he'd never forgotten: erect a scale-model of Bayeux, and as a first step, the Saint-Jean neighborhood where he'd grown up. He had the necessary materials for the buildings and street layout delivered. Then he spent hours on the internet finding figurines to populate his model. The money he now had allowed him to buy nearly anything, but the real joy during this initial stage was feverishly studying the photos of each item and hemming and hawing about each choice, which he wished to believe was critical.

As the weeks progressed, the neighborhood began to take shape in the middle of his double living room. Most of all, after placing a figurine in a scene, Jean-Baptiste loved giving the person a name, an occupation, and a valid reason for being there, information he recorded in a small notebook. Street sweepers, police officers, merchants, and tiny old people could appear in these streets and no one would blink an eye, but the reason others happened to find themselves there remained quite obscure. In particular, there was, unearthed on a Danish dealer's website, a magician mid-trick, wearing a cape and eye mask, his top hat in one hand and a dove in the other, about which one would certainly wonder what he was doing there in the middle of the intersection of Avenue Georges-Clemenceau and Rue Saint-Floxel. A few centimeters away Jean-Baptiste placed a car overturned on its roof in order to deepen the mystery.

This slow, minutious hobby—his mind intensely focused on a tiny world as opposed to great accomplishments—allowed him to stay grounded, he explained to the journalists from the website Super-H who were allowed to visit his home. It also surely distracted him from his relationship difficulties. He had scared Marion [*the young woman he was supposed to meet on 1/19 when he lifted off the ground, and whom he dated for several weeks*] by showing up one evening as the actor Brad Pitt. He thought it would make her smile, but it only terrified her. Other relationships he expected too much of followed. Each time, he was the one who left, but his heart was broken.

One evening, however, at some mundane ribbon cutting ceremony he attended, dragging his feet the entire way, he met Martha Brookes, a young English actress. The beginning was rough—he didn't particularly like the efforts she made to please him, the earrings she wore, the languorous smiles after each kiss. But then, on a beach in Croatia where he'd taken her for the weekend, he said to himself, okay, she's the one. Everything's nice and easy with her. Love bowled him over. They were to be married.

V

ONCE IT WAS established that they had all been stuck in the same traffic jam on the A7 highway outside of Valence on July 5, 1992—and lacking any other explanation, it was assumed that some unknown phenomenon happened on that day in that place that had affected all of them—Thérèse Lambert was called in. The scene had left nearly no trace. Eyewitness accounts were as few and far between as the rare photographs taken from the roadside by bored vacationers: the weather was looking stormy, and it in fact had started to rain. A young woman was seen picking wildflowers in a field along the road. Elton John was played several times on the radio, and the strike by truckers protesting the establishment of a point system for drivers' licenses dominated the news breaks.

The authorities were counting on Thérèse's hypermnesia to make reappear before this grayish backdrop some suspicious activity, a glimmer in the sky, a strange odor, some detail that would allow us to better understand how six children,[1] all born in 1983, might, twenty-six years later, unveil incredible abilities.

---

[1] It was quickly established that Saïd Mechbal was not present in the traffic jam. For him, more than for his fellow superheroes, the mystery of his origins remains absolute. Similarly, it has frequently been pointed out that other children of the same age were in the immediate proximity of the six on July 5th. Why didn't they develop similar powers? Some far-fetched explanations have made the rounds, which I don't feel are useful to evoke here.

Thérèse had not yet mastered her powers completely. Even for her, the day of July 5, 1992, was very far away. However, bedridden for two days with a migraine as a result, she found in her mind a few fragmentary images, the residue of some memories. She saw her father perspiring in a short-sleeve shirt, hands gripping the wheel of their stopped car. To distract them her mother made her and her brother sing songs she'd learned during her years as a girl scout. A car went by on the shoulder. Her father heaved a sigh about cheaters. The heady smell of creosote emanated from railroad ties that paralleled the highway. In a hollow between two hills, three towers from a shuttered factory evoked an abandoned lunar outpost.

Nothing that would come to pass in their lives was foreshadowed that day, neither their parents' divorce in 1996 nor her brother's committal several years later, unless you interpreted her father's silence, her mother's forced enthusiasm, and Nicholas's groans as harbingers. But she refused to do so. A family was leaving on vacation. It was hot. The father was irritated that they were stuck in their car, while the youngest sibling was losing his patience. That's all.

All too frequently, as she was now able to peer into her memories, Thérèse felt as if she were prophesying backward, and it was this, more than nostalgia for what had disappeared, that bothered her the most about her hypermnesia. The past, as presented by her memory, was teeming with gestures, looks, and intonations that had become heavy with significance. All the parts fit together like some bad mystery novel where the slightly-too-obvious clues lead to the final revelation.

Her memories hadn't helped the investigators determine the truth. So we heard from scientists of varying levels of rigor suggesting radioactive fallout from Chernobyl. As for the conspiracy theorists, they focused on the hypothesis that a mutated substance had leaked from a military laboratory that was located a few kilometers from the traffic jam. The fact that this lab worked on thermal imaging and not molecular biology did not dampen their suspicions in the slightest.

Thérèse's account did fascinate Raphael Zabreski and Gregory Marville, however. She remembered the following event: allowed to stretch her legs, she had walked up the shoulder a few meters and saw two boys who, each in his own car, were staring at one another. The color and make of the cars as well as the description of the kids left no doubt: it was Raphael and Gregory.

They hadn't the slightest recollection of that particular July day. It was as if that day, along with so many others, didn't exist. But in a general way they did remember the usual traffic jams in the Rhone Valley at the beginning or end of any vacation period, when the air, even with the windows open, was hot and stale, clothing seams made your crotch itch, cakes, eaten too quickly, sat leaden in your stomach, and games, as tensions increased, provoked wild laughter or sobbing fits. Raphael wondered if chance hadn't led them to cross paths in other situations. They recounted their childhood vacations and school trips in detail. They may not have been fated to run into each other, but their meeting, twenty-six years after that glance, took on the appearance, at least in their minds, of the authority of destiny.

Raphael's dour expression reminded Gregory of a kid he'd known on his high-school soccer team, a certain Sylvain Reviatti, a taciturn team leader whose silence amid the adolescent din seemed to signify a superior mind. The similarities didn't stop there: like Reviatti, the Prophet had long lashes, curly brown hair that fell down his neck, and milky white skin that made people think he had a fragile constitution. He was, however, tall and well-built. Reviatti, but all grown up.

Convinced that he was not thoughtful, that he was too impulsive, Gregory found in Raphael a right-minded individual who judged without prejudice, and whose intelligence was expressed simply. His intelligence didn't highlight your own stupidity, as some brilliant minds do.

For his part, while they were quartered in Normandy, Raphael had admired the photos on The Captain's phone of his wife and eldest daughter, two beauties who, when they weren't smiling, pierced right through you with their otherworldly eyes. You could tell that in Marseille Gregory hung around with guys like him—relaxed, in good shape, whom he'd meet up with on weekends for impromptu barbeques, or jaunts to the seacoast of the Calanques nearby. Of course, annoyances must have troubled these idyllic seas. It wasn't possible any other way, but they remained invisible—"and perhaps invisible to Gregory himself," Raphael would later say. He had to conclude, therefore, either they didn't make their way to Gregory's consciousness or he'd swept them away through his faith in the intangible truths he held. When Raphael finally asked him, Gregory took stock of his life: after eight years together, he and Jeanne were shocked they still loved each other so much. He was incredibly lucky. You have to live each day like it's your last.

Everything had changed, of course, since his powers had been revealed. But Gregory still organized little weekend trips to Corsica or Marrakech with his family, and, whenever he found the time, would meet up with his friends to grill in a buddy's backyard or enjoy a drink on another's patio. In Raphael's mind, Gregory's life ended up looking like a cheesy slideshow with saccharine music in the background, one of those advertisements that extols the charms of a destination you might not think about until summertime: CHOOSE GREGORY

MARVILLE—A CALM AND BEAUTIFUL LIFE. "It might have been a bit shallow," remarked the Prophet, "but it did make you envious."

While people his age were spending more and more time in poor-paying jobs, which one day would lead to more comfortable positions, while they were marrying or at least settling down, having children and taking care of them with the worried and all-encompassing attentiveness unique to this generation of parents, Raphael had no known plans, no enduring passion, not even a good idea of himself.

In high school he talked of astrophysics as a promising subject to pursue. Then he mentioned architecture. Finally, without telling anyone, he got himself admitted to the literature program at Henry IV, one of the best schools in the country. There, he slowly started to withdraw. After six months during which, instead of attending classes, he devoured Russian novels while lying in his dorm room and, citing ocular migraines, cut himself off from everyone else, he was summoned before the administration and expelled.

After taking courses but never completing a degree in philosophy nor in history, he got by on a series of odd jobs, sang in a rock group, studied the possibility of expatriating to Montreal or Sydney, and eventually ended up at the reception desk of a hotel on Rue Ordener four nights a week. This sleepy job earned him enough money to have a one-bedroom apartment in the twelfth arrondissement in Paris and lead a life of leisure based on inexpensive pleasures: paperbacks purchased at discount stores, an unlimited movie pass, café lungos, *L'Equipe* or *Libération* when the newspapers' headlines intrigued him. He still had a little money leftover to dress nicely in inexpensive clothes and satisfy his large appetite with a diet of quick, easy meals he'd settled on when he was a student. Rice with sour cream and curry, pasta with cheese, and couscous smothered in tomato sauce appeared weekly on the menu.

Sometimes people found him a disappointment. True friends were few and far between. His bachelordom continued. His family worried about him. But he had the life he wanted, he assured them.

The rare notes he jotted in his journal offer no insight as to what 1/19 represented for him. The following day we see a simple "Oh!" scribbled in the middle of a blank page. Nothing else for the next ten pages, or at least nothing that made it to us.

Every time he was asked a question about this time and what it was like for him, Raphael would turn the question back on the person, using the neutral tone that he'd frequently employed since donning his white mask, an oval whose eye slits and muted pallor were reminiscent of Japanese theater: "How would you have felt if you were in my place?" "Well, what did 1/19 mean to you?"

His ability to predict the future undoubtedly improved more quickly than the authorities wished to admit. According to the official version of events, at the beginning, when he concentrated, he could only see the place on the body where death would strike, the heart in the case of a heart attack, the lungs or breast if cancer was to be diagnosed, near the hand if the targeted person was going to die after slitting their wrists. The death zone would pulse with a reddish glow, he explained, while the rest, the target's body as well as the space surrounding it, was immersed in darkness laced with blue filaments.

Then a date became clear: first he could discern the year of death, then the month, then, with those who were easiest to read, the exact day they would pass.

Various witnesses confirm that, starting in August, he could more or less reconstruct the circumstances of death. He could now perceive, in the middle of a peaceful dinner, the body hit by a stroke and gradually crumpling to the ground like a hesitant actor on stage, then the alarmed dinner guests, the emergency call, the final convulsions. In December he began to see other events: divorces, births, landslide elections, sporting achievements, firings, various moments of happiness . . . He had become clairvoyant.

The consequences were painful, even if he avoided talking about them. Like Thérèse Lambert when she sifted through her memory, Raphael suffered from intense migraines each time he examined someone's future. Even so, he found himself inundated with requests, some of which were hard to refuse. Heads of state, random people in poignant letters, debtors and friends pleaded to know what would happen to them.

It was soon determined that this fate could most often be avoided. This only increased the interest in his powers. When, for example, the Prophet would discern, based on a suspicious redness in the occipital area, a future car accident—the car rolling into a ditch and the driver's head smashing into the windshield—it was not an inescapable event he was announcing, but rather the future such as it appeared at that moment. If the target were warned early enough and decided not to get in the car on the specified date, she would avoid the awaiting death sentence without fail. Rather than a prophet, a term he always refused, Raphael considered himself something like a lookout. Thanks to him lifespans were increased, tragedies were avoided. "I predict futures that won't happen," he noted in his journal as a kind of policy statement.

His predictions implied that everything was preordained. For rationalists, such an idea contradicted the concept of human existence they defended. The Prophet was not popular among this group. They criticized him for playing the religious game. Others tried to convince themselves of the opposite, that if it were possible to change the future and thwart his prognostications, then the usefulness of his ability was yet to be demonstrated. What he saw could be avoided. What he didn't see remained unknown. In short, everything was open and undecided. But that wasn't quite right. If nothing were changed or if nothing could be changed (in the case of an incurable disease, for example) what he predicted came to pass every time. This made him a terrifying and macabre personage.

Life had taken on a somber tinge for him as well. When prognosticating, the target's sweaty hands tightly gripped in his own, he was witness to scenes of agony in hospital rooms, mutilated bodies in crushed automobiles, people hanging, bathtubs full of blood, and open windows through which people were going to jump. And when he opened his eyes he had to tell them all about it.

Although no one ever understood why, sometimes the red mark would appear on people he wasn't examining, people he would pass by in the street, patrons at a nearby table in a restaurant.

He confessed that a model he was planning on spending the night with induced a scream of horror when she walked out of the bathroom nude. Her right breast was red. What do you do in that situation? Most of the time I ended up telling them what I saw, the Prophet explained. But when it came to revealing circumstances of a death that couldn't be avoided, he felt like he was ruining these peoples' lives, or what was left of them. So, more and more frequently, he just kept his mouth shut.

For him, even more so than for the other 83ers, wearing

a mask was a necessity. This was in addition to a number of very strict measures he took to protect his true identity. Knowing the future inflamed feelings. At every public appearance, the Prophet had to face hordes of weeping fans, their hands stretched out toward him in the vain hope he would reveal some or all of their future. Fringe groups of varying levels of credibility plotted his assassination. All the surviving 83ers agree that the pressure they felt from their celebrity was nothing in comparison to what the Prophet had to endure every day. "Plus, since he refused to have a team assist him, he had to face that basically alone," confided Virginie. "He stayed close to his family, but, day to day, I don't know how he didn't go off the rails. He'd kind of lose it, sometimes he'd drink too much, or have mood swings, but when you think about it, he managed to keep it together. I remember one time outside HQ there was a woman who sat there for four or five days with a lit candle and a sign that said: 'My son has disappeared. Will I find him?' You have to be really, really strong-willed to put up with what he went through."

Shortly after the birth of Marianne on July 5th, Gregory called Raphael to ask him to be godfather. He immediately accepted. The more difficulty he had thriving in his life as a superhero, the closer he sought to be with the Captain. (Sometimes we like to believe that, as if through reverberation, the happiness of others will bounce back onto us.)

He would later confess that a keen excitement invigorated him the day of the baptism, thinking not only about the idea of meeting Gregory's friends and family but even more of seeing where his friend lived and went about his daily life. It was a duplex nestled in the hills of Marseille. Glass doors opened onto a patio with a limed-wood pergola and a swimming pool.

In the living room, a large flat-screen television dominated a white leather chaise longue and a translucent coffee table on which a multi-colored crystal sculpture of a wildcat, either a panther or a cougar, took center stage—a wedding present the couple no longer dared to discard. At the far end behind the fireplace was an open kitchen of stainless steel and waxed concrete, which gleamed in the sun through a skylight. The interior was nice, but too neat and as conventional as Raphael had imagined Gregory's tastes to be. In the entryway, however, one detail surprised him. A love of old things, which he'd gotten from his mother, had incited the Captain to acquire a sixteenth-century Murano glass plate. Raphael liked to feel its weight in his hands, bringing its enamel-painted, scalloped rim close to his face and breathing in the relic's acrid odor.

There is little information available on Marianne's baptism or the Prophet's stay in Marseille. Over the course of his interviews with the journalist Patrick Woodworth, the Prophet doesn't dwell on the details of this "magnificent, emotional day, which sealed [his] friendship with Gregory much more firmly than the missions over the past few months had," during which they had risked their lives together. Turning to Raphael's journal, it offers only factual information:

> Slept on the train. Enjoyment of not wearing a mask. Extremely hot in Marseille. Gregory super happy, not because of the baptism itself, but to have all the people he loves surrounding him. Like to stay a few more days.

In his minutely detailed investigation, Alexis Bertarelli, Jeanne's biographer, did establish however, that during the course of the afternoon, when the other guests and their children were seeking refuge in the pool (the entire city was suffocating that day in the burning, still air), Raphael chatted for several minutes with Gregory's wife in the kitchen. Bertarelli and many superologists after him have seen in this fleeting tête-à-tête a moment of epiphany.

At thirty-four, Jeanne Marville, a real-estate agent and former professional tennis player, was remarkable in her delicate good looks and her shyness (coldness, some said), which bestowed upon her a dash of mystery. In photographs from the baptism she can be seen wearing a blue tunic, revealing her already svelte shape, just three months after her second pregnancy.

It is tempting to see in Raphael's brief account, as Bertarelli does, the avowal of some inner turmoil that remained obscure. Some have also similarly interpreted, carelessly in my opinion, a photo from the same day in which he has an anguished face and an evasive look. But the coincidence seems to mesh all too well with the conventions of drama: having come to celebrate the budding friendship with a man he envies, our protagonist becomes enamored with his wife at first sight, the only one he is forbidden to love.

VI

"Forget Superman"

SAÏD MECHBAL: Now what he told me was that when he got to the baptism he told people he worked for the Ministry of Defense and that his name was François Perrin. Apparently Gregory's wife gave him this "yeah, right" look, and he felt bad he had to keep bullshitting the rest of the day in front of this woman who saw right through him.

At least Gregory and Jean-Baptiste didn't have that problem. They were who they were. Period. We tried too hard to protect ourselves. You wouldn't believe how hard we made it for ourselves with our double identities. And, truth be told, it was a relief, maybe Virginie told you the same thing, when our names came out and we flipped forever into the "post" category. For me it's still a huge regret I lied to the people closest to me, especially my father. My dad was a good guy, a really kind person, and I don't think he had a very happy life, even though he said that everything was fine, that we were better off here than in Algeria. I would've loved to tell him before he died I was Number Seven—that was me. Just to see his face, to see the look on his face at that second. But, well, I made a different decision. The same as the others. We were too easily influenced.

How do you explain that?
I dunno. Drugs maybe.

Are you serious?
It sure don't seem like it, huh? I haven't looked into it, it's
not my job to know what kind of psychotropics they were
perfecting in the military labs, but me, if I'm in charge of the
country and they throw seven people with incredible powers
in my lap, I can tell you my number one priority is to get just
one thing: their consent. Later, it can happen in a lot of different ways. I'm not saying I'm 100% sure they drugged us.
Don't write that 'cause people are going to say Saïd Mechbal's
hurling accusations with no proof again. I'm just saying, with
hindsight, we were very disciplined. Good little students of the
Republic. And that I have trouble understanding.

*Becoming aware of your capabilities might have encouraged you
to act responsibly . . .*
Like Spiderman, right? Maybe. Maybe we were those kind of
people. Good people. [*He laughs.*] In any case they put you in
a very strange psychological state. Even before you shake the
President's hand or before you're whisked to a ceremony in a
special motorcade, they create this kind of atmosphere, very
pampered but still with this feeling of urgency, and just that,
that puts knots in your stomach, it makes your heart race, and
I can tell you that you don't feel like screwing around anymore.
At every briefing they keep making you feel like you're somebody important and you're going to rewrite history if-you-are-
willing-to-of-course. 'Cause you also have the option of doing
whatever you want with your powers. After all, guys, you're
free. It's management 101, but it works just about every time.
Mickaël called it the "Bruce Willis Method."

Why Bruce Willis?
Have you seen *Armageddon*? It's the movie with the giant asteroid that's about to destroy the Earth. And suddenly, I can't remember why, but the only person that can prevent this catastrophe is this guy who does deep sea oil drilling, a kind of irresponsible hard-ass who only thinks about number one, Bruce Willis. The plan's to send a team up to drill a hole in the asteroid and drop a nuclear bomb inside and blow it up. Bruce Willis, he's havin' nothin' to do with it: working for the military, following their rules, it pisses him off and he wants the hell out. But the generals explain that six billion human lives are in his hands. And that's when Bruce Willis sheds a tear and decides to be the hero everybody's waiting for.

They did the same thing with you?
In any case they showed us how we could have a purpose. And it worked. We felt invested. All of us, not just Marville. All of us, we thought of ourselves as national heroes. And that's what they were hoping for.

You seem to have regrets . . .
Not at all. For me that was probably the best time of my life. The most balanced in fact. I'd screwed up almost everything until then. I passed my baccalaureate exam, but they were kind of giving them away then. After that, nothing: screwed up my studies even though everybody said I had potential, screwed up my relationship with Leïla [*his girlfriend from 2007 –2011*], screwed up my life in the neighborhood over some meaningless shit with some dudes that were ten years younger than me. Delivery guy . . . at thirty-four . . . I had no purpose, I was really nothing. But with my capabilities, can you imagine, it was totally different. "The Colombians are asking for

help nabbing their biggest drug kingpin . . . *Yes, boss.* Pirates took three French hostages in the Gulf of Guinea . . . *We'll find 'em, boss.* Oh, and would you have some spare time for a ribbon-cutting ceremony at a hospital in Quatre Chemins? *Sure thing, boss. That's my old neighborhood!*"

Tell you the truth, I had no vision. I did everything they asked me, but I felt totally awesome. The endurance we acquired, that was the most amazing thing. I only needed to sleep, what, two-three hours a night to be in top form. And so you got time for everything. I, maybe it's kinda lame, but when I was 32 or 33 on the internet I'd found some lists of books and movies, something like "The Greatest Masterpieces of Humanity," and I'd promised myself I'd get through all of them before I was 40, just to finally get myself some real knowledge, since I hadn't got very far in school. These lists were on my phone, 30 books and 100 or so movies, but before 1/19 I couldn't ever find the time. I'd thought about it a lot, it had become like the symbol of all the shit I couldn't get done. Right when we got our powers, almost every night between one and five in the morning, I'd read. I watched all the Scorsese movies, Hitchcock, the classics.

And then there were the more material aspects. The salary they gave us, the new apartment, and even if you gotta keep the mask on, the chicks, you can pick up as many as you want . . . Now hold on, fame, being a star, people all act like it sucks, like it's really terrible, but for me it was like Disneyland: huge parties, yachts like you see on TV, celebrities that wanna take a photo with you, Bono and Angelina Jolie calling to find out if you want to do a charity thing, and in the middle of all this fake bullshit, friends I've made for life—Nico [*Anelka*], Lil Wayne, Diego [*Maradona*], who was crying on the phone with me just before his brother died . . . For a year, I had a blast.

But today you have a much harsher view of that time.
Because it wasn't genuine.

Why?
First off you have to understand we weren't invented by the Americans. I mean, this idea that superheroes have to do good, where does that come from exactly? From American comic books and the blockbuster movies that came later. Now for three minutes just try and forget Batman, Superman, and the rest. Totally. And put yourself in our place. In my place. I realize I can make myself invisible whenever I want, just like that, at the drop of the hat. Fine. And so people explain to me that that's actually going to create a ton of problems, invasion of privacy if I start waltzing in unannounced, going into people's houses, government offices, with all the state secrets, etc. I agree. Again, if I'd been the President, I wonder if I wouldn't have just outright had us eliminated rather than trying to make use of us, because it was clear we were going to create a shit ton of problems. And so Saïd, the invisible man, he's great but he might also stir up a fair amount of shit. Nowadays, I agree with that diagnosis.

Well, so they place these super strict guidelines on me for using my special powers, and me, since I'm a good guy, or because I swallow my daily dose of their obedience drug, or because I'm just a little dumb, you check the correct box, I sign all the papers. Fine. You still following me? Try to put yourself in my shoes again. I mean it's totally awesome to have the power to become invisible. It can serve the nation, sure, but above all it's exciting. Super exciting. And hanging around on the roofs of Paris, peeping in on the lives of people at home, for sure I did that a bunch at the beginning. I saw people having sex, but not all that much. Most of the time they're just on their phones, they're eating, they're playing with their kids. There was one family in particular in a duplex not far from my place. I loved going to see them. Good looking parents, squeaky clean little boy in his pajamas with his hair freshly combed. You're there, right next to them, you're spying on them, which is definitely not right, but you actually feel like you're part of the family, too, like you're there with them doing their normal stuff. You're not hurting anyone. Moments like that I found very soothing. I'd always had some issues living with others, and here I'd found my alternative to being isolated.

Okay, but I'd signed. So I didn't have the right anymore. Fine. But that doesn't mean I didn't *want to*. That doesn't mean it was *easy*. Do you get that? We were doing capital-G Good 'cause that was our role and we felt obligated, but it didn't come to us *naturally*. It wasn't our calling. And even, let me tell you, it was the complete opposite: our calling was to fuck stuff up. 'Cause when you've got powers like us, it's hard to control your desires. Even harder. Just compare, I dunno, a Hollywood movie star and some nobody with bad breath. It's a hell of a lot easier for the second one to not cheat on his wife, am I right? Nobody's hittin' on him. The real Bruce Willis, I don't know if he's married, I don't know if he's faithful to his wife, but if that's the case then he's a hero. He deserves a medal.

Here's what I figured out: we were taken for a ride 'cause everybody's seen *Superman*. They thought it was normal for us to be irreproachable. And the opposite was shocking. With that kind of setup, we had no chance.

What should've been done in your opinion?
Just the word "superhero." We actually never should've accepted it. That threw everything out of whack, everything. For the rest . . . I don't know honestly. Could it have happened

any other way? I don't think so. That's why I'm not here complaining. That's why I'm happy with my life.

[*It's a man with chin-length hair streaked with strands of grey, tanned, but weary eyed whom I meet in the imposing lobby of the Grand Hotel of Kinshasa. Saïd Mechbal says he now works freelance as a "security expert" and is currently on a "short-term mission" in the Congo. The tooled leather of his boots, the silver and turquoise belt buckle, the white-framed sunglasses pushed back in his hair confirm his taste for flashy outfits. But perhaps he simply enjoys presenting me an image that corresponds with his bad reputation. After having refused my request for an interview with a one-line email—"Ask Thérèse, her memory's better than mine"—five days later he suggested that we meet here, even offering to pay my airfare if the cost of the trip might preclude us from meeting.*]

If we'd had a bit firmer political backbone . . . if, instead of doing law enforcement we'd asked the right questions, maybe things could've been different. I'm telling you this, but I don't believe it. It wouldn't have gone nowhere. Look at the revolutionaries now. Always fighting among themselves. Probably sabotaged by undercover cops. Anyway, nothing ever changes. Really, could you have seen us with the outraged crowd at some Alter-Globalist rally? It would have been ridiculous.

When did you feel that things weren't going to turn out well?
For me it was very distinctly the day of the Courneuve operation in September. [*On September 25th of Year I, Saïd Mechbal, Mickaël Pereira, Gregory Marville, and Virginie Mathieu-Brun were dispatched to support an Emergency Response Team. They were tasked to apprehend two terrorists in their apartment who were planning a chemical weapons attack on a movie theater at Les Halles in Paris. Their neutralization was complicated by the*

men's unexpected resistance. They had in their possession a large arsenal as well as abettors in the area to help them escape the apartment building, which had been blockaded. During the chase that followed the police raid, Saïd Mechbal was taken hostage by one of the two fleeing men. According to the police report, Virginie overpowered the individual as he threatened to kill Saïd.]

Because you almost died?
No, that's not it at all. But I did figure out that some of the rules of engagement were changing.

Could you be more specific?
It's not the official version . . .

But I'm not asking you to confirm it . . .
Ok. So, Saïd's side! I jumped from the fourth floor in the dark to run after Djamal Benzekri. There's a combat drone just above me, I'm running without my invisibility 'cause I don't want it to mow me down, and I'm about to catch up with Djamal, but I slip and fall like some fucking loser, and then the dude's on top of me. The guy's jacked, and let me just say one other thing: he's driven. Ready to do whatever it takes. With maybe just a little extra motivation 'cause he's going to bag himself a superhero. It's kind of like when some rinky-dink, fifth-division soccer team wipes the floor with Paris Saint-Germain in the Coupe de France Championships, you know? He's got me on my knees right next to him, and I've got the barrel of his 9mm pushing against my skull. For a split second I become invisible, but he tells me don't be stupid, stop right now. If he could've rammed his piece into my head he would've done it. Every time he talks the barrel brushes against my temple. So, yeah, I'm following orders. Virginie and Micka move in, but Djamal tells them to back off. He yells that he's armed and

dangerous, and I remember that expression, "armed and dangerous," 'cause it seemed kind of highbrow, sort of journalistic coming out of his mouth, like when some prisoner makes a getaway and you hear on the radio, "the suspect is considered armed and dangerous." Well, there I am on my knees with a dude like that staring down at me.

What were you thinking?
Nothing. It's happening so fast. My mind's blank. I'm just terrified. The guy's gonna kill me. I can hear it in his voice. Every time he talks, that goes through my mind. I'd had a gun pointed at me before, one time by some teenagers in Saint-Denis, but that was totally different. Weapons have been pretty easy to find in the neighborhoods since the 90s, but you gotta understand there's very little ammo. So dudes have guns, they carry them around all over, might even jerk off with 'em, but they never fire 'em. Which means they generally don't know how to use 'em *at all*. So, comes time to squeeze it off and either they spray bullets in every direction but can't hit a target three meters away or they just quietly piss themselves and never pull the trigger. Djamal wasn't like that at all. That you could tell right away.

Did you know what the other 83ers were doing while he was holding you hostage?
I couldn't see them. My head was down, but I hear Mickaël, very calm, telling the guy to relax, that he's bluffing, that it's not going to work. And when I hear that I beg Mickaël to cut the bullshit. I know him and his everything's-under-control, his I'm-the-shit-with-my-nerves-of-steel bit. It pisses off Djamal, too. But Micka says the guy's bluffing again, and now he's talking to Virginie. He tells her the guy won't shoot. He can't do it.

He knows it?
He says he knows. And then Virginie's on the guy. And that's all she wrote.

You're not really acting as if you believe that's what happened . . .
Nope.

Can you explain?
I'm sticking with what I told you. At the briefing, they told us about Djamal—armed robbery at 19, a stint inside, travelled to training camps in Yemen right afterward . . . He was a bad dude. He had guts. I told you what I experienced that night. I know when he threatened to waste me, he's totally capable of doing it. He's going to do it. If he didn't . . .

It's because Mickaël manipulated his mind?
Yes.

So, you believe that Mickaël's capabilities had already evolved in September.
Yes.

Did you tell anyone?
No, not a soul.

Why not?
'Cause the shit would hit the fan. And, you know, where I'm from, you don't rat people out.

PART TWO

VII

Mickaël Pereira never rated very highly in the opinion polls. The public found his power fascinating, but he didn't know how to please people or be charming. Broad shouldered, with a wiry body and an unfriendly gaze, his hairline so low that it swallowed up his forehead, he gave the impression of a tough guy who's looking for trouble. Starting in preschool he was labeled as antisocial, restless, and mean. In middle school he was expelled several times for violent acts against other students, and, on one occasion, for shoving a teacher. On his report cards we read that nothing interests him except sports. One of his first girlfriends, Fanny G., nevertheless believes that people place too much importance on his troubled past. "People need to stop with all the stories. There're tons of guys out there who had problems in school, and they didn't all go mental. It's too easy to tell it like he was wired from the beginning to do what he did."

The Pereiras lived in a low-rise building in the Pablo-Picasso housing project in Nanterre. In the early 1980s, the area was still calm and much more welcoming than the shanty town in Massy where the couple had lived during their first months in France. Mickaël's father, João, wasn't paid much at the automobile inspection station where he worked, but he really liked it. It was at this time that he started going by the name "Joe."

His two sons revered him, even though he was strict and taciturn. He adored cars. He and his wife loved to drive around on the highways in their Renault 17. On weekends they took their children to Normandy and sometimes even as far as Lyon or Mulhouse. The ostensible goal of their expeditions—picnicking at the seashore, checking out the progress of some large construction site—was almost always abandoned during the trip. Once they had reached their destination, they'd turn around.

If they dawdled, it was at rest stops or roadside snack bars, which the family visited frequently. Sometimes the kids would get a free order of fries, and the family almost felt like the place belonged to them—in any case more so than to the haggard families passing by in the sunlight, never to be seen again.

With his father and brother Eric, Mickaël liked to scour service station parking lots looking for new models or high-end automobiles. When they found a Porsche 911 or 924 they'd wait nearby to hear the motor start up. One time a man invited Mickaël and his brother to sit behind the wheel. Joe didn't have a camera to take a snapshot of his boys in the Porsche, which he regretted. Mickaël, for his part, was relieved. He didn't like the owner's benevolent smile nor his father's repeated thanks. "Typical dago politeness," Mickaël would later say.

Around thirteen or fourteen, his grades in French improved, and he set out to write a science-fiction tale, *The Voyagers of Alfa*, which tells the story of a man and his robot who explore a deserted megalopolis. Handwritten in pencil in a school notebook, Mickaël's story trails off as the voyagers discover an immense, apparently bottomless well in the center of the city. Mickaël later claimed he hadn't opened a book since the age of fifteen and barely knew how to write, but this wasn't true. He read detective novels, scientific works written for the general public, and even poetry, including Baudelaire and Eluard. Two of his friends from Nanterre revealed to me that Mickaël liked to come across as less intelligent and cultured than he really was.

Perhaps to compensate for the lack of empathy he aroused in others, he did show a marked narcissistic bent as a teenager. He would check out his profile in the double doors of his mirrored armoire, flex his muscles, and ask his brother to take photos of him shirtless, in sunglasses, a gangster's blasé expression on his face.

At the same time, his talent as a soccer player was attracting attention. On the weekends men would stand near playing fields in the suburbs and occasionally after matches would ask the coaches for information. Mickaël knew if they were there just by glancing at the parking lot. They all drove big cars, which were always clean and undoubtedly paid for by their clubs. The teachers always said to pay them no attention, but Mickaël definitely played better when they were there. In the middle of the pitch, all of the attacks went through him. He was small, aggressive, relentless, and nimble-footed, just the type of player that helps out any team. Bordeaux, Nantes, Auxerre, and Monaco invited him to try out. The ball flew a little faster at the training centers, but Mickaël was able to show what he could do every time. He played like he'd been taught in Nanterre, simply and always working downfield. After the tryouts they'd give him a city tour and would ask if he'd like it there. He would immediately respond yes, but felt as if he should have added something, words that he could never put his finger on. Other players found him too cold. Plus, his size might be a problem. Teams hesitated.

When he was fifteen, a group of journalists came to
Nanterre nearly every week for six months to film his soccer
team. They were producing a one-hour feature on the role of
soccer in economically depressed suburbs. One of the reporters,
Sebastien Desmarets, remembers a chippy boy who wouldn't
even give them the time of day. Then, like the others, Mickaël
ended up watching for their car. The weeks the camera wasn't
there practices seemed duller and their lives drearier. Finally
he agreed to speak. The footage from his interview wasn't kept,
but Desmarets recalls the moment when, in the silence of an
empty locker room, Mickaël spoke to them about his course-
work in accounting, which he was studying without really
knowing why, the clubs he hoped would soon call him back,
and especially of a girlfriend with whom he hadn't yet made
love because he truly loved her. When speaking about her
he became completely pale, his brow furrowed with concern.
Desmarets also remembers that Mickaël shook his hand for a
very long time when they were saying goodbye. Later, nothing was retained during the editing process. Mickaël's teenage
emotions were touching, but didn't really fit the subject matter,
and the producer was of the opinion that other players had
expressed themselves more meaningfully on the problems of
their everyday lives and being poor.

At twenty-two, after an inconclusive tryout with a Walloon
club, Mickaël found himself sleeping on a bench outside the
Brussels-South railway station. The so-called agent who had
sent him there wasn't answering his phone, and Mickaël didn't
have enough money to take the train. It was there, shivering
with cold on that bench, that he gave up. He wouldn't break
through. He returned his boots and gym bag to his parents'
balcony. Soccer, he declared, no longer interested him.

He killed time at the subway station, McDonald's, or a tea room/hookah bar behind La Defense. It was during this time that his superstitions intensified. To stray cats, to birds that look you in the eye, and to odd numbers, he now added to his suspicions the number four, lit candles, knives left on the table, and, in his dreams, snakes, musicians, and crying children. To protect himself from the evil eye, he developed a series of complicated rituals that only he understood, further closing himself off. He borrowed books on guardian angels and numerology from the library. He consulted fortune telling websites. "But I don't think he really believed all that stuff," his brother Eric later objected. "It was just another one of his affectations. A way to draw attention."

Those who hung out with him heard him talk of joining the service to become a fighter pilot and then an astronaut. They pointed out that he didn't even have a high school degree, and called him Neil Armstrong or Skywalker to make fun of him. But he wouldn't back down. He'd rack up all the required degrees, he'd crush the physicals, they couldn't pass up such a promising candidate. Then he'd talk about three years of training and then about missions on the space station. "We let him blather on," admitted a neighbor from Nanterre who socialized with him at the time. "'cause he could get riled up real quick if you started pointing out problems."

It does not appear that he attempted, in any way whatsoever, to make this astronautical dream a reality. The following year, in 2007, he took out a loan to start a fast-food restaurant, which failed after a few months. Then he joined a locksmith business one of his uncles owned, proved reliable, and took over management himself three years later when his uncle retired. He branched out to other construction trades and gained a reputation in the area for upscale renovations.

Twelve years later, married, father of a young boy, and living in Saint-Ouen, he was known as an energetic young entrepreneur, occasionally too rigid, but a straight shooter. He only socialized with couples his wife knew. He no longer saw his parents or brother. Nanterre seemed forgotten.

His powers revealed themselves three days after those of Jean-Baptiste and Gregory while he was shaking the hand of a smarmy mayor from whom he hoped to receive a contract. When he touched the mayor's limp, warm hand he knew the man would not give him the pleasure of his business.

At the very beginning, according to the military reports I was able to consult, he was only able to capture certain states of mind such as fear, anger, satisfaction, or dejection. Furthermore, these feelings had to reach a certain level of intensity for him to be able to distinguish them. The other targeted individuals he probed were "gray," he said.[1]

His progress was spectacular. After a few days he no longer needed to be in physical contact with his targets; seeing them was enough. He was soon able to follow a thought by deciphering a few key words, part of a phrase, of which he could nearly always reconstruct the meaning. A bit later Mickaël gained access to his subjects' memories. He confirmed that most people were very affecting inside, even those filled with rancor or frustration. Reading the thoughts of some unknown person, he said, was like looking through a microscope and seeing, underneath peoples' faces, an infinitely complex and captivating world.

Among the existing limitations, it is not true that Geminis were immune to his powers, nor that it was impossible for him

---

[1] Even though he used a chromatic code to describe his activities, he was never convinced that the thoughts of others did indeed appear to him as colors. Communications consultants suggested these equivalents so that the public could better conceptualize how his power worked.

to read the thoughts of those whose heads were covered or who closed their eyes. However, for some reason that no one has ever been able to explain, some minds remained impenetrable to him, and a moving target or one that was more than a couple dozen meters away was more difficult to auscultate, just like a hostile target or even those who simply knew they were being probed. In spite of all this, Mickaël possessed a capability that was of inestimable interest to French authorities. They saw him as one of their best spies. The *Washington Post* contends for example that the German Chancellor was probed during the first summer after 1/19. Mickaël discreetly infiltrated the personnel at the Berlin embassy in order to be in the Chancellor's presence on two separate occasions. But the Saga of the 83ers does not square with such allegations, which France has always denied.

The lynx mask that Mickaël wore for several months was apparently suggested by Rochelle. In terms of public relations, associating an animal to a superhero seemed like a good idea— simple and striking. French authorities even went so far as to speak of Lynxman, but the name didn't catch on. Just after he announced his divorce in September, he removed his mask of his own accord without a word of warning, announcing that his name was Mickaël Pereira. For a short period of time the British tabloids named him Mental Mike. But just "Mickaël" stuck.

Although he was unhappy after the fact, he never expressed any remorse for having explored his wife Vanessa's mind while she slept. He found what he'd been looking for: how she saw him, what her real feelings for him were, if she'd had any affairs.

She loved him and had always remained faithful to him. But he also learned that she thought he had become too muscular since he'd started lifting weights. She would have

preferred some other gift than the gaudy ring he had purchased
for their tenth anniversary. And she didn't particularly like it
when, some evenings, he would kiss her neck while breathing
heavily through his nose, then slide a hand in her underwear
to squeeze her butt. Personally, she would have liked desire to
take them by surprise.

He was almost disappointed to spot no adulterous temptations in Vanessa's thoughts, whereas he on occasion had lusted
after other women and even satisfied his desires between visiting two job sites. To compensate, he felt himself authorized to
satisfy a curiosity that had been nagging him forever—Anthony
Mestaller, a driving school instructor whom his wife had loved
two years before the two of them had met and about whom
she refused to speak. To Mickaël, this refusal was like a partial
confession, the sign that some inner turmoil persisted, perhaps
some passion, which was not completely extinguished, and
which tormented him each and every time he thought about
it, filling him with retroactive jealousy. Anthony Mestaller,
who at the time had talked about opening a youth hostel in
Bali and could sing an amazing rendition of Radiohead's *Creep*
(those were basically the only two things his wife would really
say about him), today lived a humdrum life and was losing
his hair in the Morbihan region of France. Mickaël regularly
checked Mestaller's Facebook page and found nothing to make
him envious. Moreover, he was relieved to note while exploring
her mind that from Vanessa's point of view, her former lover
was a failure.

On the other hand, he winced when he accessed the memory of the first time when, in the driving school car in the parking lot of a nearly deserted supermarket, Anthony leaned over
to kiss her. Not even three minutes later his hand had ventured
to Vanessa's thigh and rubbed it with a self-confidence that

seemed crude to Mickaël, but that his future wife, who was but nineteen at the time, found very exciting. Soon, in August or September (she didn't remember precisely) at the sand dunes near Landes, Anthony forced her down in the shade, removed the bottom of her swimsuit, and took her there, on all fours. The gray sand, as fine as powder, was so cool beneath her fingers it seemed wet. She was afraid someone might see them from the path, she was afraid what people might think, but it was delightful (the location, the shame, Anthony's semi-feigned roughness), and she started to moan, and he whispered to her in a husky voice that she could scream, that he wanted to hear her, and he grabbed her breasts so hard it hurt, and she cried out like he asked her. Mickaël had never imagined that his wife could scream like that.

The 83er never admitted that this foray into Vanessa's mind might have prompted his divorce, which he presented as a joint decision, whereas it had been his alone. He cited the inevitable wearing down of any relationship and the difficulty of reconciling his schedule, his responsibilities, and his new status with his previous life.

A few weeks later he met a television host, who, it was revealed, was hermetic, impervious to his power. One day, while he was visiting Brazil on holiday, shortly after the announcement of their forthcoming wedding, a journalist asked him if it wasn't precisely this quality that had charmed him about his new girlfriend—the impossibility of completely knowing her. Mickaël shrugged his shoulders and walked out.

Over the course of the following months he frequently proclaimed that he was not happy. When asked why, he would offer two reasons that varied from day to day. At times he would say he didn't really know why, and he would mention

his age, the fact that at thirty-six (his birthday was in July) few
of life's illusions can still stand up to all its disappointments.
Other times he would state, without explanation, that he had
been "edited out" and would let the interviewer ponder over
this enigmatic response, presenting it as a metaphor. Did he
mean he wasn't given enough space within the 83ers? That the
media overdid it with the Captain, the Prophet, and Virginie?

I found an interview, published in Mexico, that, to my
knowledge, provides the only clarification he ever offered. To a
reporter from *Porvenir* of Monterrey,[2] he recounted that during
his youth a television crew had filmed the everyday routine
of his soccer team and that he had ended up confiding in the
director. Mickaël had talked to him about his feeling that he'd
never amount to anything, not just in work—that was less
important—but in life in general. He worried he'd never find
his place. One day during halftime of a match his team was
losing, the coach criticized his "erratic" positioning on the field.
Ever since, he was obsessed by this adjective he'd never heard
before. It was precisely the word he'd been missing to name
what he felt. He was errant. He felt no connection to anything,
not even himself, since he didn't really know himself, since
he'd turned away from his inner voice. He felt he was adrift.
He believed he was moving away from the center like a satel-
lite thrown from its orbit, drifting toward the empty depths
of space. Mickaël told the director all of this and thought he
had touched him (his eyes were red) because when the interview was over, the locker room, where it was filmed, was filled
with a thick, pensive atmosphere, like after certain effective
speeches. But it had been cut during the editing, and Mickaël

---

[2] Why was this Mexican daily given the right to this scoop? Starting in the fall after 1/19 we
find more and more signs in Mickaël's behavior of what appear to be unmotivated decisions.
In all likelihood, *Porvenir* was chosen because Mickaël had no specific reason to confide in
them.

didn't realize until the evening the film was broadcast.

All that remained of him was his profile among a group of adolescents running around the field and, later, a sullen face listening to the coach's advice before an important game.

He had, as he asserted twenty years later, identified this editing out as the "confirmation" of everything he feared. There would be no place for him. And he presented this humiliating event to the Monterrey paper as the origin of his unhappiness. Everything could have been different if, at fifteen, he'd been in that film, if he'd found someone to refute this feeling that terrified him. If the director had at least called him to tell him he didn't make the final cut, to tell him why, perhaps he might have been able to alter his trajectory. But the Pereiras' phone didn't ring, neither before nor after the broadcast.

And if by chance someone were to point out that this event could not have determined his entire existence, that assuredly it was more complicated, he would shake his head and say that people were entitled to their own opinions. He knew his destiny was sealed that day, following the conviction we all had when we were young that one event determined the rest. One event gave your entire life its shape and tone. After that, various joys and sorrows accumulated, each in its own column, but the overall feeling remained the same. Nothing could ever be changed again.

VIII

AROUND AGE SEVEN, Jeanne, watching Steffi Graf's victories on television, asked if she could go out on a tennis court, a request that her parents saw no reason to refuse. They did start to worry, however, when they grasped the fierceness their daughter brought to the game. Jeanne loved the salutary repetition of the hitting drills, the inviolability of the rules, and the recurrence of the same problems: landing the first service, keeping the ball in on the return, moving your opponent out of position, wearing them out. She also loved the feeling that the perfect forehand shot provided, when you knew even before hitting it that it couldn't be any better, that everything was in the right place, the body positioned so precisely at the correct distance from the ball and yet at the same time so relaxed that the movement of the racquet appeared careless and lax.

Having become a professional, but, due to a weak backhand, limited to second-tier tournaments only, Jeanne reached the high point of her career at the Athens Olympic Games. She was called up to replace the regular partner of one of France's best women's doubles players who was out with an injury. Then, at twenty-five, her winnings could no longer support her. She left the circuit and found a job in real estate. She was never overcome by the least bit of nostalgia afterward. "I wasn't able to compete at the top level anymore and so I lost the drive," she explained once during an interview. All she would say was, "it was a simple life. You knew what you needed to do."

It is well known that Raphael loved everything about her, even and especially her love of tidiness, her tight chignons, and her declared lack of originality or extravagance. At the time he'd told his friends that he'd had enough one-night stands with nutcases who really only wanted to know what the Prophet looked like and were disappointed when he kept his mask on even in bed.

When he offers a profile of his ideal woman for *Elle* magazine in November, you might think you can recognize Gregory's wife—and perhaps Raphael was already in love with her at the time of this confession: "A girl who's at ease with herself, who knows where she's going, who's not at all a character, but rather someone who loves everyday life and knows how to make you love it."

The dream partner—that's how Gregory described Jeanne. Raphael listened without comment to the joyful confessions of his best friend who was never as loquacious as when talking about his wife and the contentment her calmness, clear-sightedness, and faithfulness immersed him in every single day.

Likewise, around the same time the Prophet noted:

On the last metro, a couple on folding seats. They're sleeping, leaning against one another, heads nodding in rhythm. Painful longing to be one of them. And afraid it's too late. There's nobody left, just consolation prizes.

And later in one of the most cited passages of his journal:

Paged through Jeanne and Gregory's photo album from
their trip to Ecuador. They seem to smile at everything,
all the time. One photo came loose. Jeanne, shot three
quarters from the back, her arms leaning on the window of a train. She's tan and in a tank top. Skin soft
and warm, it must be wonderful to hold her, smell her
scent. I wanted to keep the photo for myself.

When he would spend the weekend in the Marville's duplex
in Marseille, Raphael was secretly elated to see Jeanne come
downstairs at 8:00 A.M., baby in her arm, but already dressed
for the day, hair pulled up in a bun revealing her delicate neck,
her eyes subtly made up.

He loved her disdainful frown and furrowed brow when
she'd check her messages on her phone. When they were too
long she would shake her head from side to side, smiling at
him with a half-amused, half-concerned look.

Once, the name of Jacques Brel came up in conversation.
She said he was very handsome, that he was perhaps the greatest
poet of the twentieth century, that no one had spoken about
human feelings as well as he had. Raphael, who had never
particularly liked the Belgian singer's affected diction, found
himself agreeing with her.

He took Jeanne's coldness for self-restraint and her lack of
knowledge for humility. In the beginning, love refrains from
separating the wheat from the chaff.

Everything leads us to believe that Jeanne also liked Raphael
immensely. We don't know what impression he made on her
the day of Marianne's baptism when he introduced himself
for the first time as François Perrin. Gregory soon revealed the
secret to her—this was the man behind the Prophet's mask. At
times Raphael's face took on a sorrowful expression, revealing

he was overcome by sadness. He intimidated Jeanne when, and simply because he believed it, he asserted that Magritte and Dali were overrated, or that out of all American writers Joseph Mitchell was his favorite. Gregory was constantly singing his praises, and Jeanne thought that her husband was never wrong about people.

It is possible she also learned of the evening the two were helping evacuate passengers from a sinking ferry [*On October 28th the Norwegian government called for the 83ers' help. Immense waves had been pounding the Stavanger coast for nearly 24 hours. Rescue workers could not get near the ship. Inside the Silja Star, which had cracked partially open and was listing at over thirty degrees, human beings, reduced to their savage state, were clawing their way, trampling, and killing each other to gain access to the few remaining lifeboats.*], when Raphael plunged into icy waters to rescue Gregory, who had been knocked unconscious by a container that was skidding from side to side on the upper deck.

"It remained a secret. The authorities didn't want anyone to even suspect that one of us could have a weakness, and especially not the Captain," Virginie Mathieu-Brun tells me. "But Gregory was so thankful to Raphael . . . I'm almost certain he told his wife about it."

Jeanne liked to say that her second daughter's godfather was part of the family. She worried about the risks he took, his lack of sleep, and his love life. Despite his occasional amorous conquests, whom he avoided introducing to them, it was obvious he wasn't happy. Jeanne tried to find someone to introduce him to, but her friends who were still single seemed too strait-laced to please this free agent who must desire a less mundane life than theirs. Plus he was a celebrity now. He needed a partner who could shine just as brightly—a singer, the Princess of

Wales, someone exceptional, and in Marseille, she used to say to herself, there's nobody like that.

Many times she made fun of herself in front of him, saying she was unimaginative. If he demurred, she would insist, assuring him she was boring and too uptight. Raphael began to think that she worried about not pleasing him, that his opinion mattered to her.

One day, she sent him a text: "Sounds great for Sunday afternoon. XO." He compared it to the other messages he had received from her. They all concluded, "Warm regards." In this hitherto unseen "XO" Raphael distinguished an urge, a nascent desire. He could see Jeanne's slender, half smiling face raised toward his and could feel her lips pressing against his cheeks a bit more firmly, as if they longed to linger.

As many pages of his journal attest, he now imagined her at home in bed, naked sometimes, her eyes closed. He was almost certain that she made love with her eyes closed, submissively, and he envisioned her with her cool hands pressing on Gregory's neck, her face calm at first, almost resigned to the task, but under the Captain's regular pounding, she tenses, grimaces, and finally overtaken by waves of reckless pleasure, which made her let out little moans, mews which undoubtedly embarrassed her. Sometimes he would place her on her knees, always nude, in front of her husband's rock-hard dick (which he could only imagine as being enormous and triumphant, like an ancient bronze fertility fetish), and he would watch her attentively suck him off, never changing her rhythm, a bit unimaginatively. It was this awkwardness, this desire to do it properly that excited him most of all.

It is not precisely known when he declared his love. Jeanne deleted all of the messages that Raphael had sent her during the time, and the Prophet always refused to describe what happened. We must call upon our imagination.

Ever since September, the 83ers were called upon with increasingly frequency. The successes they racked up—terrorist plots foiled, criminality on the decline, incredible rescues—led the authorities to extend their area of operations outside France. The President, people say, liked to call them "my ambassadors." On a weekend in December, after accomplishing a mission on the high plateaus of Libya, Gregory was delayed by a debriefing. He won't get back until the following day, he explains to Jeanne over the phone, and asks her to please give his excuses to Raphael who is supposed to spend Sunday with them. Raphael comes nonetheless. He is their second daughter's godfather after all.

The late Saturday afternoon skies are stormy, the wind is blowing through the streets of Marseille, and torrential rain is forecast. Jeanne's driving with Raphael in the passenger seat. They're going to pick up Lucille at a birthday party. Or maybe they're on the way home, Gregory and Jeanne's two girls asleep in the backseat.

Raphael has just turned thirty-six. He celebrated his birthday at his parents' house near Fontainebleau. While certain 83crs will insinuate that 1/19 complicated their relationships with friends and family, the Prophet on the other hand asserted from the very beginning of the events that his family was his only refuge. His parents and sisters still don't know anything. For them, Raphael's still that boy who's in no hurry to launch, who lives the way he wants to, "a bit of a poet," as his mother says. At the Zabreskis they talk more about the state of the world than personal issues, and Raphael enjoys returning to his place at the head of the table, where he shall forever be the naysayer to his father, who, mocking, never misses an opportunity to take on the air of the betrayed patriarch. This particular day, however, Raphael cannot enjoy the company, the wine, or the veal roast. He writes in his journal that he became "aware" of his age when, just before dessert, he went outside to smoke a cigarette on the patio with Judith, the sister he's the closest to. Everyone, he believes, has made something of themselves by thirty-six. Not him. He could be indifferent. All it took was one January day for his life to become legendary, but his new status weighs on him more and more. He can't get over the idea that it's as if these last ten years were lost because he was the same person just before his powers were revealed as he was when he was twenty-five, enjoying the same few things day after day, listening to the same music, voicing the same opinions, regretting not understanding anything about market economies and not speaking at least three languages, but without showing the slightest intention of doing anything about it.

The day after his birthday he wrote in his journal: "Don't do things halfway anymore."

Is it the children's regular breathing, this conventional image of innocence which, through its contrast, highlights the hidden torment they were struggling with, or the silence in the car, this silence accentuated by the back-and-forth of the wipers now that the rain is thrumming on the windshield, or Jeanne's hand brushing past him as she switches gears, or, conversely, the obvious care she takes not to touch him, avoiding any movement that might make them forget themselves? Raphael senses inner turmoil. He convinces himself that Jeanne, too, is fighting against this forbidden and fatal desire, but which keeps her senses on alert.

Eventually, he says something. We can imagine that, despite his resolve, it's not terribly clear, whatever it is. Raphael was never a gifted speaker in situations that, like you see in movies, require clarity and confidence. Or perhaps he prefers, out of modesty, to leave things partially unsaid, phrases that express better than others the confusion that passion inflicts upon us.

Whatever he says is intelligible enough for Jeanne to understand that he is in love with her. We do not know how the horror that this confession triggers in Jeanne manifests itself. It is likely that in addition to the feeling of betrayal, of an attack against her husband and behind his back, is the intolerable thought that Raphael imagined she harbored feelings for him, that she was that type of woman—everything she looked upon in disgust: unfaithfulness, weakness of character, romps that never lead anywhere, misery of unbridled desires.

Jeanne grows pale. She's choked with anger. Words of refusal trip over one another in her mouth. Unless, completely to the contrary, she remains very calm, expressionless, because she knows exactly what she shouldn't do at that moment (refute, explain, feel sorry, move one step further into this situation she's being dragged into), and what, in such situations, a woman like her must demand.

Raphael requests permission to take off at 6:47 p.m. and leaves for Paris before receiving a response. Jeanne ordered him to leave immediately. The following day in his journal, without any further explanation, he writes: "Devastated."

Before leaving however, he did get her to agree not to say anything to Gregory about what he just confessed. And, most likely too quickly, Jeanne accepted—contemptuously, haughtily, or on the grounds that what he just did was too despicable for the Captain to hear. But almost immediately she regrets this decision that binds her in a secret with a man whom she now wishes to banish from her life. When her husband returns from his mission in Libya, she can't stomach that he remains blissfully ignorant of what his so-called best friend tried to do.

Most likely she has to lie to him when he asks why Raphael left so early. She now realizes that she's trapped. Either she keeps quiet—but that would require her to become the Prophet's accomplice in some way—or she breaks her promise, but then she wouldn't have kept her word—and Jeanne makes it a point of honor of being, in any and all situations, irreproachable.

IX

THE ONE-YEAR ANNIVERSARY of 1/19 occasioned an immense celebration. Just before nightfall, nearly one million spectators crowded around the Champs-Elysées, hoping to watch the long line of dancers, actors, and acrobats reenacting, in a lavish sound and light show, the highlights of this national epic, through which, after Vercingetorix, Louis XIV, Napoléon, and Jean Moulin, the 83ers embodied a shining new example.

When they appeared far off in the tawny sky, flying in tight formation before passing through the Arc de Triomphe at full speed, a victorious cry rose from the streets of Paris. (Much later we would learn that up until the very last minute Jean-Baptiste and Saïd had pleaded for a slightly less imperious entrance.)

To their memory, the French had not experienced such elation since winning the World Cup twenty years ago. There had been, over the past few years, too many humiliations and dashed hopes to seriously shy away from, in the name of reason and good taste, the pleasure of finally being on the winning side. On the giant stage set up in front of the Eiffel Tower, singers, actors, sports stars, and celebrities appeared one after the other for five hours. Messages of world peace were delivered. The French ideal was evoked. People even went so far as to predict that it would inspire moral progress in other countries.

The President of the Republic himself embraced the seven
superheroes before belting out the National Anthem. He sang
magnificently.

A couple of weeks later, the newspaper *Le Figaro* made public
a news item that had been circulating on the internet since the
previous day: the police suspected Mickaël Pereira's father of
being involved in the trafficking of stolen metal. He was being
placed under investigation. The charges were serious and wors-
ened by the hour as revelations leaked out. It wasn't enough
for the criminal network for which Joe acted as a middleman
between a dishonest scrap merchant (the client) and some
small-time delinquents from his neighborhood (the workers)
simply to rip out copper wire and loot transformers along
railroad tracks. They had gotten into the bad habit of strip-
ping cemeteries in the western suburbs as well. Soon there was
discussion of desecrated tombs, even if this wasn't precisely
correct. Furthermore, the fact that these acts were committed
primarily by the children of immigrants, some of whom were
Muslim, ended up giving this minor local news item the whiff
of a social issue in which such diverse issues as the brutal rise
in copper and steel prices, the monitoring of railway lines,
and the alleged ill-effects of Islam were thrown together pell-
mell with the question of whether Mickaël Pereira could have
remained unaware of the racket his father was mixed up in.

They hadn't seen each other in years. Joe's dalliances and
his increasingly pronounced taste for booze had led his wife to
divorce him. His sons had distanced themselves as soon they
were of legal age. After great hesitation, Mickaël had nonetheless invited him to his wedding. But when Joe showed up at
City Hall with his glum face, as if he disapproved of everything,
Mickaël promised himself he would never see him again. In

September of Year I, when he had summoned the press to reveal his identity, Joe reached out, but Mickaël did not yield. He believed his father wanted money and placed no faith in the affectionate letter, which was the first such message he had ever received from him.

Joe was withering away in a studio apartment in Nanterre splitting time between his poorly paid job at the automobile inspection station and weekend jaunts behind the wheel of an old coupe. His checked shirts and facial features hollowed by alcohol gave him the look of a weather-beaten cowboy, which did still allow him a few amorous conquests, occasionally with very young women who would take him to deafeningly loud nightclubs where he would watch them dance. To keep one of them from getting away, a sales associate he was wildly in love with, he decided to venture into stealing metal after having read an article about it. He knew the right people. It was an easy business and almost without risk. With the proceeds he hoped to improve his lifestyle and "seem like somebody"— these are the words he uttered during his trial. As he could read people's thoughts, could Mickaël have known about his father's activities? Nothing at the time would indicate he concerned himself with knowing what was going through Joe's mind. But he was probably not surprised when he learned of Joe's felonious activities.

He was pressed to clarify his position. The vitriol of numerous commentators, both French and international, deserves our attention here. For it seems obvious that some wanted him—wanted one of the 83ers—to be guilty of something, one way or another. Was it a reaction to the national day of celebration, like some kind of delayed regret after the somewhat overblown enthusiasm displayed that day? I think instead that a sort of rancor, which had been gaining ground since

1/19, combined with the stolen metal scandal, created the
ideal situation for these sentiments to come to the fore. Saïd
Mechbal goes even further: "At a certain point people got fed
up. Especially the media. Too many triumphs. Too much love.
It was always the same thing. No plot twists. Things had to go
south because people wanted something new."

The Secretary of the Interior and the members of Mickaël's
inner circle advised him to publish a statement clearly stating
that he condemned his father's actions. He responded to both
that the affair was none of his business. He was estranged from
Joe, and his reprobation, in any case, was obvious: who for one
minute would think he supported his father? So he kept mum,
which only inflamed the debate. Mickaël became the target of
more and more overt attacks. "His offence? He was from the
wrong side of the tracks," concluded Saïd Mechbal. "He left a
bad impression everywhere he went."

It was in his character to refuse to allow others to dictate
how he should act. Moreover, the sweeping judgments con-
demning his father undoubtedly, regardless of what Mickaël
may have said, ended up injuring his self-esteem.

Several days after the start of the scandal, it pained him
to see that a video of his father had been dug up. A month
after Mickaël had removed his mask, his father was a guest on
an obscure cable television talk show whose theme was "My
Life with the Superheroes." Mickaël hadn't made the effort to
watch it at the time. Parents, childhood friends, and even middle school teachers were invited to tell their stories. Wearing
a shiny, grey shirt with a large collar, which made him look
like a bartender at some hick club, speaking in a version of
French that was even more laborious than normal, probably
because he was intimidated, Joe recounted tender and inane
pseudo-memories of their family life. What the fuck was he

doing on that show? Mickaël now wondered. Was he trying to make something off it? Could it have been that he just wanted to show his pride in being the father of a hero the entire world celebrated?

When, two days after Joe's arrest, his lawyer explained on the national news that the defendant was thinking about his son and bitterly regretted any wrongs he may have inflicted upon him, it definitely wasn't the rugged cowboy with the harsh look that came to Mickaël's mind, but a Portuguese immigrant wretch who'd been thrown to the wolves by people with their sarcastic remarks and unassailable judgments, but who knew nothing of their lives.

With pressure mounting, however, he finally approved the statement that had been given to him. It was only with anger and resentment that he agreed. And this resentment only grew when other voices criticized his harshness and ingratitude. Now that the son was rich, famous, and powerful, of course he had no use for a father who had drifted from the straight and narrow, forced by poverty to turn to petty theft, and whom he had repudiated in a few curt lines.

They were right, thought Mickaël. He should never have given in. This is, moreover, one of the final things he confirmed he couldn't forgive himself for before being neutralized. He was haunted by the idea that his father, awaiting trial in his jail cell, must have suffered after learning that in his darkest hour his son also condemned him. There was no one by his side anymore.

X

JEANNE DIDN'T KEEP her word. She could no longer put up with her husband when he would return from a mission and tell her what Raphael had done, what he had said, and what the two of them had found funny. She felt as if the Prophet notched a victory every time Gregory, through each compliment he paid, reaffirmed his ignorance about what had happened and was in some way strengthening the secret association that linked her to Raphael.

In her heart of hearts she also didn't like what she thought of her husband when he talked about the Prophet. How could he be so blind about a guy who wanted to steal his wife? Jeanne was convinced that Gregory excelled in his position as a prosecutor because he possessed the ability to see deep inside people. He could uncover a hypocrite at a glance. He was never wrong.

When he learned what Raphael had done he went berserk. He talked about maybe calling him right then and there. About going to Paris and punching his lights out. Jeanne was the one who became frightened and had to reason with him. She had betrayed the promise she'd made to Raphael. She still had one regret. She didn't want a scandal. But Gregory was determined. He demanded redress.

Be that as it may, we know that he admired, that he envied

Raphael's consistently measured opinion of people. Gregory himself wasn't like that. He felt he too frequently lacked nuance. So, finding an example in the Prophet, he had been endeavoring for a while to say new things. She's angry at the whole world, he said of a government minister who was always at odds with the 83ers. He's been brain washed, he reminded everyone of a young baggage handler who was arrested just before leaving for Syria. He insisted that even a scumbag's point of view, we had to try and understand it, and it seemed to him that he elevated himself, that he demonstrated great generosity of spirit each time he was able to attain this state of mind.

Consequently, after a few days, he felt bad about his initial reaction. Jeanne was right to have tried to stifle his anger. He knew Raphael well, and his friend must feel terribly guilty. The mind has no power over love. You do stupid things. You lose control. Nothing terrible. In spite of it all, Gregory disapproved of Raphael's actions toward his wife and the awkwardness she felt when he declared his love. All this created an embarrassing situation, what he called a "veil." He and Raphael could no longer be friends like before. He had decided to see him as little as possible. To his mind, the two would smoothly drift apart, like with old friends you don't want to see much anymore and who eventually figures it out.

Jeanne was relieved. That's what she wanted, too. Yes, distance Raphael from their lives, without any drama. Everything was going to go back to normal.

On February 15 of Year II, after a dinner during which he appeared preoccupied, Gregory spoke to her of entering politics. He'd been thinking about it for a while, he declared. Maybe since the very beginning.

At first he had thought of supporting a party or career

politician. But he'd crossed paths with a number of French politicians over the past few months: no vision, no fire, except for base political maneuvering. No one would dare say things anymore like *we must end poverty*. Everywhere was defeatism and half measures, "the more-or-less accepted acquiescence of the world such as it is," as he would soon write in his policy statement. Only cynics thrived in this barren wasteland. And he for one wasn't going to take it anymore.

He ended up convincing himself that his fame, his popularity, his own charisma, and the great hope that the 83ers brought gave him the opportunity, no, the duty, to make another voice heard. Local elections were the only window of opportunity in the near-term. He had to go for it. In Paris, none of the candidates had managed to win over voters. This would be his springboard.

The most well-informed readers, those who have read one of the numerous volumes devoted to the Captain, may perhaps say that I am oversimplifying. In the widely accepted version of events today, sense of duty plays a less important role than opportunism and appetite. Many confirm that Gregory's desire to enter politics materialized much earlier than 1/19. That after his mother's death he was already talking about seeking local election. For some of these authors, it is also obvious that the Captain's speeches, this extremely particular assortment (this hodgepodge, they wrote) of outdated lofty words, patriotic zeal, and, it must be admitted, ingenuousness and imprecisions, was never anything but pretense whose goal was to position him within the growing niche of outraged virtue.

As is frequently the case, I look to those closest to him. Hardly likely to be suspected of deference toward the Captain, Saïd is categorical: "Listening to him, you felt like he was going to save us all. And in my opinion he really believed he could do it." Thérèse states that the day Gregory informed them of his intentions she was struck by his naiveté, "the way he talked about suffering in the world . . . You woulda thought Mother Teresa had just been reincarnated. It's one of the only times I saw him trembling. He was pale, choked up by emotion. It was awkward. I think we all thought that."

Of course you can come to the conclusion that like so many others, Thérèse and Saïd had been deluded by the Captain's shtick. Moreover, you might think I'm hellbent on defending him. It just seems to me that things were more straightforward with him than most people normally say. That his own glory had gone to his head, that cold calculus and even bad faith might have guided his actions, there's absolutely no doubt—who could avoid it? But he really believed it. At least that's my firm belief. He believed in what he wanted to be.

In March the Marville family moved to Paris in preparation for the elections. The other candidates accused the Captain of being a carpetbagger, of "parachuting" into Paris (the expression made him smile, and he set the record straight during a radio interview, "I did jump into Parisian politics, that's true. But a parachute? I left that on the plane."). It was not conceivable for him to campaign in the capital without living there full-time.

Jeanne had never really liked Marseille, but she was of the opinion that continuing to live in the same house, seeing her oldest daughter, even if it was now under police protection, visiting the same preschool, socializing with the same friends as before, that all of these things safeguarded the family from the effects of 1/19. Gregory could be absent for multiple days and risk his life on missions he wouldn't say a word about. He could surround himself with a team of unknown people in charge of his messaging, his workouts, or his travel. He could shake the

Pope's or David Beckham's hand. He could, of course, cleave through fervid crowds in which younger women would not miss the opportunity to smile at him like groupies ready for anything. But nothing would really change as long as nothing changed in Marseille.

And Jeanne must have been reassured to see that Gregory himself made it a point of honor to maintain the rituals of their previous life. He still made dinner while listening to Nat King Cole, swaying his hips to make her smile. He still insisted on wearing, on mornings he was free, old athletic clothes, which he'd kept since he was a student and which she threatened to pitch as soon as he'd turned his back. They refused to hire any help around the house or allow more than one police car to be stationed outside. And they were thrilled to realize that despite the Captain's new life, they were still able to put the kids to bed and eat spaghetti bolognese at the coffee table while distractedly watching a cop show on TV.

In leaving Marseille, Jeanne left her real estate career behind. She had never been very comfortable, struggling to close sales of apartments she herself had no desire to buy. But she missed having an occupation. She had been an independent woman from a very young age. Under no circumstances did she want to become the nice but dull spouse of a national hero.

Furthermore, even though common sense repeatedly told her that her husband couldn't do anything about it, she had difficulty accepting that his new ambitions drew him closer to Raphael, who also lived in Paris. According to one of her closest friends, she in fact ended up sharing her concerns with Gregory. The conversation was painful. He didn't see the problem at all. Was Jeanne afraid of seeing Raphael again? Feeling under suspicion, she responded that she just didn't want anything to do with him anymore. Period. Gregory assured her there was no reason to run into him just because they lived in Paris. The city was huge.

Although he seemed to have lost his composure in front of the other 83ers, the Captain's first outings as a candidate revealed an eloquent man who was in control of himself. At his campaign launch at the Buttes-Chaumont Park on March 22nd, the crowd was thin due to the cold weather and also probably the location, which was unusual for this type of public event. But several celebrities were already sitting in the first rows, including the singer Patrick Bruel. "He's got something that can't be taught," he told a reporter from *Le Monde* the week before. "He's a leader. He's going somewhere, and you want to follow him."

The Captain climbed on stage holding the hands of his wife and oldest daughter. He applauded the crowd at length and then spoke of Paris, traffic problems, and exorbitant rents. Half an hour later, his speech, delivered without notes, had drifted to the future of the country and the forgotten dreams of the French revolution. Levitating a few meters above the lectern, he quoted Mirabeau as well as Bob Dylan ("Heard ten thousand whisperin' and nobody listenin'"). This mixture of erudition and pop culture became his trademark. He was still young and incredibly handsome, nice, fresh, and passionately kind. OUR BARACK OBAMA read the slightly mocking headline of one of the national newspapers the following day. The front page photo showed him smiling, his arms open wide in front of the crowd, surrounded by blue sky. He made people forget politics.

XI

MOST OF MY INFORMATION about what happened near Agadez in Northern Nigeria on the night of April 12ᵗʰ of Year II comes from Thérèse Lambert's accounts. I realize that until now she has remained in the margins of this book, perhaps because I fear not keeping the proper critical distance my story needs when talking about her. The moment has come for me to explain that I met Thérèse before 1/19, during a language study trip she had made to Santiago, Chile in 2004. I remember that her short stature, the thinness of her somewhat stooped figure, and her hair falling plainly down her face, which was swallowed up by an old pair of glasses, gave nothing away of the quick, bookish, and provocative mind she possessed. At the time I wanted to be a poet. She wrote much better than I did, and after reading a few of my texts she had no compunction in handing down decisive judgments that dampened my ambitions. Nonetheless, we became friends. I admired her and was even a little in love with her. This is undeniably one of the reasons that led me to follow the news about the French superheroes so closely, to the point of dedicating most of my journalistic career to it.

Northern Nigeria is what is known as an unstable region,

which means that no one really understands what's going on there. French special forces more or less officially defend the strategic interests of their country there—notably the mining of uranium deposits—against various Islamist fighter groups, separatist rebels, traffickers posing as rebels, traffickers posing as Islamists, and semi-clandestine business networks whose appetite has fueled a laundry list of dirty tricks. It's as if the dryness of the land here increases the nebulosity of the alliances and the luxuriance of the plots, which are so thick even the main players can't always unravel the threads. Jean-Baptiste Fontane and Thérèse Lambert were thus spared an overly detailed briefing before being sent to help free an engineer from Areva, a French multinational group specializing in nuclear power, whom a katiba had kidnapped three months previously and intended to execute. Officially this was in protest against French crusaders in the Islamic State of Azawad, but in reality it was because the hostage was suffering from kidney failure, and it had become too difficult for his captors to keep him alive. One of Jean-Baptiste's assistants supplemented the presentation with some internet research, giving him a folder with twenty or so pages of articles he'd found.

Nothing allows us to confirm, as was later written, that Jean-Baptiste initially refused to participate in the mission—Thérèse herself refutes this version of the events. But the two 83ers did have misgivings about committing themselves. They clearly gauged that the mission could go forward without them, and the special forces officers did not refrain from suggesting that as both the terrain and the operating procedures of the unit they would be joining were unknown to them, it was more for public relations that the two superheroes would be accompanying them. They were the official saviors now, without which any large-scale operation could not be imagined.

Three days before the departure for Niger an argument broke
out between Saïd and Gregory in their HQ's soundproof room,
where all classified meetings were held. Saïd claimed that the
83ers had gradually put themselves at the service of the rich. In
order to justify their salaries and satisfy the increasingly vocal
demands to see them in action more frequently, it certainly
had been necessary to add more routine operations to their
noble deeds and last-hope missions. And Saïd couldn't stand
going out at dawn any more to arrest young dealers holed up
in bad neighborhoods on the outskirts of Paris, where dealing
was the only thing that made any money. They were doing
low-level police work. They were bolstering the establishment.
The Captain freely conceded the point. France needed radical
reform, but he would not accept that their actions might be
equated to defending the "system." Jean-Baptiste was more
on Gregory's side. Saïd's baseless accusations, the bitter jubilation that invigorated him when he railed against their servility
while he, the only one with an unyielding conscience, fancied
himself able to see how things really were—but Number Seven
was paid by the Government just like they were and diligently
carried out all the missions he was charged with—all of that
eventually infuriated Jean-Baptiste. So now, three days later, he
was being asked to neutralize some Sahelian outlaws who most
certainly professed a religious rigorism for which he had no
sympathy, but who also condemned the conditions by which
Areva, and, through its majority shareholder, the French State,
mined uranium in one of the two poorest countries in the
world. Just before taking off, Jean-Baptiste read several damning articles about water reserves contaminated by radioactivity,
open-pit mines from which the wind blew radium and lead
dust over nearby cities, and pieces of contaminated metal that
were found in markets where they were sold as construction

materials. Damning as well were the repeated denials from the industrial group's spokespeople, that mollifying rhetoric for which they were certainly handsomely compensated.

They bolted out of the helicopter while bullets, spit out by a heavy machine gun mounted on one of the farm building roofs nearby, pounded the earth around them. Their night raid had not caught the enemy unprepared, they realized with regret (but was this surprising given that when they arrived in Niamey three days prior, the two 83ers, letting the unit members reach the military base incognito, were greeted in a luxurious hotel in the city center where the best suites, complete with grey granite bathrooms, an on-call exclusive concierge, and a private fitness center awaited them, after which they were invited to dine with a delegation of senior officials where they assured a group of local journalists, who were considerate but not stupid, that they were only in the region to visit the troops stationed there and recognize the authorities' resolution in combatting terrorism?).

With their 40-kilo packs on their backs they ran, darting toward the doors of the fortified farmhouse. Jean-Baptiste, either because he hadn't heard the orders amid the chaos of the raid, or because he wished to prove his worth, jumped on the flat roof to take out the gunner. In a second he was within striking distance, crushing his adversary's carotid sinus with the blade of his hand, just as his instructor had taught him in his Kyusho-Jitsu class. But he didn't see that behind him, despite his fear, a 15- or 16-year-old shepherd armed with an assault rifle was aiming at him. Jean-Baptiste's life was only saved because at that exact second an explosion from below threw them both to the ground.

The farm was booby-trapped. The first French infantryman

who entered the courtyard had just stepped on a mine. It soon became clear that the kidnappers were more fanatics than outlaws, in any case more ready to die than the intelligence officer had estimated during their briefing in Niamey.

Another explosion inside the main building confirmed this. Flames had now engulfed the banco mudbrick facade. Hit in the tail rotor, their transport helicopter was flying away, spinning around on itself. A pickup that had been set aflame (by whom?) was spewing thick black smoke, children who had just been woken were screaming, frightened goats were streaming out in every direction, an airburst grenade exploded behind them, and the assault team leader was screaming on the radio to switch to plan B. Things were not off to a good start, thought Thérèse.

She remembered to the smallest detail the buildings' layout and the maneuvers the special forces had planned. But, like every time she was sent on a mission, uncertainty seized her. Her legs became jelly as soon as she climbed into the Puma's cabin, and a vague and sickening state of weakness incapacitated her as she observed, without really believing it, the combat going on around her. The other superheroes confessed that they too experienced some apprehension at times, but it was like an actor before going on stage. In the field, feelings of elation and the intoxicating joy from witnessing their superiority predominated, which was reaffirmed with every movement, like, when an experienced player in a video game chooses a novice level to rack up points. Thérèse, for the most part, was paralyzed. She registered a whistling noise by her head. Sweat trickled down her sides and then rolled across her thighs. She couldn't move anymore, and the personal coaching sessions she'd been attending for the last six months hadn't changed a thing.

It was patently obvious that her special ability, this capacity to remember everything, for which she was dubbed "Miss Memory"—a nickname she despised, perhaps because the "Miss" unflinchingly highlighted what she believed to be the failure of her personal life—was not the most indispensable of the powers the 83ers possessed. Entertaining and even astonishing, yes, but of limited strategic interest in an era of unlimited data storage and widespread surveillance, when you can reconstruct just about any human being's movements by examining cell tower data, and a drone at 8,000 meters can determine within a 15-kilometer radius the model of a rifle slung across the shoulder of a mujahid crawling on the ground. Thérèse, after spending the day at an intersection in Paris, could describe to you how every vehicle and person that crossed her field of vision looked without a mistake. Entertaining and even weird, yes, but not all that different from what a high-quality camera mounted in the same place could record.

Her other abilities also proved to be inferior to those of her comrades. The diagnostic tests the French superheroes underwent every six weeks bluntly reminded her that she ran slower and that her punches inflicted less damage. The Captain, the superhero who displayed the most impressive physical abilities, had a vertical leap that was 43 centimeters higher than hers and could lift weights that were three times heavier. The only other woman in the group, Virginie, also obtained results that were far superior to hers. As the American reporter Shawn Blanchard, author of the most thorough biography devoted to her came to write, "Lambert was a superhero, no doubt about it. But second tier."

And even if since 1/19 she surpassed the most accomplished athletes, every time she exercised her capabilities she felt she was doing it wrong, that she didn't fit the type. Her parents considered sports an idiotic pastime, one in which you risked injury to boot. She'd grown up in an apartment full of books and political discussions. The boys and girls she'd liked were puny and cultured like her. "You have to believe in yourself," this sort of gurvi, whom she met with weekly, repeated while massaging her scalp. Therein lay the problem: she still didn't.

Even before attending the briefing in Niamey, she had clearly understood that if she were being sent to join this special unit it was precisely because there was nothing for her to do. Watching a squad of over-trained soldiers disarm some bush-league kidnappers didn't present any danger. Her inevitable breakdown would not put those fighting by her side at any risk. The commander had found a concealed landing zone, a sure victory that would unleash a torrent of positive press and would also delay the discovery of what she was—an old maid, she thought, endowed with incredible powers, but too anxiety ridden to ever be able to use them.

She looked for Jean-Baptiste through the curls of black smoke now billowing in the courtyard. She made out a soldier on the roof of the building breaking a weak adversary's arm before leaning against the edge and jumping twenty or so meters toward the burning entryway of the main building. That was him. For a second, witnessing the self-confident magnificence of his movements, she felt a pang of jealousy, which regret immediately squashed.

Of all the 83ers, she liked Jean-Baptiste the most. Their love of reading brought them together, and they had pieced together something like a common history at the National Library where, a few years before he started working there, she'd done research for her doctorate. With Jean-Baptiste she shared the experience of spending whole days in that caliginous building where readers, cloistered away in monastic silence, piled volumes around themselves which they would never have the time to read, and, looking feverish or at times catatonic, seemed like mental patients plotting an escape. Together Jean-Baptiste and Thérèse could draw up a list of everything that had become unbearable to them at the library, from the hand dryer in the bathroom that shot out glacially cold air to the obdurate sniffling of the stuffed-up readers, which social etiquette forbade you from interrupting by offering them tissues.

But more than anything she loved Jean-Baptiste's sense of self-mockery, which never abated. He had changed immensely since 1/19—huge muscle mass, transplanted hair, love affairs exposed in magazine spreads—but he remained, like her, convinced that he was an impostor. They got the wrong person, he claimed. It was Jean-Baptiste Fontang that the Gods of Olympus had originally chosen, and he would make her laugh cataloging the imaginary life of this poor Fontang devil—handsome, brilliant, athletic, and a true patriot, that some stupid typo on the list had deprived of an heroic destiny. "One day or another I'm going to be recalled," he would add.

The Puma helicopter that had dispatched the unit crashed against the side of a mountain. The fireball it emitted when exploding briefly lit up the courtyard, followed shortly by a muffled detonation. When Thérèse looked at the burning building's entry again, Jean-Baptiste was no longer there. She walked around a bit in the courtyard and nearly tripped over the dead body of a Tuareg, whose face, she could see, had been distended by an expanding hollow point bullet. A blackish, clotted substance was leaking from his ribcage.

Horrified, Thérèse crawled behind a row of rusty barrels. Her gasps for air echoed in her ears. It seemed like her chest was being compressed. She felt the air, trapped inside her body, harden like metal and slowly penetrate her skin.

She was going to die right there from suffocation, she

thought, her head heavy and buzzing. After removing the night vision goggles that were affixed to her helmet, she lay down on her back.

Screams and moans, punctuated by the rat-a-tat of automatic weapon fire, kept her apprised of the ongoing strike. Once the nasty surprise of the first act had passed, the French troops got back on the script conceived in Niamey. Arms out to the side, knees up, Thérèse was slowly regaining her composure. Warm sweat was irritating her neck, and she could see herself, as if her eyes could look down at her own body, massive in her combat gear, grotesque and bovine. Captain Franchi was calling on her communicator, but she was afraid that her spasms would start up again if she responded. She listened to the soldiers' chatter in her ear. The hostage had been located. The superhero had recovered him from a hiding spot in the basement. They were making their way through the fire toward the exit (oh, she imagined Jean-Baptiste Fontane, a dark silhouette against a wall of fire, a comic book hero whose outline was highlighted by the red sparks from the flames).

A bit later Captain Franchi wanted to help her stand up. They were now searching the farm, looking for any terrorists who'd been cut off. "You're injured . . ." he said to her gently, almost with embarrassment. Thérèse stood up and noticed large dark circles staining the legs of her fatigues. Perspiration, she thought, ashamed to find herself soaked through with anxiety. Then the pain coursed through her, a burning sensation so intense it took her breath away, before causing her to let out a long howl. That was her last memory of the mission: her mouth wide open with a scream coming out, a scream that she thought would never end, even as she gazed upon Captain Franchi's handsome face right next to her, smudged with soot and eyes widening. I'm awful, she thought, before passing out.

Until the military reports are declassified one day, in order to know what happened next it's necessary to refer to the books published by several of the operation's participants whose accounts are consistent, save for a few details.

The unit's snipers took position on the rooftops where the Tuaregs had been and were keeping watch on the surrounding area. In a corner of the courtyard a soldier had detained a group of about twenty men, women, and children, their hands bound in plasticuffs. The engineer from Areva waited in a chair, wrapped in a space blanket like a runner after a marathon, while from the valley came the rumble of several allied helicopters. They would soon be evacuated.

It appears that Jean-Baptiste was the first to notice, at the far end of the courtyard, still thick with smoke from the assault, a young man emerge from a building, most likely a barn or loft. He was a thick-haired, barefoot adolescent wearing a ripped tunic. His arms were spread wide.

Several days later the hostage would claim that the unknown youth was smiling. But the silent expression of fear frequently pulls the closed lips of the local inhabitants outward, soldiers had learned over the course of their missions. In his published account, one of them even went so far as to guarantee that the young Tuareg was not smiling, that this detail had been invented in order to make what happened next more logical, and that no one had expected it.

Jean-Baptiste advanced, slowly and slightly bent over, his semi-automatic pointing at the adolescent. Several soldiers saw him start frisking the youth—cautiously, they said, but they neglected to note, out of respect for the superhero, that a full body search is conducted by a two-person team, one with his gun trained on the suspect while the other moves in to perform the pat-down.

Some believed that the two men then embraced each other. The two were squeezed together, one against the other, and it seemed as if the young Tuareg was struggling to dislodge something that had stuck in the superhero's combat gear. His right hand twitched as Jean-Baptiste let out what seemed like sigh of fatigue or satisfaction. He fell over flat on his face, having been stabbed.

During the press conferences she gave afterward, Thérèse said next to nothing about the three days in the intensive care unit where they were transported. She would maintain that, isolated in her room, wavering between states of hazy, feverish waking and long periods of unconsciousness, she'd had no direct contact with Fontane.

She would not relate that at the end of the second day, while still intubated, she had managed to enter her friend's room. Jean-Baptiste seemed much thinner. There were dark rings around his eyes. His skin was pale and shiny. It was as if a heavy-handed makeup artist had painted an agony mask on his face.

Agitated, Jean-Baptiste mustered up enough strength to smile at her. His breathing was labored, and his body emanated a sour odor that he himself may have smelled since he said, "I stink of death." Thérèse took his hands and found them icy. The tube down her throat made it difficult for her to speak, so she stroked his cheek and the back of his hand.

She would not say that Jean-Baptiste cried that evening, terrified at the idea that death might take him away. Staring into the distance, he kept running his hand across his face while mumbling that he wanted to see his mother, that he so wished she were still alive. Thérèse would also not relate that from her room the following day around noon she heard him moan and even scream in terror as they took him one final time to the operating room. And if she remained silent about all of that, it wasn't to protect some secret, but rather because no one wished to hear of it. Jean-Baptiste died an hour later. The news was made official that evening.

Funeral vigils were organized nearly everywhere. Vast crowds gathered in all the large public spaces, but also in Bayeux where he was born, along the highway where he had probably attained his powers, and around the Réamur-Sébastopol subway stop he had flown over on 1/19. In homage to Jean-Baptiste's transformations, many put on costumes. From a distance you might have thought it was a masked ball, except for the falling tears. In Paris, among all the candles, bouquets, and children's drawings, anonymous people left DVD copies of the film *A Self Made Hero*. [*The plot had no connection to the 83er, but the title seemed appropriate. In the following days sales skyrocketed.*]

There was almost no space for controversy surrounding the exact conditions of Jean-Baptiste's death and the near fiasco of the operation that saw the two helicopter pilots as well as a foot soldier die and Thérèse gravely wounded.

The tale of the 83er's final acts during the assault, the young assassin's apparently smiling face, and the admirable resolve he demonstrated during his final hours in the hospital doubtlessly helped flame the zeal of these gatherings. It was alleged that on his deathbed Jean-Baptiste made a number of important declarations, mantras that were soon emblazoned in English on T-shirts, coffee cups, and posters: "Life is simple." "Stop overanalyzing." "Do what you love."

To many, it seemed that a man had died whom they'd always loved, who wasn't different from them, who knew how to keep it real. But people at these impromptu gatherings also felt a deep-seated guilt rising to the surface. They'd been savage with Jean-Baptiste Fontane. And now opinion writers were laying blame. Would he have acted the same way if he'd been left alone? Did he not put himself into harm's way as a means of responding to critics who never stopped ridiculing his pathetic attempts to look like a superhero from a Hollywood film? Their columns concluded by deploring the singular modern affliction which consists of burning one's idols, this penchant for denigration that the French, more than any other people, unsparingly demonstrated each and every time one of them rose above the rest.

XII

RAPHAEL ISN'T SLEEPING any more. He's spotted at the most exclusive VIP parties, he drinks too much on occasion, he's in love with his best friend's wife, and he hates himself. It's like some kind of curse, a role he didn't want in a play he can't quit now that the performance has started. To avoid thinking about her he asks to be sent on missions as frequently as possible, tells the future to those who ask him, and goes out into the streets to offer his services to anyone who asks. He wants to work until he can't think anymore. Every morning he hopes he'll wake up cured. The days drag on, brutal and empty, and he keeps checking his phone for a message that she'll never send.

Jean-Baptiste's funeral service forces Jeanne to see him again. At first she thinks she can avoid the ceremony, but Gregory's advisors persuade her that this absence, which will not go unnoticed, will hurt her husband's campaign.

As a million people throng the streets of central Paris, pagan chapels are erected on sidewalks, and loudspeakers installed outside Notre Dame broadcast the eulogies delivered in the nave, Jeanne forces herself to look straight ahead so that she will never see the Prophet, who is sitting, she's completely aware, in the same pew as her, a couple meters to her right.

She saw Thérèse, Saïd, and Virginie crying when she walked

in. Everything bothers her—the faces on the sidewalks convulsing in sorrow, the quaver of the President's voice during his
funeral oration. Her husband remains the most dignified. He
was asked to speak, but refused. During an election he doesn't
want people to suspect the candidate of providing himself a
platform here to give a campaign speech.

Jeanne doesn't know that Raphael was chosen to replace
him. On her right she suddenly discerns a tall figure climbing
the stairs toward the lectern and the bright spot that his mask
makes under the chancel lights, now that he is standing before
the congregation.

As Raphael is searching for words, overcome by emotion,
Jeanne harshly stares at him. Perhaps she is hoping to unnerve
him now, and make him suffer in front of millions of television viewers the same type of distress he'd inflicted on her a
few weeks earlier. But the white mask protects the Prophet.
He doesn't look in her direction. And his voice, strengthening, booms throughout the nave, as if, she thinks in disgust,
he just found some perverse reward—she finally turned and
looked at him.

Now that Gregory has decided to distance himself from
Raphael, Jeanne can give way to her anger. And everything
about the Prophet's personality disgusts her. That self-assur-
ance, that vainglory, the pleasure he gets from remaining a
mystery. How could his fans let themselves be taken in? His
mask seemed to her the most cocksure of them all. Is she
the only one to find the face he chose to present the world
unseemly and even nasty at times?

When the Prophet shares with the crowd that if his ability
to see the future could have saved one person he would have
liked it to have been Jean-Baptiste, Jeanne, bitter, softly clears
her throat. She'd heard him many times in Marseille make fun
of poor Fontane, this guy who was so convinced he was a loser

that all of his choices seemed to be guided by the need to fail.
He announces his marriage with an English actress and three
months later she's photographed on a yacht in Croatia in the
tattooed arms of a former soccer player . . . Now the Prophet
laments: Jean-Baptiste wasn't taken seriously. *I* didn't take him
seriously. *He* didn't take himself seriously. But was that, in
fact, the most wonderful thing he taught us? Jean-Baptiste was
funny. He was honest. He refused homages. He was suspicious
of consecrations.

Jeanne has to sit down. She's suffocating.

Raphael's doing better, Gregory announces to his wife several
weeks later. He's found somebody.

She shouldn't care. She swore to herself not to do it, and
then she looks up Sonja Bachmann on the internet. Former
German model, born in 1990, television host for a period of
time, a jetsetter. Jeanne examines her in photo after photo.
Obviously a boob job, penciled eyebrows, an clear taste for
absurd dresses at photo shoots. About as refined as a porn star,
she concludes. That only confirms what she thinks of Raphael,
she tells one of her friends. Way below the high and mighty
airs he puts on. "He thinks with his dick," her friend opines.
Jeanne laughs, but uncomfortably. She doesn't like that word.

"We should invite them to dinner," Gregory suggests one
night.

He's joking, of course. Raphael with a girl like that, it just
seems so implausible. What do they talk about?

"They probably don't do a lot of talking," Jeanne replies.

At the end of April she visits a friend who just had a baby in
the maternity ward at a hospital near Nation. Noëllie and
Jeanne experienced the hell of life on the circuit together—
stuck, waiting for hours in no-name airports, crappy hotels

with drunk guys knocking at your door in the middle of the
night. They spent entire mornings hitting together, afternoons
encouraging each other from the stands. Yet Jeanne never really
liked Noëllie. She always found the girl a gossip, and not very
clever either.

Since the end of their careers, Noëllie has become increasingly affectionate. She's the first to send Jeanne a birthday
message. She even started calling her "sis." Since for the last
year now Jeanne has arranged things so she doesn't see her or
ever talk to her on the phone for more than a few minutes,
she feels obliged to go to the hospital. Noëllie will be mad
otherwise. In Jeanne's mind, one must be beyond reproach,
even with people one spends time avoiding.

She passes fifteen minutes with Noëllie in an overheated
room that smells like clammy skin and hospital meals. The newborn is sleeping, but Noëllie insists on waking him up. They
take a photo, the baby screaming, apoplectic, in Jeanne's arms.
Noëllie give updates on people they knew—a former player has
become enormous since her divorce, one of the directors of
the Federation is cheating on his wife with a girl who's barely
eighteen. His wife knows, but doesn't say anything.

Noëllie also compliments Jeanne, who has kept in shape
and has never let herself go. Jeanne shrugs her shoulders while
Noëllie repeats it. Just before giving birth, she watched one
of her husband's speeches on YouTube. She'll vote for him.
She adds that Gregory's handsome, that they're so attractive
together, and suddenly tears start rolling down her cheeks.

What am I doing here? wonders Jeanne. While Noëllie
sobs, her chin drooping into her neck, Jeanne mumbles that
she doesn't feel well, and it's not far from the truth. Smiling
weakly, her friend opens her arms for a hug, but Jeanne finds
herself adding that she has to leave because the room smells.
She notices Noëllie's stunned look—need to sort that out

later—but leaves the room without saying another word.

She almost runs across the large hospital lobby area. Telephone wedged between her ear and shoulder, she calls a taxi. There's a cafeteria on her right, with some café tables and a newspaper rack. And there's the Prophet, sitting alone at a table, a plastic cup in front of him.

She would like to believe that this is some fan dressed up like his idol—the white mask is the top seller, by far—but a young nurse walks up to the Prophet, finger pointing at his phone, who appears to be asking for a photo together. And even behind his expressionless mask, Jeanne's sure she recognizes Raphael when she sees his body move, tall and thin, carefully impassive, his large hands clasped on the table, the white oval covering his face tilted slightly toward his admirer.

She froze in the lobby, a hand at her throat. So, he'd started following her. He came all the way here. He waited for her here so that she'd see him when she went by. Jeanne would like to walk right up to him, press her hands on the table, and belt him with an "It's over. Leave us alone," or another one of those thrilling, definitive phrases that would lay waste to him. But her legs are wobbly and can hardly hold her up.

The fact that he's here, here in the flesh, that he's got this audacity and brazenness smacks her with a kind of dizziness tinged with fear. Oh, she gets it. Sonja Bachmann, the grotesque German who'd been exhibited to the public for the past several weeks, was nothing but a lure to make her jealous—which almost worked, she could now admit.

At that moment a man in a suit and tie enters the scene. He joins the Prophet who gets up, greets him, and follows him. They leave the cafeteria.

In the following weeks several newspapers will mention the Prophet's discreet visits to sick children two or three times a month. It's his sister, Judith, a nurse in the hospital, who

encouraged him to get involved. Inevitably, there will be someone on social media who will insinuate that the Prophet is
playing the good Samaritan to make up for his chilly reputation. Jeanne will think that the French are malevolent.

At the moment she feels like an idiot. What's she doing
there, trembling, looking helpless, spying on him like that?
It's hard for her to catch her breath. It seems like the lobby is
vibrating around her, like a painted backdrop that's about to
topple over.

The Prophet and the gentleman walk off. Jeanne's not sure
he saw her. Then he looks over his shoulder, flinches, and leans
toward the other man to say a word. He finally turns around.
He comes toward her.

"What are you doing here, is everything okay?"

"Is that your brother?" she asks, short of breath.

"No, he's the hospital director."

"And Sonja . . . Sonja . . ."

Raphael's eyes must definitely be widening behind his mask.

Panic-stricken, Jeanne steps back, waving her arms about.
She runs off. In the taxi, sobs make her body convulse the
whole way back.

Gregory didn't think there would be so many occasions, but
his campaign needs the 83ers. His advisors are saying it, and
they're right. Without them it's just ordinary, it's just like
what's been done before. When, prepared to apologize, her
husband tells her she should expect to see Raphael in the days
to come, Jeanne makes sure to heave a sigh of resignation or
pucker up her lips in annoyance. Gregory tries to figure out
ways for her to avoid seeing him. Each time she finds good
reasons to be obliged to.

Now, believing it pleases his wife, Gregory makes an
effort to speak somewhat ill of Raphael. It must grate on his

character. Slanderous talk doesn't come to him easily. She listens, nodding her head.

Jeanne and Raphael cross paths at the Captain's campaign office, backstage at campaign events, and at various inaugurations and openings where candidates must be seen. As soon as she arrives she searches for the white mask among the guests. And when she finds him, there's always the same jolt (stupid, she thinks afterward), that turns into a shiver of dread. She lowers her gaze and forces herself to turn her back. On the way home she will congratulate herself on having ignored him.

All I need is a little self-discipline, she realizes. Especially at night when there's nothing to impede her ruminations. She'll be her own judge and will remain unyielding—childishness, empty thoughts that lead nowhere, that's what's upsetting her. But they're just thoughts, she immediately justifies to herself. Feelings, but fluctuating. Torment, but passing.

Now Jeanne's the one pleading Raphael's case before her husband. She'd been too harsh on him. She always takes things so seriously. But. What can we do if. He's over it, isn't he? Gregory concedes; things would be simpler if she pardoned him. We'll forget the whole thing and pretend it never happened.

Raphael and Jeanne reconcile. They exchange text messages. The words are cautious and reserved, always distant. They wait nervously for them. They write "XO" without seeming to think about it.

And Sonja? Jeanne asks maybe one more time. How that name obsesses her, how her vulgarity both vexes and fascinates her.

Oh, the German, she was nothing, nothing but a rebound to get over all this. It would never have worked. She was wasting her time, he ended up telling her.

Now they see each other a bit, with the family at the

Marville's or at the 83ers' HQ. Out of the public eye, without his mask, Raphael reappears. During those moments, Jeanne doesn't tire of examining his face, which remains hidden the rest of the time. His dark hair with thick curls, languid, falling on his neck and forehead, his watchful gaze under thick eyebrows, his incredulous frown with his plump lips—that doesn't do anything for me, she decides. Some women might find him handsome, but not her. And she clings tightly to that idea.

The joy of talking to each other is even stronger than before because they really thought all was lost during those months of contention. She didn't know he'd studied in the US for two years. He listens to her talk about her father, whom she's only seen once since he left her mother. They recall the boredom of being a teenager in the country, and since they've hit thirty, the feeling that everything goes by more quickly.

But it's nothing, Jeanne continues to believe. Nothing but some turbulence. A test, like everyone goes through. Her friends will confirm it. Welcome to the real world, Jeanne Marville. She laughs in shame and relief. She listens to them reveal similar troubles, temptations, some straying from time to time. Most of the time it goes away all on its own. That's what she thought, Jeanne concludes, trembling with joy now that relief is in sight.

In the middle of the night she strokes her sleeping husband's wrist. She listens to him breathing very low right next to her ear. He's the best man in the world, she thinks. She'd like him to take her in his arms and carry her up there, above the clouds. They'd never come back down to this dirty city where everything's a mess. If they were far away from Paris she would forget Raphael, and nothing would happen.

XIII

The Captain avoided going into the details of his platform. They were more or less nonexistent, agreed most observers. But that was also surely related to the fact that his candidacy was an "act of vision," as he himself repeatedly said.

When giving a stump speech he frequently ended up, buoyed by his words, elevating above the floor. His gaze thus extended out over the crowd, and his voice beckoned them toward the world to come. Another France would emerge. In renovated schools, better paid teachers would educate students who would be better understood. The number of people at food banks and in prison would diminish, while hospitals, where new wings would be built, would be hiring. The young would help the elderly, the elderly would like the young. Stupidity and racism would diminish. From the ruins of industry would spring forth clean factories where virtuous objects that are yet to be imagined would be produced. Redistribution would finally take place. And, simply stated, Paris would be the lungs of this new revolution, the intersection, the forum, the beachhead, the beacon.

It's going to be hard, he warned. They won't let us do it. But each generation in France has risen to great challenges. Nazism. May 1968. Abortion and the death penalty. Gay rights. Each generation prevailed. We're going to roll up our sleeves. It's not my campaign, it's your campaign. He would quote Martin Luther King, Jr., Saint-Just, Lou Reed. A beam of light would descend on the audience.

It's all very nice, said a few journalists, screwing up their eyes, but how much is it going to cost us? And what's his plan for public transportation in and around Paris? What's his analysis of rising rents?

There were some hiccups. He frequently got confused when citing numbers, mixing up million and billion. Economics wasn't his strong suit. His main opponents inventoried his inconsistencies and scoffed at Gregory Marville's naiveté. They were old-fashioned politicians, people retorted. Numbers say what you want them to say. What we need are lofty principles. The Captain frequently said: he would provide the initiative, and the experts would hammer out the technical details. France was a rich country, yes or no? We know where the money's at. And to those who underscored his lack of experience, he remarked that the experience of others hadn't really gotten us all that far.

The polls were contradictory. Less than half of those polled believed he could keep all of his promises. But more than three-quarters saw him playing a central role in the upcoming years. And the same proportion were of the opinion that he "inspired confidence," that he "seemed honest," and that he "gave France a positive image." He pleased idealists, young voters, the retired, those calling for new blood, newspaper editors, and even the disillusioned who found his foray into politics amusing, at least.

The team around him was sparse, volunteers for the most part—die-hards, but clueless. The support of celebrities and the 83ers made a major impression, but he's the one people wanted to see on stage. He's the one they wanted to hear quote some rock song and chant "Stronger Together," which had become a slogan.

He lost his voice. Sometimes he stumbled over his words. And thus, out on the horizon, great hopes faded.

One day, while visiting a public school, driving rain pushed the candidate and the press corps that followed him everywhere under an awning. It was never clear whether the words had been prepared by his advisors or whether they just came out, unexpectedly, in a moment of exhaustion. And why did he say it? The most likely answer is he was responding to a new attack: the previous evening a lawmaker from Paris had described him as "abnormal," which unleashed the usual back-and-forth of indignation and then protests against the hypocrisy of those claiming indignation. Did the Captain mean to suggest that in order to really change things exceptional people were necessary? With his habitual conviction he asserted: "Normal people will never be extraordinary."

The sea will never be the land. Fire will not make us wet. Wheels must not be square, declaimed newfound comics on the internet, imitating the Captain's sententious tone. In and of itself, it wasn't a big deal. There'd always been barbs aimed at the superheroes. The idea that Gregory was naive, even a bit of a simpleton, was nothing new. But from that day forward the Captain was under pressure. He was gripped by doubt. Every one of his speeches would be scrutinized. He was advised to stick to scripted remarks. Up to this point he'd convinced himself that he only needed to state with the necessary energy the lucid ideas he defended. From now on he would watch his words when speaking. He would strive to find the right word, the right expression.

XIV

SAïD WOULDN'T SUPPORT the Captain's campaign. Their relationship had deteriorated further since Jean-Baptiste's death. Number Seven had appeared in a march with a group of mourning citizens demanding an investigation of the circumstances surrounding the tragedy. He mentioned the commander's "likely negligence." The other 83ers criticized him for feeding the flames of controversy, and Gregory lamented the fact that Number Seven hadn't consulted them. A meeting was called to smooth out their differences; they left on bad terms.

Thérèse was in a rehab center fighting to recover the use of her legs. She nevertheless published an op-ed piece calling on people to vote Marville. She did it in her own style, always with what may have been a hint of irony, specifically lauding the Captain's "innocence" and "faith."

Virginie appeared next to the candidate at all of the most important events, but she never stayed long. Everything quickly bored her. Plus she was having a tempestuous affair with a former athlete, and the relationship's various ups and downs frequently took her to the other side of the Atlantic.

Mickaël was more available, however no one made any special effort to seek him out—his appearances didn't go over well. Every time he leaned toward Gregory to whisper something in his ear, you wondered if he hadn't just identified some secret thought, some base desire in your mind that he was now divulging to his friend. People felt naked around him.

The Prophet appeared next to the Captain more frequently. Together they wound their way through outdoor markets, shook hands at café counters, appeared on subway platforms, led town hall meetings in gymnasiums and small theaters where their supporters shouted themselves hoarse, and obligingly squeezed next to voters for photos.

Among Gregory's entourage, it was Raphael who offered the kindest words, the nicest messages of encouragement. But at times he also showed disappointment or annoyance. You should have said this. You forgot that. This campaign looked like the others', he regretted. The leaflets, the rallies, the campaign stops—people have seen all that before. At the beginning Gregory welcomed the Prophet's comments. He was insightful, he should be listened to. On several occasions, however, he detected in Raphael's tone an aggressiveness, a flash of exasperation directed toward him. He seems unhappy, he confided to his wife. And maybe Raphael was mad at him too for some reason or another. Didn't Raphael envy him a bit? I've been so lucky, thought the Captain.

It was said that Raphael showed himself to be disagreeable with Gregory because, deep down, he'd always disdained the serious and self-assured hero, or even because he dreamed only of one thing since he'd started sleeping with his wife—making Marville disappear.

After reading his journal, I believe the exact opposite. Overwhelmed by remorse, he intensified his support in the confused hope of redeeming himself. But he also couldn't stand the easy-going flow of their friendship, nor the peaceful smile Gregory flashed when he looked at him, with his pale, blue eyes that perceived nothing. Now, in the cars transporting them toward a street march or a meeting with supporters, the Captain liked to lean his head back, cheek pressed against the seat, and softly talk to him about the fun they'd have after the campaign. He employed a special tone during these exchanges, a low murmur, underneath which coursed the cheerfulness of old friends. Raphael wanted to destroy this. He was picking fights with Gregory to taint their relationship, and without daring to tell him the truth, to get him somewhat closer to it.

Virginie confirms: "Raphael was distraught. Not at all happy." It appears that the Prophet regularly spoke to her during this time. For herself, she was making a considered effort to have better relations with the other 83ers. Her addiction to speed had first given her a scare when one February night she felt herself compelled to borrow a car from someone she didn't know and drive on the beltway around Paris at 180 kilometers an hour.

Since her powers were revealed, she had participated in forty or so missions, streaked across the sky in every direction, had a couple dozen lovers, and shaved a couple tenths of a second off her hundred meters, which at the beginning of Year II she was running at a little under seven. There was now something a little pathetic about seeing professional sprinters clumsily giving it their all to make it under ten seconds. These athletes' performances didn't really interest many people anymore. Stadiums were emptying, and the Sultanate of Oman, which was to host the next Olympic games, had just pulled out. An angered sporting association pointed the finger at Virginie. In particular, they criticized her racing against a Lamborghini Centenario at a charity gala. She made records look ridiculous. She put careers in jeopardy. She destroyed lives. To diffuse the situation Virginie met with the head of the association,

Clayton Moore, a decathlete who had lost his sponsorships, with whom she became infatuated. He treated her poorly. She couldn't get herself to leave him, and no one really understood what was stopping her.

Now, in the various hotel suites where she lived, memories would float back of mundane events from her everyday life with her daughter Emma and her husband Julien that no longer seemed so unpleasant—their overly cluttered apartment in Daumesnil, quiet walks in the park where she'd be annoyed with Julien, so easily amused, circling Emma with his camera or shuffling along in his shapeless, grey coat splotched with stray white hairs while holding Emma's hand. She recalled him falling asleep watching *Dexter*, and, in the inexpensive restaurants they would visit occasionally, concluding after eating too much, "It was basic, but it was good." She remembered dinners with friends where they'd talk about movies they'd seen, and about the day they'd leave Paris for the country to find a simpler, healthier, fuller life.

Her daughter Emma, taking her father's side, currently refused to see her. Devastated, Virginie wanted to convince herself that she had to accept it, that they'd reconcile later. Around her there was now only a self-effacing assistant, a hair and make-up stylist, a wardrobe consultant, taxi drivers, receptionists, customer care representatives, diligent servers, brown-nosers, men who wanted to sleep with her, and the dumbfounded faces of unknown people who recognized her—but no one to talk to.

Virginie sent messages and photos from her phone nearly every day to the 83ers, even to Saïd and Mickaël whom she didn't really like. They were the only people close to her now.

The Prophet didn't tell her the entire truth, but did broach the subject of his relationship with a married woman. Their

hands would touch in the shadows of hallways, in the back-
seats of taxis, and shivers ran through them each time they had
the opportunity to be near one another. This secrecy increased
the buzz of an embrace and the rhythm of their hearts.

Raphael rented an apartment under an assumed name in
a building with two entrances in the heart of Paris located
within the "Quartier de l'Horloge," one of those urban islands
developed in the 1970s, where, in place of the luxury bou-
tiques originally planned for the space, only copy shops, shady
cybercafés, and a couple clothing stores on final closeout survived. The few people in the neighborhood walked quickly as
if instinctively motivated to leave the area as soon as possible.

Their time together was limited, and always went by too
quickly, injecting each day with a stultifying boredom, which
put them in a daze. Assignations foiled at the last minute
caused disappointments, which they treated like calamities,
but radiant calamities. Their secret emitted the intense scent of
storybook romances, of spies. Each encounter was anticipated
with bated breath.

"Except Raphael was stuck with this deep-seated guilty
conscious, which came from his Jewish education," Virginie
believed. The 83er remembers a man on the road to ruin,
gaunt like a junkie looking for a score. "Guilt was eating away
at him physically. But that didn't have anything to do with
marriage or monogamy. He didn't give a shit about any of
that." Virginie figured out that his distress was due to the
husband, a man he knew and admired. "I never would have
thought it could've been Gregory. Everything seemed so simple with them. So laid back. And Raphael, in his own way,
was very honest. He took friendship *very* seriously. He was
literally the last guy I would have imagined sleeping with his
best friend's wife."

Jeanne always refused to comment, but there is no lack of others' accounts. Her former friends seem to all have a precise idea about what she was going through and especially the reasons that pushed her into the Prophet's arms. The number of articles, essays, and forum discussions on this subject is also immense. From this varied catalog the reader will recognize the adulterous woman's typical motives: the desire to put an end to her Emma Bovary-like boredom, escape the Captain's asphyxiating perfection, alleviate the sexual void of their married life. It is obvious that the public reveled in the most sordid explanations, and that they expected as much. Jeanne's beauty itself and her bourgeois coldness encouraged this. Paradoxes derive their persuasive force from the feeling of intelligence they provide to those who formulate them. The model wife, but who's insatiable. It was an obvious and basically irrefutable fact.

XV

FORMER COLLEAGUES SAID Gregory Marville was a poor prosecutor. Despite the time he spent and the fact he remained convinced the opposite was true, his investigations proved to be a mess. He excluded evidence that contradicted his original opinion. He didn't go into detail.

If he did perceive some sign of the relationship between his wife and best friend, he chose to interpret it following his own convictions. There can be no doubt that Raphael's desire for Jeanne, or what remained of it, still surfaced in certain glances, certain smiles that he'd let slip out. But that his wife might please other men and stir their lust, this was an idea Gregory more than tolerated. In the vastness of his happiness, he liked being the object of envy.

In the month before the first round of elections he launched an intensive ground campaign. Spurning elevators and bounding up stairs with a lightness that his out-of-breath advisors begrudged, he would knock on doors, clear his throat, and make his appearance. Sometimes, rumors of his impromptu visits proliferated. People would wait, not really believing it, and this impatience mixed with incredulity gave rise to a number of touching scenes, tears of emotion, embarrassed laughs, small cries of delighted surprise, hands on mouths like an unexpected reveal on a reality show. Photographers and film crews couldn't get enough of these well composed scenes: the superhero illuminating half of the frame while in the other half stood weary-faced Parisians, ghastly as they frequently are at the end of winter—women with dull, thin hair; nervous, rubicund old ladies; dads blinking, looking fragile and child-like now that the Captain's power radiated in front of them.

In the end, he arrived at voters' windows and balconies by flying. He was encouraged to emphasize the spectacular. It better illustrated his promise to embody politics differently. His rivals protested, criticizing his showboating. They cited the interdiction of 83ers flying outside of combat missions. The authorities turned a blind eye to these infractions. They were accused of conniving with a rule breaker. This was only partially true. The President derived no pleasure in seeing this independent rise in popularity.

In order to silence his critics concerning his incompetence, his advisors decided that Gregory would be specific. He announced more preschool openings, new bus lanes and green spaces. In their doorways, Parisians nodded their heads. When asked, they mentioned neighborhood issues and would timidly formulate suggestions for the area, then they would move more enthusiastically to photos, autographs, stories, and finally loud kisses on the cheek when it was time to leave. At moments like this, the Captain seemed bound to win.

The latest polls placed him in a more precarious position than originally thought. It was also necessary to select candidates for the ticket from each arrondissement who would represent his interests. For the most part these people were conscientious, but inexperienced, lacking guile and name recognition. They obviously benefitted from the Captain's

charisma, and he tirelessly put all of his energy into helping them on the ground. However, faced with career politicians who could rattle off an intimidating number of statistics
and who knew the local merchants by name, a way forward
remained uncertain.

The traditional parties now trained their fire on Gregory. As
his past, which was hopelessly virtuous, couldn't be attacked,
as his lack of knowledge of the capital didn't bother anyone
and the charges against his inexperience had had no effect, they
stated over and over that Gregory's life was just too far removed
from that of Parisians. Too different, too strong, too attractive.
This was definitely more cunning. Since he first took to the
skies above Marseille, the Captain seemed from another world.
You can't deny his day-to-day life has nothing in common with
that of the men and women he's talking to. He *flies* to work!
And this had an effect on wary voters, for whom success inevitably breeds suspicion.

One day, as he was leaving a retirement home in the
Belleville neighborhood accompanied on this occasion by
Mickaël and the Prophet, he decided to visit a few nearby
apartment buildings. As hoped for, they came across some
poor people, women, and immigrants, who were all delighted
by this surprise, smiling and committed to voting for the
Marville ticket.

In the middle of this outing, while, galvanized by their
welcome, the Captain was joking with his advisors, a reporter
noticed they had just entered the lobby of a building where a
police officer had been wounded during a scuffle with some
neighborhood youths three days previously, one of whom had
just been released from prison.

"I tried to hit reverse," remembers François Scherwiller, one
of Gregory's advisors. "But too late. Ever since his little gaffe

about normal people, some reporters were waiting for a gotcha moment. They were biding their time."

Microphones extended, a question was asked. Gregory undoubtedly remembered the calls for caution he received after the first incident. According to several witnesses, his smile dissolved and a wrinkle of concentration formed on his furrowed brow.

In France during that era, the correct response would have been: all forms of violence were strongly condemned; the security of Parisians will never be compromised; it was shocking, to say the least, that a judge would grant early release to an individual who was obviously apt to relapse into crime. In France during that era, the following could have been added: we needed to stop finding excuses for the inexcusable; we'd had enough of these scum, these kids who do nothing, and these people who are French in name only.

Instead of which, the Captain mumbled: "It's complicated for them too . . . Living here . . . Constantly stigmatized . . . You have to put yourself in these kids' place."

Later, he had let it be understood that the Prophet's presence, the influence his friend held on him and his pernicious way of wanting to nuance everything, was probably the source of this disastrous response.

It all went very quickly after that. Rather than trying to backpedal, he attempted to justify himself. The right, who already accused him of being irresponsible, proclaimed he had become dangerous. He encouraged people to act out. For a supposed defender of the public order, wasn't that worrisome? So, trying to catch them in a lie, he railed against the illegal encampments on the outskirts of Paris and deplored the lack of authority in families. The left became inflamed: behind his humanistic speeches, he was nothing but a supercop. He thought he could escape the pack by claiming we needed to put an end to old divisions. Right and Left no longer meant anything. The word "depolitification" came out of his mouth. People didn't wait for the other shoe to drop. In every article written about him, besides stating the blatantly obvious, they now created portmanteau words. Celebrities who had supported him were now more furtive. Even among his ardent supporters people were shaking their heads. Poor guy. What was he doing there? His adversaries, dull, but low profile, merely stated that politics needed professionals. It's disappointing, but that's how it is. At this level making it up as you go along is inexcusable, the commentators concluded.

During his last speech in front of a sparse audience he stumbled over his words. It seemed like every sentence was a tightrope on which he wobbled forward.

At the rate that news flies, since he'd been expected to lose for ten days, the elimination of the Captain's ticket on the evening of the first round of voting went nearly unnoticed. It was just a confirmation of how things were bound to turn out. A non-event. A professional mistake no one really would hold against him.

The election didn't captivate many people. Participation was very low. The special election night coverage was constantly interrupted by news bulletins. For it was that same day, June 10th of Year II, around 6:00 P.M., that Mickaël Pereira, depressed after separating from his new wife, unable to endure any more, sick of being who he was, purchased a ticket at the Trocadéro metro station, walked down to the platform, let three trains pass, and threw himself under the fourth.

XVI
"The Naive Years"

SAÏD MECHBAL: The revolution ain't gonna come from these small-time far-left students letting their beards grow out on campus. I hate sayin' it 'cause I like those guys. I really tried to look like them when I was twenty and was bumming around at the University of Saint-Denis. Julien Coupat's my hero. He's the invisible man, not me. But anyway, you're not going to end capitalism derailing trains. The people that can really change things are savvy entrepreneurs in Silicon Valley or billionaires seeking respect. Even today I can't stand hanging out with them. Their clear consciences, you know, it's kind of sketchy. I have trouble believing it. But their actions, you have to admit those guys sometimes do great things in spite of themselves. The ruse of history . . . that's what they call it, right?

I don't really see how you make the link between your participation in an advertising campaign and some revolutionary project . . .
'Cause just the idea of advertising blocks you mentally. Saïd starts hawking some food product, that's just wrong automatically.

You were quite well paid for that advertising campaign.

So what? What's the problem with that? The money I got, was it stolen? Was it dirty? If you've got proof of that, okay. Otherwise, you need to stop your two-bit anti-wealth morality. What I'm trying to tell you is that Ambrosia was revolution in action.

[*That day—this was the second series of interviews he granted me, this time in Nizhny Novgorod in an even more outrageously luxurious hotel than the Kinshasa Grand—Saïd and I discussed his personal involvement in the commercialization of Ambrosia, a meal replacement product developed by a university student from California by the name of Josh Quanton. This product, combining rice protein, oatmeal, maltodextrin, canola oil, and several dozen other chemical ingredients—zinc, magnesium, folic acid, vitamins, etc.—which meets all of the human body's nutritional needs, had the goal of nothing less than replacing all other forms of food.*]

Was Josh Quanton aware of the revolutionary significance you attributed to Ambrosia?
What he liked was the idea that with Ambrosia you would save money and time. When he started making it himself, ordering raw chemicals off the internet, he reduced his food budget by 80%. It fell to 50 euros a month. At the time he was a broke college student, but he was also a workaholic. He was finishing his thesis in biochemistry, and what he liked in the Ambrosia project was the act, the simplicity of it. By adding water to the nutrients and shaking vigorously—don't even need a blender—in three minutes you've made yourself something to eat that will sustain you for the whole day. Way better than choking down a frozen pizza.

Except it had no taste.

So what? You'd rather have the kind of dead rat taste that McDonald's leaves in your mouth? I for one saw that kind of criticism coming from way off. Especially in France. It doesn't take long for someone to pipe up and explain to you, thanks all the same, but food is a way of life. We're not going to sacrifice that, blah, blah, blah . . . And I was happy people said those things 'cause they let me get to the heart of the matter. How much does it cost today to eat good food, to eat healthy? Fresh fish, chicken that's not factory farmed, good vegetables, who has access to that stuff? The so-called gentleman who tells you about his latest meal from some big-time celebrity chef, who's happy with himself because he's under the impression that eating well is like going to a museum, it's proof of his class, his refinement . . . Now how much did he spend? What does the proof of his refinement cost? Sixty, one hundred, a hundred and fifty euros? That's the problem right there. For the poor, and even for large families that aren't that poor, all that's left is the supermarket shit—saturated fats, fruits packed with pesticides, nasty orange juice, stuff that's been tampered with. It doesn't taste good, and it's not good for you. There's your refinement. Ambrosia signaled the end to all that. Now poor people could eat decently, so their health care costs are reduced, and they could save money for other purchases. A revolution.

But did you seriously believe that people could stop eating regular food?

Josh did. 'Cause him and his buddies, that's what they did. Each day they drank their bottle of Ambrosia and that was it. And they were in amazing shape, really. Now I thought that, on the one hand, there'd still be relaxing dinners now and then, nice family meals for the pleasure of being together at the table and eating, because I won't deny that it is a pleasure sometimes, and then on the other hand, 90% of the time, Ambrosia. Lots of people made fun of the project because, obviously, explaining to people that food's going to be eliminated, that made Ambrosia more disturbing. That made us these kind of food Nazis.

How do you explain the project's failure?
First off, there was the proportioning error with the first batches released. [*In the first packages of Ambrosia sold to the public in May of Year II, the sulfur quantity was too high.*] And you know, as much as I may be a conspiracy theorist, this was an error, not sabotage. It was an epic fail, and since the press was already pretty set against Ambrosia, the effect was disastrous. Customers were farting all day long, and farts like that, excuse me for getting into detail, but they're really unbearable. You can clear out a whole movie theater in less than five minutes. I stayed at home for three days and didn't see anyone. Also, deep down, man learned to chew meat millions of years ago, or put berries or roots in our mouths. It's not a habit you're going to stop just like that. You can keep telling the public that it's not milk that they need, it's the lipids and the amino acids that milk contains. Culturally, like bread, it's some kind of need . . . People need their hit. I was very naive. Like Gregory, who was totally convinced he was going to change how people did politics. It was, let's just say, the naive years in the history of the French superheroes.

What's your diagnosis of Gregory and his unfortunate municipal campaign—error or sabotage?
What's certain is they basically succeeded in planting the idea

that he wasn't playing his part, that he didn't belong there. Superheroes are great, as long as they stay in their place. I never believed in the man, his Moral Father bit, the grand speeches, but out on the campaign trail, I almost want to defend poor Marville. Everybody made things hard for him. 'cause the established order didn't want the 83ers. Would he've changed the world? No way. He was a social-democrat, a nice moderate. But with his head at the top of the ticket, mayor of the capital, a guy with no party affiliation, that would've stirred up some real shit, that's for sure. The other parties knocked down, the rules of the game totally changed . . . The ruse of history, once again. I would've liked to have seen that. Except stuff like that don't ever happen. Ever.

There won't be a revolution?
Riots, maybe. More and more acts of violence, but isolated, suicidal, like the mass shootings in American high schools. No rising up around some common goal, no. We have to speak the same language to create a goal. And we lost it. Or it never existed. I don't know. In any case, when we talk, we don't really hear each another. We don't understand each other. Community doesn't exist anymore, only coexistence. In areas that are more and more isolated. In relationships that are more and more strained.

So is there anything left one can do?
Besides seeking pleasure, I'm not sure . . . Seek pleasure with the time that's left. Enjoy it selfishly before the end of the world. At least that's what I've decided to do. In the court of public opinion I've become fat and vulgar with all my dough, the Cadillac Escalade I gave my brother, the 3,000 watt sound system, my girlfriends who look like hookers, my friends who

are oligarchs or warlords. I've shaken Vladimir Putin's hand.
I almost married Shevchuk's daughter [*Yevgeny Shevchuk, former President of Transnistria, or the Pridnestrovian Moldovan
Republic, an autonomous territorial unit to the west of Ukraine*].
I offer my services to police states. I'm a pariah. Fine. If you
prefer Barack Obama, if you'd prefer to convince yourself that
Good is on the side of the Americans, that drone assassinations
approved by Obama don't exist, that the way American capitalism is fucking up the planet isn't really all that bad, that its
intentions, or appearance of intentions, count, well good for
you. I think there ain't much difference between any of 'em.
And I don't think our actions really matter, in the end. I just
don't believe it anymore. So now, yeah, I do commercials for
whisky and cars. I take money where I'm offered it. And I do
the best I can with my free time. You got a problem with that?
I don't. You think it's because of people like me that your life
sucks? Good for you. If I can do that for you, if being your
scapegoat helps you put up with who you are a little better,
I'm sincerely delighted. It's proof I can still be of some service
to my fellow humans.

PART THREE

XVII

AMONG THE SCREAMS of horror, gasps, and vomiting, some witnesses glimpsed, as he got back up, his face dripping with blood, his stomach ripped open, and an arm that had not quite been severed hanging from his side. Others swore that nothing had happened to Mickaël, not the slightest scratch, when he took off running down the tunnel. Later a surveillance camera would confirm this: only a few seconds after his suicide attempt, his body had regenerated.

During the hours that followed, people looked for him in the subway tunnels, and his presence was reported in multiple locations. A dozen or so dumpy, brown-haired Parisians must have been apprehended erroneously because of this unorganized search.

Saïd was the 83er who got along best with Mickaël. He was asked to assist. Based on his latest diatribes against the authorities, people feared he would refuse. There was great relief when they learned that within the hour he would be taking off from Miami, where he had taken a few friends from his old neighborhood to party with escorts. He wanted to avoid the worst with Mickaël, but it's also likely, while he was preparing to take his case before the court (with his legal advisor he was already contemplating a means of breaking the exclusive contract that held him, hands and feet tied, at the disposal of the French State), that he had the good sense to show himself beyond reproach each time he was solicited.

Around 10:00 P.M. Mickaël set himself on fire and jumped onto the beltway around Paris, where a delivery truck hit him. Half an hour later he was swimming in the Seine and diving underneath tourist boats, whose passengers testified that he had responded to their greetings with insults. At midnight, beaming, he jumped head first from the top of the Eiffel Tower.

What's he trying to tell us? wondered expert superologists, psychoanalysts, and public intellectuals who'd been invited on various television shows. Yet at the same time, fearing other mentally unstable actions, the chief of police received the order at midnight to apprehend him.

After smashing to the ground at the foot of the Eiffel Tower, his face still swollen from the impact, Mickaël snatched the cell phone of a young, horrified woman, curtly chastised her for not having filmed his fall, and took a selfie, his fingers making a V-for-victory sign in the foreground. He immediately tweeted it with the caption "IMMORTAL!!!" He then stopped a car on the Quai Branly, took control from the driver, and disappeared again.

In the early morning, a news flash announced his death. This was soon refuted. A source close to the investigation had only stated that the 83er had given no sign of life since the middle of the night.

What was he being accused of exactly? objected those who were outraged with the manhunt and the frenzy surrounding it. He hadn't hurt anyone. In the parking lot of a far-flung suburban service station where Mickaël had left him, the driver of the car taken near the Eiffel Tower had just been found. Although groggy, the young man was completely ready to recount the 35 minutes he spent with the superhero—a moment of incredible intensity, he said. They had hardly spoken, however. Mickaël proved himself to be gentle and understanding. The driver stated that he was very happy to have let him borrow his car. He now wanted to give it to him.

It was revealed that there were reasons for concern after all. The general public would discover, as frequently happens in these situations, that inside sources were in the possession of information, which they had deemed prudent to withhold. For several weeks Mickaël's behavior had proved to be "dysfunctional," an article published mid-day on the *Guardian's* website claimed. Several times the 83er had withdrawn from crucial missions without giving any reason, sometimes without advance notice. At sea on a long-distance patrol, the submariners aboard the *HMS Vanguard* had the surprise of detecting his presence 400 meters below the surface on the hull of their ship, where he carved, using the special brand of humor he loved, the words, "MICKAËL WAS HERE." Over the past three months he had gained eight kilos. He was probably on drugs. And they especially suspected him, in addition to being able to read the thoughts of others, of now being able to direct them. His gifts had not stopped developing.

Emmanuelle Mercier, the legislator who left anonymity behind after describing Gregory as "abnormal," had become the champion of all those in France who felt the superheroes represented a threat to their security. A poll indicated that 28% of them already believed this before Mickaël jumped in front of the subway train at the Trocadéro station. Mercier railed against those who "knew"—the ministers and the President, the journalists, the magistrates. They had let an unstable person free, and he was out of control. Quoting Montesquieu out of context, she concluded that absolute power corrupts absolutely. In this way she was voicing general opinion: Mickaël's powers made him go off the deep end.

He was located. Thanks to the markings on his car and an analysis of video recordings from the highway system, it was possible to follow his route to the commune of Trégastel in the Côtes-d'Amour department, where Mickaël forced entry into a seaside cottage without knowing precisely why. Two British expats were living there, a mother and her son, who woke up when Mickaël entered. He ordered them to remain in bed and close their eyes. But the command had no effect on the boy, who didn't speak a word of French. Mickaël knew it. This was the limit of his powers of suggestion. He had unsuccessfully tried to obtain the favors of some Brazilian dancers he'd accosted several weeks earlier in Praia do Sonho. In order to be obeyed, he had to be understood. So he tied the boy up, typed "anglais tais-toi" on a laptop he found in the living room, and repeated "Be quiet!" with his very mediocre accent until the boy understood him and submitted.

Seated near the window, the superhero gazed at the sandy beach, flooded by drizzle in the gray half-light. The tide was low, exposing rocks with dull forms among puddles and patches of washed-up algae. From his observation post, behind the thick window that salty sea spray had left constellated with pale spots, the immobility of the landscape seemed more complete and its silence more painful. Every now and then, one or two silhouettes would appear in the distance, lingering on the rocks or pointing at them, engaged in some thought, headed toward some adventure. And Mickaël drifted off, vaguely stunned by such immense tranquility.

Five hours later the house was surrounded. Two helicopters were flying above the coastline, and elite snipers were lying in position among the surrounding dunes. A negotiator approached. He and the 83er parleyed for several minutes through a closed shutter, then he came back to the police chief to tell him that the superhero was demanding a biographer.

For the past several years in the neighboring commune of Perros-Guirec lived Hugo Desprez, a young history professor and author of three science-fiction novels. After some information was collected regarding this person, he was deemed reliable. He entered the house with a laptop computer equipped with a hidden microphone, a secret camera, and even an explosive charge, which he only learned of later—given that Mickaël could read people's thoughts, nothing could be said to Desprez of the maneuvers underway.

The 83er didn't seem incoherent or agitated, as had been occasionally reported. Hugo Desprez remembers the clammy handshake and dark rings under the eyes of a man who seemed exhausted. Mickaël claimed he hadn't slept for twenty-nine days, which was probably false, but he liked to appear superhuman on all levels. He wished to take stock before getting some rest, however. His life, he confided to Desprez, had grown dimmer by the day. "Like all lives . . ." he finally added.

He pursed his lips with doubt. Perhaps he suspected that what he'd just said was trite or debatable. In any case, Desprez was struck by the frequent signs of indecision that interspersed his remarks—puffed out cheeks, lifted eyebrows, unfinished sentences riddled with ellipses. "He seemed completely adrift," summarized Desprez in a steady voice. [*When I meet him—by his invitation we meet at his house to recollect this episode—he seems to have come out of his relationship with Mickaël unscathed. His face, a bit fuller than before, exudes a feeling of solemnity and control, but to hear him talk about the life he's returned to as a more-or-less anonymous faculty member, it's hard to believe that for four weeks he was the person closest to the 83er.*]

Mickaël explained that he needed someone to help him

put some order in the chain of events, starting from the very beginning, maybe—he refused, we know, to consider 1/19 as anything other than a station in the strange and unfortunate journey he'd been allotted by some superior power, perhaps God, or the hand of destiny. And, just as ancient kings retained official chroniclers, Mickaël wished that some sort of remunerated journalist would follow him from day to day.

"That's when I understood that he wanted to live, that he had plans," Hugo Desprez stated. "Even if I believe that, in his mind, things were still rather confused, kind of all or nothing. Either he would find a way to die before the end of the day or he would accomplish great things, feats for which he wanted to have a fairly trustworthy observer at his side."

At no time did Mickaël enter his mind, Desprez assured me. That day they spoke of long-lost ambitions, tacit abjurations, and lives that were failed without people realizing it. Mickaël unbuttoned his shirt and showed him the rounded shape of his breasts and thick torso. He wanted to explain, through these extra kilos, something that according to him went beyond the problems of being overweight. "But it wasn't very clear that day. It was better defined later," Hugo Desprez remembers.

This conversation was the beginning of the *Lightness Pact*, for which Mickaël would formulate the precepts over the following days. By aging, he pointed out, humans get weighed down in every sense of the term. While their bodies became these abdominous masses that were increasing difficult to move (it's in bed making love that one most realizes this, every movement requiring an effort, eliciting a sigh, leaving one to lament the layer of surplus flesh in which one is trapped), their minds became stuffed with morose ruminations, arrested judgments, or more rarely, sagged under the conviction of their own importance. Why did our laughs no longer produce the same ethereal sound? When did we give up scampering around in the grass? What happened to the feeling of weightlessness that lifted our souls on carefree days? People wanted to rid from their minds the idea of living like cattle. It ended up imposing itself on us.

Around 11:00 P.M., following a police request, Mickaël allowed the mother and son to leave. The Prime Minister hugged them in front of the cameras. Someone started to applaud, which was immediately echoed by the emergency responders, the police, and even a few reporters. But boos covered this up, bursting from the beach parking lot where the crowd of gawkers had been cordoned off.

Now and then they had crossed France to gather along road barricades where you could see nothing but the comings and goings of a few silent police cars. It was a diverse group of neighbors, retirees, student activists, busybodies with binoculars, libertarian bikers, teenagers sporting T-shirts with the slogan LIFE IS SIMPLE who were skipping class, and street vendors offering fries, doughnuts, crepes, and small bottles of water. Many had come to show their support for this superhero that some wanted to take into custody. Very few of them could have claimed a long-standing affection for Mickaël, but they had probably been shocked by his suicide attempt in the Paris subway, and now that the police had surrounded him, it once again seemed to them that justice would be ignored. Others, however, worried aloud about the 83er's deviancy and hoped he would be captured. On both sides tempers flared.

The applause that greeted the mother and son's release triggered the hostilities. Kept up to date on the events through their phones, the pro-Mickaël camp remonstrated with the journalists and their biased reports. Why were they talking about "liberation?" What was really known about what had happened inside the house? Who could say that the 83er had mistreated anyone? The anti-Mickaël camp refuted these arguments, and fists flew. Barriers were knocked over. Police retreated as well-organized demonstrators pelted them with various objects while using burned out cars for cover.

A unit of the CRS riot police had to be deployed. On television, a constant loop of armored police and rioters whose faces were hidden by scarves evoked incidents that were thought to be limited to Paris and its outskirts. To this were added distressing views of motorhomes in flames and retirees crying in a fog of tear gas. The Côtes-d'Amour are burning, announced the news updates.

Desprez received permission from Mickaël to use the bathroom. There he was able to communicate with the police. [*For reasons of strategic confidentiality, he is not authorized to explain by what means.*] They reminded him that he was in danger and that he could mention the late hour as an excuse to ask Mickaël's authorization to leave. "Not one single second did I think they'd launch an assault. It's weird, because that's actually how it usually ends. But maybe I was under Micka's influence so much already, so at ease talking with him . . . I imagine that everybody thought the same as I did—they'd leave him alone. They wouldn't dare upset him."

Hugo Desprez walked up to the 83er, whose tired eyes were fluttering. He asked if he could go home, and Mickaël smiled before walking him to the door. He should go get some rest, yeah. Tomorrow would be a busy day.

Finally alone in the house, Mickaël turned on the television. He saw demonstrators dispersed, police in riot helmets, and the horizon, red and yellow with flames, behind special correspondents. Perhaps this gave the 83er, as people have said on occasion, the feeling of having the masses behind him, of being wanted.

He would later reveal to Desprez that at that point in the evening he no longer really understood what had brought him to this location on the seashore. The events of the previous evening formed a blurry and fragmented sequence in his mind. Transitions and segments were missing. Julie, his second wife, had called in the morning to tell him that, after the trial separation they had agreed upon to think things over, she would not be coming back. He had, which he never did, taken out a notebook to jot down what she said right then and there: *she loved him. It was too complicated. All her life she's been hounded by regrets. It could've worked. She had to piece herself back together. Ending their relationship seemed like the only solution.* How had he reacted? Did he really try to change her mind? He could only remember the words she'd said.

Afterward his cheeks burned, and he cried for awhile, his head in his hands. Then a torpor overcame him. And it was toward his first love that his thoughts led him. She was the one, Fanny, the Fanny from when he was fifteen, whom he never should have left. He looked on the internet to see what had happened to her. One single photo, too small and blurry if you enlarged it, revealed that she now had short hair. She worked for the Ministry of Transportation, according to LinkedIn. She hadn't changed her name. She wasn't married. Perhaps happiness had escaped her, too. He could have her brought here, and she would lie down next to him. She would lie her head on his knees, and they would love one another like long ago.

He remembered the little trailer behind Fanny's parents' house, where they'd slept during the summer. All night long they would rub against each other. They would sigh with pleasure, half asleep, and would wake up around noon, soaked

with sweat and heads heavy. The scent of patchouli perme-
ated everything, including the books and CDs she would lend
him. The books, he didn't open. The CDs, yes. She listened to
Renaud, Bob Marley, Noir Désir, and Manu Chao.

Having decided right then and there to rekindle their relationship, he made a few calls and eventually secured Fanny's
number. Life is full of surprises, he thought while contemplating this wonderful series of numbers that would erase all this
lost time. A lump in his throat, he left her a warmhearted message (*He'd thought of her this morning*). Twenty minutes later in a
new message he was more specific (*Was she free for coffee today?*).
The third time, as Fanny didn't pick up, he tried to express his
disappointment (*She had decided to ignore him. Fine*).

She wouldn't call back anymore now. And to make her love
him would be excruciating. He'd have to force her.

Before walking down to the subway platform he spent
the afternoon watching YouTube videos of his adolescence.
A melancholy enveloped him, which seemed to come from
far away—from old humiliations, mistaken expectations, and
changes that never happened.

Toward five o'clock in the morning, the decision was made to
neutralize him. Scenes of the burning parking lot had brought
consternation all the way to the highest reaches of government.
It became imperative to act before daybreak and the cameras
returned.

At no time did anyone attempt to obtain the maniac's surrender. Mickaël, given the state he was in and his behavior over
the last several months, would refuse any cooperation. But after
they had reached the south wall of the house, the first three
members of the strike force turned toward their colleagues, laid
down their assault rifles, removed their balaclavas, and froze,

arms down to their sides, eyes ahead with a neutral expression, mouths partially open—department store mannequins.

Rather than joining them, their two colleagues pointed their guns to the sky and emptied their clips without a word. Behind the police vehicles, officers started to undress. The reporters, alerted to the situation, phoned their producers: are we filming this? are we broadcasting it? Then in turn, they fell under Mickaël's control, who ordered them to stop speaking and disrobe.

Police officers set their vehicles on fire. Once naked, they held hands and slowly circled the pyres. Their features were hollowed, their eyes bulging slightly staring straight ahead as if they were unbelieving. A menacing chant came from their throats. Low and very drawn out, people recognized Darth Vader's theme from *Star Wars*. Mickaël had already shown his penchant for dark humor. He would soon offer other examples.

Amid this chaos, some minds proved to be impenetrable, hermetic. The 83er had no sway over them. They were free to act. Among the strike force, two members, Julien Brard and Gauthier Corduroy, conferred behind a vehicle. They were two young, exceptional officers, valiant beyond reason, who were determined, as much by their moral sense as by their taste for action, to put Mickaël where he couldn't do anyone any harm.

They skirted a group who were singing and coughing in a circle around a tire fire and then crawled along the side of several CRS transport busses that had just been set aflame, their windows exploding like spattering fat. Having spotted their advance, Mickaël dispatched two pugnacious officers in their direction, whom Brard and Corduroy took care of after several minutes of intense fighting on the ground. By some miracle they finally rolled into a ditch, just as a machine gun was activated behind them and started firing.

They were only 20 meters or so from the house Mickaël occupied when, alerted by some metallic grating, they turned their heads and saw four flaming police cars rip themselves from the ground. The officers were overcome by fear. Slowly, hoods pointing downward, the vehicles cut through the curtains of smoke to head toward them in procession, like they were being pushed by the hand of an invisible Titan. Soon these creatures of metal and fire were swaying while turning above their heads, motors rumbling. And so, brought back to reality, Brard and Corduroy lay down their weapons, spread out their arms, and kneeled head down on the ground to clearly show their surrender.

XVIII

XAVIER FISCHER, presidential advisor[1]: Devastation. Fear. An immense fear. And not even the shadow of an idea. That's what I remember of the first day.

STÉPHANE HUYGHE, Director, Central Operations at the Central Directorate of Interior Intelligence (CDII): We thought of killing him right away. But technically, how would we do it? He could reconstitute himself. We knew what wouldn't work: a bullet in the head, stabbing . . . That would irritate him. That's all that would do. So, starting the following day we explored two directions: poisoning and pulverization. But it remained very speculative. We had no idea what might work. The President simply told us: "You have to try something."

CÉDRIC G, salesperson: The twenty-seven best days of my life. I should be ashamed to say it, with all the hell that broke loose like nobody'd ever seen, except in disaster movies—cars abandoned in the middle of the road, people fleeing to Germany and Spain, streets full of trash super quick . . . Panic. That's for sure. Even us, we'd flip out sometimes. Starting on the second

---

[1] I have indicated here the profession or post of the interviewees at the time of the events.

or third day you'd see these gangs looting stores, going into apartments, waiting in front of makeshift roadblocks for cars. Obviously people got out of control. But at the same time, being able to do whatever, not out of spite, but still sort of whatever, was amazing. For us too, I mean. We could do it, too. You get it? With some friends we'd found a deserted airfield out east of Paris. We forced the lock to go in at night with our cars. The runway was about 600 meters long. We turned off our headlights and put the pedal to the metal.

MATHILDE HENRY, Deputy Public Prosecutor in Bobigny: The lowest-level perp who got arrested looting a supermarket would put his hands up and declare that Mickaël had manipulated him. Same thing with the violent ones. They were all under his control, if you listened to them.

JEAN-PIERRE GUYARD, President of the association Eyes on Power: The President's address to the French nation, that's what I'll never pardon Mickaël for. You can tell me he did much worse. That there were deaths that, directly or indirectly, were his fault, plus the damages that cost billions of euros. But what he inflicted on the President, wreaking havoc on his speech, making him stutter, making him say those absolutely salacious things, sentences that made no sense, it was in such bad taste, so gratuitous . . . Through the President, he chose to humiliate the entire French nation.

HUGO DESPREZ, Official Chronicler: He'd always been clear about this. From the first day he said, "I'm going to be an African tyrant." He wanted it to be like that, a huge farce, something rather excessive, and in fairly poor taste.

CONSTANCE HELTZ, researcher in political science and author of multiple articles on the Twenty-Seven Days: Still, there was a vision, a kind of program. Later, of course, you can say that his pact was kind of nonsense because it was unlike anything you could recognize. But if you closely analyze the decrees he passed in his New Republic, it's rather coherent. Required gymnastics courses, free liposuction, projects for factories to make hang-gliders and hot-air balloons, the kite as the national symbol . . . It's all organized around an idea he's formulating on a fairly rudimentary level, which he's trying to implement in nearly every area. A problem has been identified, weight, and reforms are imagined to correct it. Lightness becomes his social project.

EMMANUEL DREYER, lawyer, founding member of the French Heroes Defense League: And in the middle of all this, he still promulgates several revolutionary decrees, like the pure and simple elimination of inheritances. No more passing wealth and property down. The State recovers everything that's left when you die. What Mickaël called "posthumous socialism." For the first time in France everyone will be born equal. Now you'll tell me there are still differences—more educated families, cultural capital that will continue to be transmitted from parents to children. Okay. But there's still more equality than before. As long as inheritances exist, as long as there are people who only have to be born in the right place with their family name and a good bank account, democracy remains a fiction. With Mickaël, it was all going to start for real.

BRIEUX FÉROT, reporter for Super-H: Sure, so he asked legal experts to work on a new Constitution, he signed tons of decrees, he had official letterhead printed, but in twenty-seven days, he didn't have time to get very far. Nothing was put into action. And even if it had lasted longer, I'm not sure he really wanted to go beyond his declarations of intent. At no time did he try to control the country. Paris and the departments surrounding it became a kind of chaotic no man's land, lots of people fled the country, and the government took refuge in Bordeaux, but if he'd wanted to, he could've imposed his law everywhere with cops and soldiers, whom he could have easily taken control of. He also could have eliminated, or at least tried to eliminate, the President and his adversaries, starting with the 83ers. But he didn't do any of that. I think what got him off, on a fundamental level, was to be in the "Salon des Arcades" in the Paris City Hall, gaze upon his court, and give interviews. The rest, the political work in and of itself, was too concrete, too laborious for him.

ANDRES KOEPP, director of the documentary film *Micka*: Were there people who genuinely supported Mickaël, or did he manipulate all of them? Nowadays, you'll practically only find victims. But scientifically that doesn't hold water. It's believed Mickaël was never capable of taking control of more than 10,000 people at a time. So, when, on June 15th, you've got almost a half million people in the streets of Paris, completely nude, yelling these sort of Dadaist slogans, when you see them, for example, praying for the resurrection of the comedian Coluche, it's just off the scale. There was a ratchet and a joining-in effect. A moment had clearly come when French society needed chaos.

MICHEL SABARD, psychiatrist at Percy Military Hospital: It's more complicated than that. With Mickaël's powers of suggestion we must distinguish between two phases. The contact phase, during which he takes possession of your mind: with this, there's nothing you can do. He tells you to jump out of a window, you jump out of a window. End of story. Free will is eradicated. And then there's the phase people called "post-presence," in which judgment is still highly impacted. Mickaël's left, he doesn't control you any more, but you continue to experience feelings of attachment, which can go as far as a kind of love, and even provoke withdrawal symptoms, a rather intense melancholia. At times parallels have been drawn between this experience and Stockholm Syndrome, and I basically agree with that analysis.

SÉVERINE F., law student: There was a rumor going around that he was organizing these sort of orgies at City Hall, that all kinds of crazy shit was going on, and I wanted to see what. I remember how strongly I wanted to. At the time I was really the model good little girl, school first, not very adventurous, sexually totally average. And so this theory that you loved Mickaël because you had the need for disorder, because you were too uptight, too straight-laced, I don't know how much it's worth when it comes down to it, but for me there's no question, it totally applies.

The subway had already stopped running, so I walked toward City Hall. At the Seine the cops wanted to stop us from getting any further, but every thirty seconds or so someone would start to undress, sing, and jump around in every direction, so it wasn't too hard to break through by running into the police cordon.

I don't know when I took off all my clothes. There was a huge crowd on the other side of the Seine, almost everyone naked, bodies intertwined, people making love. It was rather shocking for someone like me. It didn't make me want to join in, but only because that's not what I wanted. I wanted him to take me. Me. And at some point, because I was pretty back then, really quite above average, they let me get all the way to this kind of throne room he'd had set up in the City Hall.

He saw me. He looked at me. Just that, it was . . . I spread my arms open and started crying. But then nothing happened. Nothing. He couldn't get in my head. His gaze hardened. Two or three guards pushed me to the ground, and then they threw me out. Next, I walked around aimlessly in the streets. I was so ashamed of myself. And suddenly of my nudity, too. And I remember I went in the Gap on the rue de Rivoli, which had been totally ransacked, and I grabbed all the clothes I could find. I know everything that happened later. All the bad stuff he did. But I felt like I was disabled.

STÉPHANE HUYGHE, CDII: There was that girl, and there were others . . . He could exert control over approximately 90% of people—precisely how many, we'll never know for sure. But 10% of the population that eludes you is still quite a lot of people. Plus, and we saw this with the hostage situation in Trégastel, since his power passed through verbal language, it was very difficult for him to dominate foreigners who didn't understand French.

He showed signs of paranoia starting on the third day. What was he afraid of since he was most likely immortal? Being spied on. Being poisoned, too. He was convinced poison could kill him. Plus that was his nature. Since he was a little kid he only saw things that way, him against the rest of the world. You didn't have to push him too much for him to start seeing enemies everywhere. So, the mood changed. After two days of jubilation, things became more heavily securitized. At least around him in the center of Paris. For us, no doubt that complicated our approach, even if we were able to continue working. The poisoning attempt had taken place the night before—a total fiasco that prompted us to take a bit more time before the next attempt.

JOHN CONYNGHAM, strategic intelligence consultant: To tell you how badly the poisoning was screwed up: still today we believe Mickaël didn't even realize the girl had sprinkled in cyanide salt. His organism was so resistant to toxic substances that he just simply didn't feel a thing.

MICHAEL SABARD, psychiatrist: All of the Hermetics' accounts mention an attempted intrusion that ended up failing. The image that comes up most is sexual. The subject is aware that something—some said a "finger," others were more vague and spoke of a "force"—tried to penetrate their minds. I remember attending the Prophet's debriefing after Mickaël's attempt on the other 83ers, who were all Hermetics, luckily. He had the feeling that a dog's mouth was searching through his head and ran into an "elastic" surface that it couldn't rip through.

VIRGINIE: But at no time did I feel like I was resisting. It wasn't up to you. This needs to be pointed out because there are people who blame themselves, exactly like women who have been raped. Those that Mickaël didn't manage to possess were just incompatible, like opposite poles of a magnet. It's not that on one side are those who fought and on the other those who gave up. Just those he possessed and those he couldn't possess.

STÉPHANE HUYGHE, CDII: That the 83ers ended up being Hermetics, yes, that was a huge relief because no one would have wanted to see them under his command. But that didn't

take care of the Mickaël problem. This time they were as powerless as we were.

STEVEN ERLANGER, reporter for the *Boston Globe*: There are several reasons why the United States entered the scene. First off,
an incontestable technological superiority. Next, after 9/11,
we developed cutting-edge targeted assassination techniques.
It's something our elite units carried out regularly, everywhere
jihadists had support bases. For the French this was still
uncommon. So on the level of expertise, advantage USA. In
the medium term, it's always useful for a power like the United
States to provide this type of service. We know what it can
mean for negotiating, advantageous business agreements, etc.

But for me, the main reason is something completely different. Between 1/19 and when Mickaël cracked up, you'll notice
that we didn't talk much about the 83ers here. The Captain's
or Virginie's achievements rarely made it in our newspapers.
Not one time did Washington ask Paris for support from the
French superheroes. Someone like Saïd, for example, with his
invisibility and his mastery of Arabic, would have been very
useful with certain antiterrorist operations. However, our politicians never asked for a thing. And that's because, in my
opinion, just the existence of the 83ers themselves was hard to
accept. It was unbearable, you know, that they hadn't appeared
in the States. We're the strongest sumbitches 'round, yes or no?
But our heroes, Delta Force or SEAL Team Six, who eliminated Bin Laden and all that, what are they worth next to the
power of the 83ers? All of a sudden we looked pathetic. Except,
from the moment your superhero started smashing stuff up
and it became a tactical advantage vis-a-vis Mickaël to *not*
speak French, it was a real pleasure for us to lend you a hand.

EMMANUEL DREYER, lawyer: The June 20th operation was completely extralegal, but that, even today, is something that few people dare bring up, and I have to point out that it gets little coverage. The decision to kill a man was made without any debate in Parliament and, this goes without saying, without consulting the public. The state of emergency that the Council of Ministers decreed in no way authorized Mickaël's assassination. Regardless, it's an open and shut case: in France *nothing* authorizes you to eliminate an individual in that manner.

STÉPHANE HUYGHE, CDII: We always knew exactly where he was, and, even if I can't get into the details due to security reasons, there were always contacts within his entourage who could keep us apprised of his actions. That's how we discovered that he slept, and from what time to what time. Sleep was his only weak point. He was well aware of this and didn't shut his eyes for very long. Never more than three or four hours. Nevertheless, that gave us a fairly good window to act. Surrounding him, of course, there were alarm systems and bodyguards, but nothing insurmountable, technically speaking. I would say that, once you have a military objective and it's been located, it's only a question of means and timing. In a situation like this one, the means are limitless. As for timing, the fact that we didn't act immediately was highly criticized, but by people who don't understand very well how these types of operations function.

FRÉDÉRIQUE SALVARESI, Assistant Director, Central Operations at the CDII: It was a typical elite unit: shaved heads, beards, tattoos, highly trained, self-confident, real war dogs. We didn't know where Mickaël's English stood. He was teaching himself online, but his New Republic didn't leave him much time for that, of course, and his speed of assimilation, contrary to what may have been said and written, was never that great. Mickaël was like just about everyone at that same level, not especially gifted, kind of slow.

It would have been better to deploy Hermetic soldiers, but we had no way of determining those individuals. The only way of knowing if you were impermeable to Mickaël's powers of suggestion was to face him. At some point, I remember, someone suggested we assemble a commando unit of people who passed the test. Like the girl Séverine F., for example, the student you interviewed. And others we'd identified. So here we are, we're going to take these regular people, train them in a couple days, and send them into the wolf's mouth to deliver humanity from one of the most extreme threats it's ever known? You know, like in some Hollywood movie? We didn't consider that seriously for more than two seconds. We took an American SEAL team that was highly trained and basically protected by their total ignorance of French. It was the best we could do.

Colonel Jean-Philippe d'Haussonville: No operation is ever perfect. This one was run from beginning to end exactly as required.

Christophe Balssa, Editor, *International Defense and Security* magazine: Air-blast bombs, which are also called thermobaric weapons, are a bit less powerful than a nuclear ordinance, and they have no secondary effects, if I may put it that way. So, in comparison to conventional bombs, in terms of cost/efficiency, you're not going to find a better option. The destruction happens in two stages. A first explosion disperses a flammable gas into the air, a kind of cloud (now, I don't know precisely what the commando unit used, but it's frequently a RDX-aluminum mixture). Then, several milliseconds later, a second explosion ignites it. The overpressure that the blast creates, combined with the combustion, is absolutely devastating. If you're in the center of the area of effect, which was the case for Mickaël, you're immediately disintegrated.

Colonel Jean-Philippe d'Haussonville: He was disintegrated. I'm absolutely categorical on the matter.

Andres Koepp, film director: He had no idea what he was going to do next. At the beginning he made it up from day to day. It's true he had that obsession about weight, but that was more of a source of inspiration that anything else. Then, as he was a bit short of ideas, he started to take himself seriously. Revolutions are frequently like that: they start like a carnival, and end like high mass.

Thomas Wieder, reporter for *Le Monde*: When I met him for the interview on the seventh day, the first thing he wanted to talk about was Quentin Meillassoux's speculative materialism. That was the last thing I expected. He was sitting in the mayor's office, a very calm room, insulated—quite a contrast with the libertarian den of thieves that had been established in the large ballrooms of City Hall—wearing a freshly ironed grey shirt. I remember you could still see the creases the iron had left on the sleeves. Several times he repeated, "the only necessity is contingency" and implied that this principle would guide the New Republic. I'm far from being an expert in philosophy, but after five minutes it became obvious he didn't understand much either—and Quentin Meillassoux, whom I later met, confirmed that to me. Since he didn't have a college degree, I think Mickaël was especially proud to give his policies some kind of philosophical underpinning. He wanted to legitimize himself.

HUGO DESPREZ: No, the Meillassoux thing was just another joke, I can assure you. I'm not convinced being serious was something that ever drove him. For a time he just found it funny to cloak himself in highly respected cultural touchstones. Claiming to adhere to factual ontology, having his photo taken while annotating *The Gallic War*, or ordering a giant statue of the writer Patrick Modiano were just ways of prolonging the farce.

PHILIPPE GENÉVRIER, Chief of Police: You know the old adage, in nature nothing is lost . . . His body was pulverized. From that point of view, the operation was a success. The commando unit entered the Hotel Lutetia, the thermobaric charge was affixed to the ceiling of the room underneath the one where he was sleeping, the unit exited, and ten seconds later, boom, no more Mickaël, no more hotel room, and, given the bomb's magnitude, practically no more Lutetia. And then his cells reassembled. It seemed very quick to me, I'd say about a minute, but it could have been three or four. He reconstituted. From that moment on, what do you expect . . . We'd made him very, very angry. This wasn't going to go unanswered.

WERNER HERZOG, director: I found it an interesting challenge. And even today, I can say that if someone asked me to do a film on his life, I'd sign in a second. Okay, so the ideas he had for the script weren't great. I told him that, and he replied that in any case he was planning on hiring someone to write it. Next, I remember, he wanted to talk about casting. That's what excited him the most, imagining who might play him, who could play Fanny, the first girl he loved. For his character he absolutely 100% wanted Vincent Cassel. I told him he was a bit too old for the role, but that didn't really seem to bother him at all. He said, "We'll make him younger." We had two four-hour meetings, and everything was like that: pharaonic, intoxicating, no limits. Now, would that have made a good film? I don't think so. He wanted to be involved in everything. He would've made it into something honoring his own glory, buffing out all the rough edges. Still, I would've loved to work on it.

EMMANUEL DREYER, lawyer: He retreated into a defensive mindset. Which was perfectly normal. People try to assassinate you . . . There's no justice you can turn to, 'cause it's held by those who attacked you . . . So you respond to violence with violence. There was no less reason for him to do it than anyone else in a similar situation.

ERIC PEREIRA, Mickaël's brother: I would just like to say that that wasn't like him. Seizing power, playing President, that wasn't at all something he wanted. Even after 1/19, he never talked to me about it. Some people are diabetic. Others are schizophrenic. Okay, with him, he became a complete megalomaniac. But it was a sickness. I'd just like people not to forget that when they talk about him.

SEBASTIAN LALLEMANT, law enforcement officer: As soon as he emerged from the rubble, as soon as you could see the silhouette of a man walking in this sort of fog the dust from the explosion had created, I pulled back and got in a car. There's no doubt that saved me. When two of my fellow officers started firing at us, I ducked down, and the car body protected me. Later, during the shooting spree, I stayed curled up in the same position. I could hear screams, shots, but didn't see anything. It was really hard. Today, I tell myself it was better that way. Truly. It would have fucked my head up to see my fellow officers killing each other. Especially the stranglings. I know there are videos out there on the web, but never, never, was I tempted to watch 'em.

XAVIER FISCHER, presidential advisor: This is France. There's no national unity, especially in situations like this one. No one agreed on what needed to be done. The only consensus was that the authorities were out of control, that we were a disgrace.

STÉPHANE HUYGHE, CDII: We said to ourselves: so, he's not going to die. It's simply not going to happen. Ever.

STEVEN ERLANGER, reporter: He managed to find each member of the American commando unit. It wasn't very difficult for him to identify them. All he needed to do was comb through the minds of those responsible for the operation and find the images of the soldiers and their identities. Like a lot of French, I think he was very anti-American. And so he made a special effort to hunt them down. And make them suffer when he killed them.

The only one who survived, Matt Hurst, lives in Florida. He's got a little fishing boat, and for a couple hundred bucks, he helps make ends meet by selling his story to publications that are still interested. Hurst's got an interesting theory when asked how he survived the 83er's manhunt against the Navy SEALs. He's convinced, even though he lived in hiding until

Mickaël's neutralization, that he could have been killed at any time. But according to him, his astrological sign saved him. He was born at the end of November. He's a Sagittarius, like Mickaël. And, according to him, Mickaël can't kill Sagittarians. It seems far-fetched, but the thing is, no Sagittarius has ever been killed, at least not directly, on account of Mickaël. When he took control of the soldiers in front of the Lutetia, in Marseille, in Rome, and later in New York City, none of them killed a single Sagittarius. Why? No idea. Hurst thinks it's because they're Mickaël's "cosmic brothers." And he's assembled a little militia around him of committed Sagittarians who train on weekends waiting for the 83er to wake up. Because, if it could all be done over again, Hurst would fight alongside Mickaël. Like quite a lot of people, in fact.

HUGO DESPREZ: When he learned that hundreds of thousands of the faithful had gathered to pray in Saint Peter's Square, because now there was nothing left to do but pray for him to have a heart attack or a ruptured aneurysm, I could see that that gave him pause. I'm not really sure why. He didn't believe in God. It wasn't superstition. But to see himself through their prayers and their tear-stained faces as the great evil, some kind of new Hitler or Sauron . . . did that just simply touch him, their helplessness, the panicked fear he inspired in them? In any case, he stayed a good twenty minutes in front of the television, pale and expressionless. And when he created the riots in Rome by taking control of several thousand of the faithful, I got the impression he did it because it was what was expected, because that's what people dreaded. Not because he was angry with these people.

ANDRES KOEPP, film director: When you think back on the

Twenty-Seven Days, it's incredible how quickly we went from this wacky, exhilarating event to something downright sinister, even for him. It didn't make him laugh anymore at all. Even The Big Whatever was the same old same old. What people expected him to do. What was left for him, if even this had become predictable? That's how you need to understand the individual: a guy who's uncomfortable in his own skin, who, fundamentally, is trying to escape. If there's no exit, you're going to see him implode.

STÉPHANE HUYGHE, CDII: The only thing we needed to think about was that now, since it had been determined that nothing, absolutely nothing could destroy him, was how to prevent him from definitively doing harm. The Prime Minister was very taken by the idea of sending him into space. You see the idea: we imprison him, put him in a rocket, and then *sayonara!* We send him off to drift in the depths of space. The problem was the first part. No certainty that we could make him see reason. We considered different scenarios, and nothing held water. And even once he was in the rocket ship, what guarantee did we have that he wouldn't be able to turn it back to Earth? We're talking here about a man who made cars dance. No laws of physics were still guaranteed since what happened in Trégastel.

SOPHIE CHASTEL-MORAND, President of The French Heroes Defense League: At no time did anyone truly consider a negotiated settlement. It was always the same: we must rid ourselves of this monster. We must kill him. He's a dictator. It'll be the end with him around. Now I would like to ask you a question: what would have happened if we'd let him do what he wanted? Would he have raped women and killed little kids? Seriously? Would we have lived in a horrible world? In a less just world?

SAÏD: We gotta stop the bullshit. All these people telling you what happened . . . The theory of the enlightened despot . . . Gotta stop this melancholic revisionism, where all of a sudden he becomes the savior we missed out on, the socialist prophet, Fidel Castro with superpowers and who wouldn't have turned out too bad . . . Let's cut the shit. He wouldn't have redistributed wealth. He wouldn't have taxed capital, financial transactions, or I don't know what else. He wouldn't have rid the world of evil corporate overlords or polluters. He wouldn't have done any of that. Not because he was against it. Simply because he had no plan. He had no idea what he was doing or where he was going. His brother was right. Mickaël was sick. If we had let him continue, frankly . . . we would have held on what, twenty more days? And then, at some point, just to see, he would've blown it all up.

HUGO DESPREZ: Nobody knows anything at all. No one can say what would have happened.

MICHEL SABARD, psychiatrist: We must be careful with reconstructions. Many people do and say things without really knowing why. It's even, one could say, one of the most common modes of action: you act, and it is only afterward that you find an explanation to justify yourself. But the process that leads to the action, even a very simple action like smiling politely at a saleswoman when you enter a store, is quite complex and very difficult to dissect. In spite of all of this, one can surmise that a feeling of relegation as they call it in soccer and a desire for societal revenge dominated with Mickaël. He never formulated it that way, but I would be ready to state that he seized power because he didn't become a soccer player. Mickaël Pereira, the soccer player, even with his mental suggestion capabilities, would most likely not have taken the same path.

ANDRES KOEPP, film director: He seized power because he was depressed. Completely broken. By several factors: immediate and unbearable fame, an intense feeling of already being too old, of having missed lots of things, and the belief that something's wrong with the world. It's revenge, yes, but it shouldn't be reduced to a personal dimension. But rather, revenge on the world as it is, a desire to reset the playing field. And to make the world leave this playing field at the same time he does.

EMMANUEL DREYER, lawyer: He wasn't given a choice. He was hunted down, and he was confronted by a completely iniquitous State. He took power to defend himself, more than anything.

SAÏD: When you can seize power, you seize it. End of story.

NICOLAS FLORY, nurse: He entered me on the ninth day. I could try to describe what I felt, but I am not going to for two reasons. First, you can't understand. Even if I found the right words. Even if there were words strong enough to describe what I felt—for you these words wouldn't mean a thing. The other reason is that it wouldn't be good for me. The person I see advised me not to talk about it. And even to try, as much as possible, not to think about it anymore. That kind of joy won't come around again. Except if Mickaël comes back and decides to possess me again. But he'll have so many things to do . . . There's so much more important stuff than filling me.

ISABELLE P., teacher: He took me on the third day to stop the police who were trying to flush our brothers and sisters from the place de la République. I was shot in the eye by a Flash-Ball riot gun. So, I frequently hear people say that I was a victim twice over: the first time because Mickaël possessed me, and a second time because I can no longer see out of my left eye. Nothing irritates me more than that word, victim. Let me tell you, I'm only waiting for one thing—Mickaël's awakening. My mutilated eye, I'm proud of it like a war wound. He took me, and I gave him my eye.

DAVID V., tobacconist: The other 83ers, for their sake I hope they'll already be dead. Because there's no place on Earth where they can stop us from finding them. There'll be hundreds of us, thousands, and that day they'll pay for what they did to him.

XIX

THE SCENE TAKES place in the spring of Year II at Courseulles-sur-Mer, where Gregory, perhaps to be nearer to the Marville family seat (the dynasty is from Cabourg), just purchased an imposing farmhouse, almost a château, surrounded by an English-style landscape garden. On the second floor, to fill the center of a separate *fumoir* with inlaid parquet floor, he installed an eighteenth-century globe nestled on a mahogany three-footed stand, a recent and prohibitively expensive acquisition of which he is not certain Jeanne approved. Although he quickly grew tired of it, the first two times they came for the weekend he enjoyed making the corrugated paperboard sphere, darkened by time, spin under his fingers, noting cartographic errors and surprising captions like a *steep coastline* to the west of Australia or, in the empty waters of the Indian Ocean, a "Whale," which was a Tibetan Mastiff with the hooves of a goat and the tail of a lion. He sees this house as his seigniorial retreat, where his wife and children can find him—him, the best father and husband in the world, the one who will always have time, in spite of his overbooked schedule, to take a meandering walk on the immense beach, learn how to ride a horse at a nearby training ring, and watch *The Lion King* in the home cinema he had installed on the first floor.

His hypersensitive hearing must remain restricted to professional uses only. This is consistent with his adherence to the contract he signed, but also, he believes, it's essential for his own peace of mind. He feels if he were to eavesdrop on conversations that were supposed to be outside his range, he would face embarrassing discoveries and even revelations that might hurt him. It's better not to be cognizant of the secrets, desires, resentments, gossip, and slander—of this viscous brew in which most human conversations were steeped.

Since the beginning of Year II, there have been situations where his gift, like Raphael's, engages by chance. Each time he cuts off the sound. It's a very simple action, he explains, like moving your hand away from a flame that could burn you. You only need to make yourself do it. Faithful to his principles as well as the contract he signed, Gregory immediately ceases to use his power.

This is more difficult the day when a sound, emitted from the far end of the grounds, behind the bougainvillea and aucuba beds, reaches his ears—a sigh of weakness, heavy and drawn out, followed by the furtive rustling of lips gliding against skin. "No . . ." whispers his wife, alarmed. But a languorous note floats in her voice and diminishes the concern. A second kiss resonates in the Captain's ear followed by another sigh, after which he detects a smile of consent. He moves in closer.

His wife is snuggled against Raphael's chest, as his right hand, which has hiked her cotton dress to her waist, has slipped underneath her beige underwear while he gently caresses her rear. "Stop that," says Jeanne, and he continues. "Stop. . ." He turns her around and presses her body against his. From his vantage point hidden in the shadow of a copse, Gregory can see the profile of Raphael's face, surprisingly grave, concentrating, as well as Jeanne's, whose mouth is open and eyes are rounded in a distracted expression whilst, bent over, she rubs against his pelvis, which slowly sways.

What does Gregory do in the seconds following this discovery? Despite the shock that just punched him in the gut, a kind of shame prevents him from acting. He doesn't want to be seen, pitiful, spying through the branches. And he refuses to move in and make his appearance in a scene he barely understands the meaning of. It would be too disgraceful. So, lowering his eyes, he silently returns to the other side of the yard where his youngest daughter, Marianne, is waiting for someone to help push her on a swing.

He saw the lovers again at dinner time around a garden table set on the terrace. He does not know that the following day Raphael will attempt a last-ditch effort to neutralize Mickaël, but for several days he has suspected that something of this order was in the works. In addition to his taciturn mood, which is more intense than usual, and the tension, the near brusqueness that drives him, one can definitely sense that Raphael's thoughts are fully absorbed by Mickaël's tyranny. And it's not hard to imagine what's preoccupying him: how to put an end to it.

Stationed in Bordeaux for the past twenty-five days, the 83ers have been reduced to reading news flashes and listening to reports in rooms filled with downcast officers. As the days accumulate, so does the awful certainty that the country's main city will never be recaptured, that for many years, forever, in the place of the capital there shall exist a carnivalesque enclave, a place of secession and debauchery. The images coming out of Paris are harrowing: naked or slovenly dressed glassy-eyed revelers bellow, urinate, vomit, stumblingly dance, and kiss frenetically. It looks like a *feria*.

Even though, since he tried to take over, it had been determined that the Prophet, like the other 83ers, was a Hermetic, any operation against him is bound to be as dangerous as it is uncertain. So, since he fears for his friend—the idea that he might lose him has tied his stomach in knots ever since he suspected Raphael was going to attempt something—Gregory entreated Raphael to spend the weekend in Courseulles. We won't talk about Mickaël. Even if the world's in danger, we'll forget about it for a couple hours. It'll be relaxed family time.

He's now contemplating Raphael. He could almost admire the nonchalant manner in which he cuts his meat and quaffs the Côte-Rôtie. He's not even pretending, thinks Gregory. So this man nonchalantly came to drink my wine, eat at my table, and, if possible, fuck my wife. He came to help himself and have a good time.

If he felt bitter satisfaction at having finally pieced together the farce that's been played before his eyes, little by little his mind fills with another feeling, more crushing, more urgent. It's not exactly hate nor is it yet sadness, but rather rage tinged with repulsion at the idea that he can never take back from this man the kisses, the hugs, the softness of his wife's open arms, the tingle in her loins, the smell of her sex. All that, Raphael took. All that, Raphael has tasted as well.

He presently follows his friend's gaze which, wherever it lands—on his wife, his daughters, him, and even on the trees around them, the garden putti dappled with lichen, the basket of summer fruits—is a taint. Night falls on the park, and everything appears as if it were painted in garish colors, violently emphasizing the irony of this tableau: the innocent look of the garden cherubs; Lucille, who asks if Raphael could read her a story (it must be him and no one else); even the suddenly obscene contours of the apricots.

Every now and then apathy comes over him. Gregory breathes more easily. His mind drifts. This couldn't have happened. Things like this don't happen in his universe. But he saw, he can still see, the man's tense face and the profile of the bent-over woman. From Raphael's and Jeanne's mouths come words that he does not hear clearly.

He promises himself that tonight, while Raphael's asleep, he'll plunge a knife in his heart. He'll slit his throat. Yes, that's what needs to be done. But when he pictures the headlines, his daughters' lives without him, Mickaël still at large and crazy, the all-too-hastily imagined revenge quickly becomes a blistering defeat. It is possible that he also remembers Jean-Baptiste's death—candles lit in front of churches, cries of despair, and the President's emotional tribute. He won't kill Raphael. No. He will have to find something better for his vengeance.

Toward the end of dinner, he also scrutinizes his wife. Later will come the regrets of what might have been avoided if he'd only been more attentive or more frequently by her side. For the moment, his head slightly cocked, he looks at her, and his astonishment increases while this face, which he knows in the slightest detail, remains just as familiar as it always was. He would like the orangey glow of twilight to unveil, like in some tale of the supernatural, the horrid features of a monster or a demon lurking in his wife's body. He would like to discover a stranger.

She gave in to Raphael because he had failed, Gregory thinks at first. During the last days of his campaign, when no one around him was pretending to believe any more, she saw him prostrate in an armchair like after the death of his mother, head in his hands, brooding over his defeat in a monotone voice. At that instant he believes she could only love him triumphant. He never should have left to conquer Paris. He, who even after seven years of marriage always makes sure his hair is combed when he wakes up and sucks in his gut when he has to be shirtless in front of her, showed himself in the worst light, ludicrous with his grand statements about the future of the human race and exasperatingly weak when, worried about committing another gaffe during the final two weeks, he started stammering in front of the public like an impressionable boy.

He then reviews the few images in his memory of Jeanne and Raphael during the campaign. In light of what he now knows, their smiles, their silences, their way of lingering close to each other gives off suspicious signals. The cuckolded husband understands that this affair has been going on for a while. He's been lied to for weeks and maybe even months.

So he thinks about their married life. When was the last time he made love with her? After Lucille's birth, between the unavailability of Jeanne's convalescent body and the young parents' fatigue, which accumulated over the course of nights without enough sleep, something ended. All that remained, at longer and longer intervals, was a chore, without release for her and with nothing urgent for him, recalling memories of emotions that no longer existed, raging and lost appetites, and desires from another era. But Jeanne had always told him it wasn't a big deal. And Gregory concurred. That was normal: all couples, all relationships, all women. He'd started watching videos on the internet to take care of his more pressing needs. He was ashamed, on occasion, especially as his preferences nearly always leaned toward the same dishonest scenario: a young woman, eager to launch a career in porn believes she's participating in a casting audition and allows herself to be taken advantage of by a fake recruiter, who films the interview and then "tests" her. In the second part of the scene the gullible young woman, an eager job candidate, puts every effort into satisfying the impostor, who will never call her back. When it comes down to it, they were rape videos, but fake—they never would have been put online otherwise, Gregory assured himself. And the urge that drove him to them, he also believed, did not contravene in any way with the code of conduct he had always strived to respect. These secret sessions took place in a parallel time, a kind of limbo where he wasn't really himself, where he simply purged everything that wasn't exactly him, the persistence of the animalistic part of himself, debauched desires that needed to be gratified so they didn't resurface elsewhere, in the Captain's *real life*. It was quite healthy in fact. He was convinced.

Although pleasure had become a solitary occupation, he wanted to keep in mind that it hadn't vanished from his life. The caresses he exchanged with his wife when falling asleep and the tender embraces they shared each morning separated their love from a passion whose flame had died out.

The rest of the time he resisted temptation and congratulated himself for his valiance. At the time when he was working as a prosecutor, on several occasions he had already sensed, through certain lingering smiles and phrases whose lines were blurry, that flings were being suggested, yet he struggled to believe that they were indeed within the realm of possibility. The intern, had she really said when he was dropping her off, that she lived "right over there," her finger pointing to the narrow street and her slightly vague look perhaps indicating both her studio and the place she'd give herself to him? And at a conference he'd attended two years previously, the hand of his Spanish counterpart leaning on his arm while he ordered two mojitos at the packed bar, did it have the meaning he'd attributed to it? He blinked his eyes like he was in front of a mirage.

Since 1/19, however, even a man with a mind as obtuse as his own could not ignore the advances that were made on him. Women as well as men were only waiting for a sign on his part. Rumors of the superheroes' alleged sexual potency had their role in the interest he elicited as well. Gregory received several emails from a group of "Norwegian Breeders" affiliated with the *Norsk foreningen for seksuell og reproduktiv helse og rettigheter*, which proposed in explicit terms he impregnate any one of the beautiful women featured in the attached catalog in order to, as it was written, improve the human race in the spirit of "sharing benefits arising from genetic resources" (*fordeling av genetiske ressurser*). No account has come to light that would contradict the idea that the Captain, as always, ignored these calls with the resolve for which he is known. Nevertheless, after feeling pulsing bodies rub against him during walkabouts, after seeing wide, toothy smiles and hearing unambiguous propositions whispered in his ear, he had reached the opinion that his contemporaries were obsessed with sex, that people at any time and at any cost wanted to screw, and if possible, to screw indiscriminately—their coworkers, their sisters-in-law, their babysitters, strangers—secretly, illicitly. When nice weather returned and bodies once again started to shed clothing, when women's dainty feet appeared in strappy leather sandals, and when discreet but lascivious smiles were exchanged at cafés, Gregory had pictured the world as a huge marketplace of screwing, frenetic and sweaty, from which he continued to exclude himself because he had made, and this promise was what was most precious, a sacred pact that elevated his faithfulness to the level of mystical discipline.

Except Jeanne had lied. She'd also had desires. And when the opportunity presented itself, she'd grabbed it. He, on the other hand, he'd denied himself. He'd wanted to, but he'd denied himself. Not her. Gregory was firmly convinced of but one thing, which he would soon find printed in the papers: Jeanne Marville was a slut. He would not forgive.

Raphael has left to tell Lucile a story. In the garden's blue-green shadows, husband and wife remain alone at the table. "This is nice," says Gregory, for the painful pleasure of seeing Jeanne agree, sounding the depths of her duplicity, for each sentence where she does not confess what she's hiding now seems to him like an additional lie.

So they're going to separate, he thinks. Other couples have overcome more sordid incidents. But their own love only existed by being a celestial passion, a source of amazement next to all it avoided—petty arguments and money problems. Gregory will not comprehend how to live in this landscape opening before him. Jeanne will plead with him several times, but he will refuse. Jeanne will tell him it's possible, but he will never want to learn how. Jeanne will repeat that she loves him, that she loves only him, but he will respond that it's a lie. In a few hours it will all be nearly over.

They will make love one last time. Gregory will take her by force if he has to, but he won't let her get away before having felt, one last time, his sex inside hers. But then he knows very well that no, of course he could never make her endure that. Never could he tolerate seeing a look of fear or repugnance that he'd provoked on his wife's face.

Then images of the aftermath come to mind: splitting time with the children, consulting a lawyer, papers to sign, moving boxes, Jeanne's future body and face, which will quickly, he knows this, take on something like another hue, first subtly but then more and more obviously, another texture when, under very rare circumstances, they exchange the traditional *bise* when she comes to drop off their daughters, and he feels her near him. You become strangers again so quickly.

Raphael comes back and sits down next to them, and Gregory believes he can discern Jeanne's relief when his friend rejoins them. When will he surprise the lovers? At the beginning of the meal he thought of the triumph the few simple words he would later pronounce would bring him. Presently, his throat is caught, his mouth has the cold, tingly taste of metal, and his courage is lacking. Later, in his bedroom, he thinks he will simply say, "I saw you," but instead he'll scream, "How could you do that to me?" He thinks he won't go find Raphael, that never again will they cross paths, but he'll knock on the door of Raphael's room and yell at him to get the hell out right now and to take his wife with him if he needs to drain his balls. He wants to believe the lovers won't take his dignity, but there will be neither dignity, nor restraint, nor generosity of spirit at that time of night.

For now, he takes Jeanne's hand. She looks at him with surprise and embarrassment, but he keeps her hand in his. He wants to feel her warmth one last time. His eyes fill with tears as he smiles tenderly. "I'm going to bed," says Jeanne, who wants her hand back. He holds it and continues to smile. Then, as he senses that the lovers are uncomfortable, and as the dinner will soon be over, he begins, looking alternately at Jeanne and Raphael, to tell the story of his ancestor François-Juste Marville exploring the hinterlands of Eastern Siberia. Jeanne already knows this story, but not in its tiniest details, which he's currently making up, which he tacks on to the descriptions so that this tale lasts a bit longer, so that this hand still remains in his. How, in 1854, François-Juste, a mere attaché at the embassy in Moscow, resigned and embarked with Admiral

Nevelskoy on one of those expeditions he had always dreamed
of. How he lost his bearings in the frozen mists aboard his
baidarka (a kind of kayak most frequently covered with sea-
lion skin). How he was saved from imminent death by a con-
voy of Manchurian merchants, which he noticed were transporting arms in order to quell insurgent Gilyaks. How, despite
the remorse he felt in betraying his benefactors, François-Juste,
accustomed to taking the side of the underdog, fled in the
middle of the night to warn Chief Nakovan and his cousin
Chief Patken of an imminent attack. How he, so cultured by
nature, hit it off with these cruel men who wore dog skins,
reeked of seal fat, and got drunk on arrack. How he learned
their language. How he overcame the regrettable superstition
that prevented them from digging in the ground and taught
them the benefits of agriculture. Finally, how he explored the
banks of the Amgun, Ussuri, and Zeya Rivers accompanied by
a young woman named Sakoni whom the natives had offered
him. On the banks of Lake Kizi, summer proved to be warmer
than had been predicted, and it seemed as if it would never
end. In the shade of the cedar and larch trees, they fished, they
frolicked, and they made love.

XX

DEVASTATED BY THE incident, regretting everything, but more than ever anxious to prove, as he writes in his journal, that he wasn't a "bad guy," or in any case not just a bad guy, and prove that his determination could make something marvelously good happen for once, Raphael pulled into the Saint-Guirec beach parking lot, about two kilometers from the place where, four weeks previously, Mickaël had broken into the house of the English woman and her child. He walked a bit on the promenade and sat down to have a drink on the fairly deserted terrace of a restaurant. The low tide revealed a jumbled field of lumpy, copper-colored rocks, spewn from the depths of the Earth during the time of the great saurians, thought Raphael, or maybe even before that—yeah, maybe even before that, when the Earth, at least in his mind, was a kind of uninhabited, convulsing planet, covered with toxic fumarole, impenetrable jungles, and molten lava.

As he was a good 15 minutes early, he scrolled around on his phone with the idea of quelling his concerns by filling in any insufficient geological knowledge. He recognized the terms *feldspar* and the *Variscan orogenic belt*, which he'd already come across somewhere, in middle school probably, and then turned to pondering the number of years that separated him from the moment when this landscape of bizarre shapes, which he didn't find particularly attractive, was formed. Three hundred million years, huh, he thought, nodding his head respectfully as if watching a weightlifter compete.

A small cluster of walkers who were wading in the water interrupted, just before they turned somber, his musings on the length of telluric time and the brevity of human existence. A pot-bellied swimmer in red trunks was being arduously carried while, out of nowhere, three firefighters loaded with large backpacks trotted toward the shore.

Raphael anticipated that Mickaël would be extremely attentive to the nature of his arrival, and he looked, in what increasingly appeared to be a desperate attempt to resuscitate a drowned man, for signs that would indicate he was there. Was the swimmer going to sit up, become thinner, dry off, and as he started to walk determinedly toward him, change his countenance to reveal the tyrant's, delighted by his joke? Were the extras preparing to transform the macabre scene into a dance number, whose finale would be a tableau vivant in which they brandished placards above their heads reading out the name M I C K A Ë L?

Even though the firefighters—athletic, solemn, and attentive—seemed perfect to him in their roles, Raphael struggled to understand the significance of this prologue. But soon, as they slowly carried the body on a stretcher toward the parking lot, he came to the conclusion that it was, without a doubt, really and truly a beach accident that had no relation to his meeting. Someone must have died there. These things were still possible. A chill went down his spine as he remembered how at age twelve he'd learned of the death of a first cousin his same age. He'd been found at the foot of a tree in his parents' yard. He'd fallen off a branch, hit his head on the ground, and that's all she wrote.

He suddenly felt a presence behind him. Mickaël had arrived. He was wearing an Emporio Armani cap, oversized dark sunglasses, a fake beard, and a white double-breasted six-button blazer that made him look like a terrorist on the lam dressed for a night at the casino.

"He thought about a crab."

"Who did?" asked Raphael.

"The guy who drowned. His last thought, just before dying, was about a crab."

In order to draw Mickaël in, Raphael had needed to operate solo. Letting someone into his confidence would risk seeing his plan exposed, now that the tyrant had access to just about anybody's mind.

The day after the botched operation at the Lutetia, the Prophet had, in veiled terms, expressed delight in Mickaël's survival. But this message of solidarity had to be discreet enough to seem credible. He decided to confide in his sister Judith, whom he regretfully recognized—life sucks, there's just so much ugliness in the world—for the past several months was the one, his favorite sister, the one he called to have coffee near Les Halles on Sundays when under a gloomy, leaden sky, everything seemed dreary and a waste, who was leaking some of his indiscretions to reporters. He let it slip over the phone—in order, if his line was being tapped, as he believed, to increase the chances of seeing the information intercepted and peddled—that even if for obvious reasons he could not state the contrary, the operation's failure had relieved him. Didn't there seem to be a rush to judgment with Mickaël? If he'd possessed the same powers as Mickaël, he probably would have done the same thing. We all would have. Because (but this too his sister could not repeat) could you really deny that jealousy obviously played a role in the condemnation of Mickaël?

Several days later he launched phase two of his plan. He

proposed a secret meeting with Virginie, who had been hearing about his soap-opera love affair for many months and therefore seemed to be his official confidante. This time, he explained, he needed to talk to her about a matter related to Mickaël. They met on a Monday evening around midnight at a gas station on the A10 highway. Raphael seemed agitated. His hands shook, and he changed his mind three times in front of the coffee machine.

He started his confession so obliquely, which was not typical, that Virginie, who easily lost her patience, pressed him to get to the point.

His powers of divination had increased, Raphael claimed. He'd remained silent, fearing they would ban him from using his powers, but he was now able to perceive his targets' future without them knowing it. Several months ago he had learned that Mickaël's powers would increase tremendously and that one day he would create some sort of a tyrannical regime. Virginie shook her head. When did he discover this? October of last year, responded Raphael. He didn't explain why he'd remained silent so long. Perhaps, when the day came, he hoped to get some benefit out of it. Mickaël would need allies. And that's it? asked Virginie, dismayed. He'd set up a meeting to let her know that he'd behaved like the biggest fuckwit on the face of the Earth?

In a hushed voice Raphael said there was something else. While scanning Mickaël's future, he'd also glimpsed a neutralization attempt. Hermetics, enlisted by a foreign power, were infiltrating the tyrant's entourage. They would soon act. As of right now the Prophet could see that the operation was going to fail. But it could succeed if contact were made with these men in time. There were just a couple details that weren't that hard to fix. Raphael preferred not to talk about it out of fear of compromising their idea, but it's the right one.

Virginie would talk. She would tell Gregory she'd met the Prophet and he'd told her a confused story, undoubtedly sprinkled with lies and omissions, one that needed to be verified. An operation was being prepped. Apparently, it could work if, of course, everything remained a secret.

It was necessary to wait for the following pieces of information to be leaked and make their way up to Mickaël: 1) the Prophet was not vehemently opposed to him, 2) he knew Mickaël's future and had foreseen an important event that could change everything, and 3) he could be corrupted, because he had hoped, not all that long ago, to profit from Mickaël's omnipotence.

Not even two days after Raphael had spoken with Virginie, a fake employee at the hotel where he was staying in Bordeaux delivered a handwritten message. Mickaël proposed a meeting in Paris the day after next. Raphael, as a matter of course, let the day pass without showing the slightest intention of attending. He needed to appear reticent and even proclaim his hostility toward Mickaël a bit too virulently so that the tyrant would have an incentive to provide details about his offer and woo him. Other messages were delivered. Mickaël proposed meetings and promised compensation in exchange for specific knowledge concerning his future. Raphael finally accepted a meeting, but outside Paris, praying that no one from his own side knew anything and that they didn't unexpectedly mount a regrettable operation that would put his own life in peril.

They sat on the restaurant terrace. Mickaël looked around, brow furrowed, mouth slightly open. The beach emptied as he commanded the walkers to head back to their cars, to move along. The 83ers had the whole area to themselves, and this rocky theater, with the sea currently at low tide, seemed even more lugubrious, like the decor of a far-away planet after the extinction of the last colonists.

Of course, thought Raphael, the tyrant must have posted sharpshooters around them, in the windows of the nearby hotel and among the rock piles. From how far can they still hit their target? A kilometer, he'd been told long ago.

When Mickaël collapsed, Raphael would have a second, maybe less, to get away. And it was still possible that, in spite of the element of surprise, these men, specially trained for any eventuality, would not be distracted and would immediately shoot him. But he couldn't figure out a better plan. There was no plan where the chances of success seemed reasonable.

A blank-faced waiter brought them two platters of oysters. Mickaël made him dance a volta every five steps, most likely with the idea of making his guest laugh, but the Prophet didn't brighten up. He ordered a glass of wine. Mickaël preferred to stick to water.

Since the founding of the New Republic, he admitted, his powers had shown no signs of increasing. He'd peaked. It was so disappointing. Now he only saw impossible feats, every-thing that remained out of reach, what would never change. He couldn't reverse day and night, for example. Or even, on a smaller scale, command the sea that was sparkling below in the Channel to rise before its normal time. He was incapable of creating the slightest thing. He dreamed of a chimera, a lit-tle, bright pink crustacean with the tail of a scorpion, which he would introduce to the animal kingdom and would bear his name. That was not within his capabilities. Our world—he could disrupt it, he could destroy it, but he couldn't add anything to it. "Superman was on a whole other level," he said after a moment.

And Raphael, who found it difficult to follow this tirade,

later told how he so badly wanted to hear the tyrant's voice become wooly, thick, and meander under the first effects of the sleeping agent that he was trembling in his chair.

In the movie he'd seen when he was a kid, Superman reversed the direction of the Earth's rotation in order to rewind the course of time. Raphael remembered water flowing backward, surging toward the demolished dam that instantly re-formed. Since the catastrophe had been undone, Lois Lane had never died. He mustered the force to recount the scene to Raphael, but his trembling was increasing. He couldn't control it any longer.

Mickaël looked at him, without saying a word.

And in comic books, Raphael went on, Superman leaped tall buildings, dug through mountains, and all that stuff without the slightest effort, without even breaking a sweat. He wasn't like them.

The two men remained silent. Raphael looked for something else to say now that time was on his side.

"Why did you want to see me?" he asked.

Mickaël shrugged his shoulders.

"Your ring . . ." he said.

"Is it about the Hermetics' plot?" continued Raphael as if he hadn't heard.

"Is that a new ring you got?" said Mickaël vaguely reaching out to grab his hand.

But at that moment his hand swept through the empty air and with it the top half of his body slumped over.

The Prophet gripped Mickaël tight to him and took off. A bullet grazed his shoulder. Another pierced his thigh, but two seconds later he was already high in the sky. Since Mickaël couldn't be destroyed and since he lost all influence when he was asleep, the only solution, Raphael concluded, was to keep

him in a prolonged coma. And, in spite of the blood he was
losing, in spite of the pain that was making his head spin, he
knew he'd succeeded. The sleeping agent had been adminis-
tered in Mickaël's drink. The drug had acted in under three
minutes. Now the tyrant was sleeping, and, in the pitiless cold
of the high altitude, the air he was cutting through seemed to
scream around him. Raphael held Mickaël's body close to him
like a shield to stop other shots. He squeezed this strangely
limp and soft mass with all his might, believing he could hear
his enemy's heartbeat, but no, it was his own. He felt his heartbeat vibrating in his temples as he headed toward a barracks
that he'd spotted the previous evening. The maze of granite
islets that line the coast was disappearing below him and, in all
its modesty and its grandeur, a landscape opened, riddled with
roofs and striated with roads on which silent vehicles smoothly
moved, following a well-ordered rhythm—that indolent cho-
reography that the affairs of the world take when examined
from high above.

XXI

THE TYRANT WAS now sleeping in the depths of an overdefended base under the influence of an extremely powerful sleeping agent.

Charles de Gaulle Airport opened the following day. In the streets of Paris, with army support, municipal workers and volunteers collected the detritus in record time. Train traffic returned to normal in less than a week. Plus, the 83ers had taken the measures the public expected: they would undergo psychological testing monthly, the evolution of their abilities would be measured weekly, and they would indicate their location every twelve hours.

Finally, people could tell where they'd spent the Twenty-Seven Days. The majority of the French hid at home. Some became hungry, but neighbors helped. The more adventurous ones fled to a neighboring country where migrant camps welcomed them. The food there was awful—and the promiscuity. But nothing too terrible. They could laugh about it now.

At first everything gleamed brightly. Just before turning off the light people would kiss passionately. Then this brilliance itself faded. In the evening, at dinner time, other subjects nudged their way into conversations. People starting treating one another poorly again, jostling each other in the harried back-and-forth of the subway. What's the big deal? The world didn't end. Nothing really happened. I think the French even made it a point of honor to tell themselves: Mickaël wanted to destroy the old world and start over, and he failed. Everything kept going. Thanks to the Prophet, France had indeed resisted.

The final holdouts, those who'd held a firm distrust concerning the Prophet, those who found him haughty and felt he overdid it with his secret identity, even they were won over by the masses singing his praises. He had ended tyranny. *All by himself!* The world was back on the straight and narrow. *Thanks to him!* People bowed before the courage and audacity of this unknown man who, behind his mask, had the most noble of souls. Western governments decorated him with medals. He was promised a Nobel Prize for the following October as well as a place in the Panthéon the day he passed.

On July 25 of Year II, unmasked, anonymous, he was walking in Paris when some way or another—coming across a headline in *Le Monde* at a newspaper stand, overhearing a conversation outside at a café—he learned that Gregory had betrayed him.

The Prophet was named Raphael Zabreski. Photos appeared on the internet. They showed him without his mask at the baptism of the Captain's daughter, for whom he was the godfather. Gregory always denied posting them online. But all signs pointed to him.

Raphael left his two cell phones on a bench at the Palais-Royal. He withdrew €1,000 from an ATM in a nearby street. Then he threw out his credit cards. He never again connected to his email. His Twitter and Facebook accounts remained inactive. No border post signaled his crossing. No air traffic controllers spotted him on their radar screens. He had vanished into thin air.

First hypothesis: the end of a love affair. The week following the incident at Courseulles-sur-Mer, Jeanne and Raphael were supposed to meet up in the same Bordeaux hotel as their previous encounters. Raphael suspected she wouldn't come. She canceled two hours before, but didn't claim something came up. It is not even certain there was a final goodbye between them. It was already over. They knew it ever since the night Gregory had confronted them. And maybe it had been ending for a while. After the rush of the beginning had followed feelings that were more confused, even if neither of them, for different reasons, would admit it. When Raphael heard her breathe a heavy sigh or when a remorseful rictus formed on her face between two kisses, he would sometimes suspect Jeanne of reveling in her role as the lover led astray by a passion she couldn't control. Jeanne couldn't stand the Prophet's complaints about the overwhelming number of pressures his masked life imposed on him. She didn't like that he talked to her about abstract paintings or old movies from the 1930s either. The strange pleasure he got pointing out her contradictions—she was afraid of their being discovered, but wanted to make love in the living room with the curtains open; she would always announce she needed to cut their rendezvous short, and yet at the door, already running quite behind, wouldn't stop pressing herself against him—revealed trouble on the horizon to Jeanne, for there stood a man who reveled in his hold on her, and, perhaps, who especially liked the state of agitation and weakness he found her in. Sometimes, with certain cold smiles he gave when she sighed next to him or talked about impossible getaways to some Greek island dotted with deserted brooks, she felt he looked down his nose at her.

When the affair was over Raphael wanted to escape to the other end of the world. At least that's what he told Virginie,

just after he'd tranquilized Mickaël, when she attended the
Prophet's Roman triumph along the Champs-Élysées atop a
double-decker bus festooned with the tricolors of the Republic.
It wasn't over because her husband had found out everything,
Raphael had explained to her, but because it wasn't actually
going anywhere. Once again he'd been fooling himself. And
what was the result? A lost friendship, suffering on both sides,
him as the bad guy. It was a real shitshow. And it was absolutely more than heartache, Virginie asserted. It seemed like
he was tired of himself. The reason he disappeared, following
this hypothesis, was because he'd messed up everything.

With the second hypothesis, he flees to eliminate his character. One can follow the roots of this desire almost since the
moment the Prophet appeared. Speaking of his special power,
which gave him excruciating headaches, Raphael had said on
multiple occasions that he would have preferred not to possess
it. When he was a guest on an evening talk show nine months
after 1/19 we see him confessing that he envies his colleagues:
Virginie does everything fast, Saïd can make himself invisible,
Jean-Baptiste can change his face . . . It's different, he asserts,
for Gregory who hears everything, for Mickaël who has access
to our secrets thoughts, and for him, since he can see the
future. We inevitably know too much. "The deck's stacked."
This became a nagging concern. What if he stopped? What if
he gave it all up?
     Since Mickaël had been neutralized, there was talk of a new
sect that venerated Raphael, young girls who slit their wrists
because he would never look at them, and incredibly heavy,
colossal replicas that various governments were planning to
erect on esplanades and hilltops. Journalists distinguished
omens in his life before 1/19 announcing his glory. A teacher

confirmed: at four he was already very conscientious. When another student had problems carrying his bookbag, he would rush over and lend a hand.

One day he heard on the radio a French writer, whose short, minutely detailed, and frosty novels he admired, explain why he had accepted to write the libretto for an opera about the Prophet. There was no place for cynicism and irony anymore, the writer declared. His work should be heard as "a declaration of love to the most exceptional man to appear on Earth since Jesus Christ. Plus, with the Prophet, we're sure he exists."

Several times Raphael confided that it was unbearable. He wanted to be left the hell alone. That the end of this relationship with his best friend's wife served as a catalyst is quite possible. But I believe that the salute to the crowd pulsating with affection on the Champs-Élysées, the surrounding streets thick with people who belted out the *Marseillaise* from tear-streaked faces, the homeland's love for its favorite son, and all which that portended—more missions, more achievements, more awards, more ovations—as well as the impossibility of leaving the stage, of escaping the role of the Prophet now that his face had been exposed, and the heart-wrenching knowledge he was amassing about all those who were going to die, about their plans, their future children, their failures, and the bitter years they still had left to live, it was indeed all of this, even if he did not completely understand it, that led him to leave everything.

He was not seen again until the day of his death.

I shall write the next part of his story, but it is not absolutely certain.

PART FOUR

XXII

GREGORY'S ACCOUNT OF what he had seen that day never varied. Everything appeared before his eyes with the clarity of a painting, like a moment frozen in time.

In its center, a man with a scarred face and squashed nose, the quintessential suspicious-looking delinquent, was escaping, helmetless, on the scooter he had just stolen. Behind him, the woman he'd just assaulted was running in the middle of the street, her yellow helmet gleaming in the bright sun, nose bloodied, her mouth contorted in a cry of distress. On the sidewalks, the passersby, quite numerous at this time of day, watched on, powerless, as the distance between the aggressor and his victim increased. At the top of the painting the September sky was filling with swollen storm clouds of an undeniable beauty, but which seemed out of place (one would expect to find them above a frigate with ripped sails facing a turbulent sea). At the edge of the frame to the left in the crosswalk the fugitive was about to cross, a stroller appeared.

At that very moment Gregory was leaving a newspaper stand located on the embankment only a few feet from the entrance to the Ménilmontant subway stop. An assistant was with him. A copy of *L'Équipe* was tucked under his arm. He was planning on eating at one of the couscous restaurants in the neighborhood whose walls were covered, he had learned, with paintings of his likeness. In the distance a church bell was striking one o'clock.

That same morning, a bit before 8:00 A.M., he'd ousted, from the restroom of a neighboring café, a drug addict who was shooting up. He gave him two spectacular slaps before lifting him by the collar and throwing him out, threatening that he would do much worse the next time he found him mainlining in a public place.

He spent the rest of the morning as the guest of honor at a soccer tournament organized by an association fighting against social exclusion, visiting a retirement home where the photo session dragged on forever, and finally trying to reason with a group of adolescents who were terrorizing neighborhood residents by perching on the handlebars of their minibikes and following behind them on the sidewalk. This profusion of good acts must have made him forget the absence of his children who were spending the weekend at their mother's. But the smiles seemed reserved. The handshakes lacked warmth. As for the neighborhood adolescents, they'd just given him shit, and he'd had to hold himself back from smacking one of them upside the head when he asked why the Captain hadn't come in tights and a cape.

Over the course of the past few weeks he had increased the number of missions outside Paris and was overjoyed to rediscover the unfailing pleasures the life of a superhero offered. Flying at 400 kilometers an hour, screaming anything that came to mind while up there, nosediving into a corkscrew spin, pirouetting among the clouds, slowing down and drifting wherever the air currents took him when he had an extra fifteen minutes before his next mission—each and every time this was guaranteed to be an adrenaline rush, giving thrills as intense, why deny it, as sex at its best. And fighting evil, taking down heavily armed adversaries in two blows, incarnating justice and seeing it triumph, and even just glimpsing the incredulous and dismayed look on the bastards' faces when he appeared—day after day this boosted his self-esteem. He convinced himself that, in spite of a painful divorce that deprived him of his children part of the time, he could be happy as the first servant of the nation, as the saintly man who dedicated his life to the triumph of good. He simply needed the French to be grateful. Well, people still loved him, but probably not as much as he would've liked, and less than the Prophet.

In three quick strides he reached a bench and launched off it so that, in a parabolic leap, he could collar the escaping fugitive, holding him firmly with one hand, and, while his scooter skidded down the road in a trail of sparks, give him a devastating blow with his free hand.

Behind the emphatic force of this action were the fatigue from the morning, the certainty of dealing with a delinquent with whom it was not necessary to hold back, and probably also the overflowing frustration and anger that had accumulated since the day he'd surprised Raphael and Jeanne in Courseulles.

Now that they were separated, and even if Gregory, out of pride, hadn't wanted to tell anyone the real reason for the divorce—he'd made do with "growing apart" in a statement—those close to him said they saw it all coming, fanning the flames of the Captain's resentment by telling him all the major and minor wrongs committed by that ex-wife he'd thought he knew so well.

Fifteen days after the statement was published, when the public learned that she had cheated on him with Raphael

Zabreski,[1] the criticisms were freer and the anecdotes more spiteful. Gregory got no joy in hearing them, and deep down what made him the saddest about what people were saying was the story itself—the idea that there had been a beginning, a middle, and an end, hidden themes, portentous signs, delayed reactions, and a logical conclusion. This love, which he'd believed he could remove from the course of time, those seven years of marriage which avoided any kind of waning or weariness, now seemed like a chunk of wood that had been eaten away by the patient work of worms. Just another chunk to heave on the pile of failed marriages.

Noëllie Rodriguez, Jeanne's former friend, offered her own little vicious story. Here Gregory learned that there was at least a precedent for what he henceforth only called his ex-wife's "perversity." At the Athens Olympic Games, Noëllie revealed, Jeanne found herself in the same locker room as Corneliu Bobesco, a Romanian tennis player who was floundering at the bottom of the world rankings. There must have been an error in space assignments (these Games were a bit of a mess). Bobesco had just lost a match in three sets, and when Jeanne walked in the locker room all that remained on his battle-tested, sweat-covered body was the thin swatch of fabric of a tight-fitting pair of underwear. Either it was a momentary lapse of reason, the joyous and unbridled atmosphere of the Olympic Village encouraging her nearly spontaneously, or she had wished, for reasons that her character allow us to imagine, to escape from herself by a unexpected act: Jeanne walked up to him. Her doubles match was scheduled for forty-five minutes later. She kneeled down in front of Corneliu Bobesco, slid

[1] It is probable, despite the lovers' discretion and extreme precautions, that some people had learned of their relationship—inopportune witnesses who at one time or another were able to see them together, be it government employees who monitored the 83ers' communications or potential confidants either to Jeanne, Raphael, or even Gregory. The source of the leak was never determined.

his sweat-soaked underwear to his calves, exposing his shaved sex, and grabbed it with her cool hand.

Gregory listened, barely shaking his head. As soon as the confidante had left he grabbed his phone. "I only gave him head," protested Jeanne when he wanted to know if this story were indeed true.

It wasn't jealousy that was torturing him at that moment. The circumstances were from a time before he knew her. How could he be jealous? But the thought of his wife having sexual relations with that Romanian tennis player was still unbearable. The Jeanne he'd known for all those years couldn't have taken part in a situation such as this, neither before they'd met nor after. And then the word "head," that she'd uttered made his stomach turn. Moreover, she must have figured that out, for she added, laughing: "Is it the word that bothers you?" *Head*, was it too concrete for him? Shortly after he thought she was getting revenge by showing him how different she was from the image he must have had of her. Perhaps this was her own way of leaving him—of showing him, now that he could view her from a distance, from the other side, that she was someone else, someone he'd never seen.

Out of control, the scooter continued forward, hitting a pedestrian, Alice Letellier, who had just calmly pulled a mother and her stroller back from entering the crosswalk. But Gregory, eyes trained on the delinquent, at first saw none of this collateral tragedy. Bullheaded, the man got on his knees, trying to catch his breath, mouth smeared with blood, while the 83er felt the eyes of the bystanders fixed on him. So, doubtlessly giving in to his vanity, Gregory allowed himself to show off with a circular kick that he had only previously attempted in training, a delicate maneuver, requiring dexterity and explosiveness.

He executed the move perfectly, his heel smashing against the aggressor's temple at the right moment. The impact drove him through a billboard ten meters away.

Still rapturous, the pleasure of such a clean action became even sharper when remembering the previous night. Having had too much to drink, Gregory had left a dinner organized by one of his advisors in the arms of an aide, a pretty girl he'd never taken the time to look at. Once in bed, the jubilation of getting back at Jeanne by fucking the first person who came around gave way to doubts. He wasn't sure he really wanted to, he hesitated, and after a couple thrusts he decided to pull out. A bit later, as an uncomfortable silence had settled around them, he started caressing her again, but uncertainty overcame him, and he soon pulled away. She looked at him, confused. He started to talk. He was going to explain. He couldn't find the words. Tears ran down the young woman's face. She sharply turned away when he held out his hand to wipe them away.

Neither clamor nor applause greeted his intervention. Not even an approving murmur, one of those faint rustlings in the air that since 1/19 Gregory's ear was used to detecting as he passed by. When he turned back toward the crowd that had amassed along the embankment, everything froze again. Dumbfounded faces scrutinized him. His young assistant's hand was covering her mouth. In the street, the woman with the bloody face was running, bathed in tears, toward her aggressor, whose legs were hanging from the advertisement he'd just passed through.

There had been a misunderstanding.

After a dozen years doing walk-on roles and stunts, Karim Benaddane had started to pick up a few lines as a gangster or bodyguard. He'd recently started playing a secondary cop on a popular police drama, nothing amazing, but it did give him some exposure, and he spent the fees he'd earned polishing his craft in workshops designed for actors such as himself, neither beginners nor seasoned vets. For a little while now he'd felt the world had taken a turn for the better and was more welcoming. He was navigating life effortlessly; even his body was more at ease. One day he would be famous and in demand.

That Sunday he'd left an apartment building near Alexandre Dumas where his new girlfriend lived, an actress who was amazing and a bit crazy, whom he'd recently met at a workshop. They were both on his scooter headed for brunch near Saint-Louis Hospital, when a large SUV suddenly pulled out in front of them. Karim hesitated between swerving and breaking, and did both at the same time. His scooter hit a parked car. A dull thud jolted him. He saw his companion on her knees, wailing. Blood trickled down her face. Karim got scared, forcefully yanked her to her feet, which he immediately regretted, and turned toward the SUV, which had slammed on the brakes. Inside he saw the panic-stricken look of a man about his age, his chestnut hair tastefully swept back above his overly-tanned face. The perfect mugshot of the consummate asshole in his Audi, thought Karim, taking off his helmet to yell and maybe thump him more easily. But from the departing SUV a conclusive-sounding "Everything okay?" was emitted. The vehicle was leaving, the guy was getting away. Then, after this moment when everything slowed down, it all accelerated again. Insults poured from his companion's mouth. Karim hopped on his scooter with the idea of catching the reckless driver. Coming back to her senses, his friend tried to hold him back. He took off. The SUV took a sharp turn disappearing in the maze of tiny streets to the north of the boulevard. People on the streets froze, their faces tensing up. Benaddane continued to speed up, helmetless and angry, without a care for the rules of the road. His companion ran behind him yelling to forget it. In one glance Gregory believed he understood everything, and, above their heads, rolled the epic contours of very un-Parisian clouds.

XXIII

MANY PEOPLE ARE convinced that it is nearly impossible to disappear today, that States, and especially the United States, know everything about us, or are at least able in just a few short hours to locate us, follow us, and maybe even eliminate us. Our phones, it is well known, have become snitches. Cameras are everywhere. The emails you send can be read as you write them. Every year, however, approximately 80,000 people vanish throughout the world and are never found. It is certainly necessary to remove from this contingent those desperate people who, after jumping off a bridge, sink unnoticed to the bottom of rivers. Victims of perfect murders, lying under concrete slabs or three meters underground at the far end of some isolated dell should also be struck out. Finally, we must delete those unfortunate prisoners, languishing in windowless rooms, locked away by their fellow man, for whom they are slaves. Yet nonetheless you will still have on your hands thousands of fugitives eluding investigation.

As former spies have publicly lamented, progress in surveillance technology has narrowed the spectrum of intelligence gathering. Even though machines are less costly to maintain than agents in the field, and less temperamental, they will always have difficulty uncovering the impostor pretending to be an ordinary person. Henceforth, to be discovered, the individual must prove to be imprudent. Proud of their deception and eager to boast about it, they must be impelled by the desire to promulgate subversive ideas, associate with semi-clandestine networks, return to places they loved, or call family and friends to catch up. But if they distance themselves from their past and informants who have infiltrated criminogenic environments, if they've given their neighbors no reason to worry about their mental health or criminal record, the chances of being tracked down are infinitely small.

Obviously the Prophet was not a typical fugitive. For various and sundry reasons a number of intelligence agencies and private sector groups had an interest in locating him. But Raphael knew how to stay disciplined. Unsure as to whom to contact and concerned about running into untrustworthy intermediaries who would inform on him, he didn't even risk obtaining false papers. It was simplest not to need them. He decided to never drive again for fear of being pulled over. Other measures were also necessary: he would never have more than one drink per evening, he would insult no one, and, if necessary, he, the superhero, would let himself get worked over without fighting back. Of course he would avoid areas near mosques, anarchist bookstores, and street corners where illegal substances were procured. He'd never access the internet again. He would claim to have no interest in politics. He'd make up a vague and credible resumé for himself, which he would avoid discussing as much as possible. He'd grow a beard. He would move to a cosmopolitan city with an understaffed police force and wouldn't leave. To survive he'd work off the books in a restaurant kitchen or else on a construction site. If necessary, he'd supplement his wages by collecting bottles and turning them in for cash. He wouldn't keep track of his efforts to erase himself.

People believed they saw him just about everywhere—in Lyon, Rio, New York City, London, Australia. They claimed that, overcome with remorse concerning Mickaël, he had committed suicide. That he'd been committed to an insane asylum. That he'd been taken prisoner by Russia, or ISIS, or a sect that worshiped him. That the CIA was hiding him, or Cuba, or Benedictine monks in a Tuscan monastery. People said he'd changed his appearance and was living in the suburbs of a large German city with a childhood sweetheart. Or else, on the run, he had been reduced to hiding in the interstitial spaces of large cities—vacant lots, train yards, buildings scheduled for demolition—and committing petty crimes to buy food.

I was still a reporter with *Últimas Noticias* in Santiago when my editor sent me to discreetly check on one of these rumors. For several weeks in the hills above the port in Valparaíso a tall, bearded Frenchman going by the name of Samuel Vernet had been staying in a hotel for hard up travelers. He had red hair and grey eyes, but these details were no reason to give up. The Prophet could have changed his appearance, especially if his escape had been supported by a foreign government, which remained a plausible hypothesis.[1]

For three days I followed Vernet around the city. In the mornings, taking advantage of the still soft colors, he took a few conventional photos of colonial houses, rusted old train engines, and outdoor murals in the Bellavista neighborhood. During the warmest part of the day he flipped the pages of a discount paperback edition of *Moby-Dick* in various cafés. In the evenings, bellied up to the bars in the upper city, eyes half closed, he seduced tourists who were younger than he with

---

[1] In fact, a popular theory claims that he was rapidly located by the American Secret Service, but they protected his clandestinity. The reasons for this decision were drawn from the usual grab bag of contemporary conspiracy theories: Raphael was working for them, Raphael was Jewish, Raphael knew when the world would end, etc.

his nice smile, prestige as a photographer, and polite but firm refusal to say where he was from.

Two of those tourists were able to confirm this: he had something to hide. In his room a heavy, metal suitcase rested on the desk, which he slid under the bed as soon as they entered. At night his sleep seemed agitated. At times he murmured strings of numbers. Finally, to one of the women, he had confided that he was a wanted man, and, to avoid putting her in danger too, they should not see each other again, ever.

On the morning of the fourth day I approached him outside his hotel. When I declared that his suitcase contained nothing important and that I'd say nothing about his rather crude song and dance routine if he agreed to have coffee with me, he put up no resistance in revealing his true identity.

His name was Corentin Dumont, and he had been a part, just after 1/19, of the hordes of *superligans* who neglected their studies, their jobs, or their love lives to dedicate themselves to their passion for the 83ers. With other supporters Dumont ran White Heat, a discussion forum dedicated to the Prophet's feats. Shortly after the superhero's disappearance, he had gathered his savings and had gotten the idea of finding him stuck in his head. Having read somewhere that in the summer of 2011 Raphael had travelled to South America and had a fond memory of Valparaíso, Dumont had started to think that maybe, if the 83er wanted to restart his life, he would decide to hide here, far, far from Europe, in this large, poor, and chaotic port, where the locals, who were used to both foreigners passing through and lost souls, would not ask any questions.

Dumont started looking for the Prophet on a whim, electrified by the promise of considerable fame if he were the first to flush him out. But he had no idea how to proceed. Although the days progressed, the investigation did not, and Dumont simply ended up attracting the attention of a waiter who had noticed the Frenchman's proclivity for talking about the 83ers, albeit cautiously. One night the server and his brother-in-law accosted him and dragged him to a parking area, which had become a vacant lot, or vice versa. There, they demanded money and threatened to tell the press everything. Even though Dumont vehemently denied it, the waiter remained convinced that this thirty-six-year-old Frenchman, traveling alone, was the superhero everyone was looking for. Only the fortuitous arrival of a bus full of drunk Chileans allowed the makeshift detective to escape this hornet's nest.

The pieces were then put in place.

His savings drying up, merchants offered him credit. In exchange, once the storefronts were closed, he claimed to call upon his powers of prediction and foretold his creditors of their generally magnificent futures. These men and women who were in on the secret were half convinced this was the Prophet—but in Chile we love a good story, and I know plenty of people who would pay the check for a liar as long as his story's captivating.

In public, Dumont played the role of a man on the run, enigmatic and reticent, which he endowed with the deep voice of an adventurer and a partiality for travel photography, having noted that with some seducers who worked the bars popular with Europeans, these attributes always got results. As the weeks passed and the range of his role expanded (he'd just had a weathered white mask fabricated, which he poorly hid in his closet), the profit he was gathering enflamed his audacity and persuaded him that this was the best possible result to his investigation. He was enchanted by his own deception. Now he dreamed of piquing the interest of spies and mystics, who, having left in quest of the Prophet, would flock around him and closely scrutinize his slightest move.

Among those who proclaimed to know the whereabouts of Raphael Zabreski, the Brazilian Luiz Gustavo Mora is the only one who seems credible in my eyes. Twenty-five years old when he started his search, he had never shown but a modest interest in the French superheroes—like everything, moreover, which was his problem. The only son of a wealthy mining entrepreneur from São Paulo, after studies in metallurgical engineering, which were brilliant but superfluous given his annual allowance, he returned to the life of leisure typical of young people of his caste. Although he tried to take an interest in the modernization of gold mines in Mato Grasso, the construction of a children's hospital, or offshore powerboat racing, in which his impetuosity brought him renown, each time he was overcome with boredom.

He would elude it temporarily by reading detective novels and acquiring new objects for his personal collections: diving helmets, vintage skis, and early wooden tennis rackets. According to him, the mystery of the Prophet piqued his curiosity at a time when, more idle than ever, he was contemplating an early death.

Like Dumont and so many of his rivals, Luiz Gustavo started by traveling to places that tickled his imagination. He had the means and didn't spare any expense. Among the places the Prophet had mentioned, Luiz Gustavo favored the exotic: a hostess club in Manilla, a Guinean montane forest, and even an island in the South Atlantic which had been described to him as the most remote place in the world whose ice cap, uninhabitable except for a few birds and marine mammals, seemed to him ideal for satisfying the wish for solitude of a superman in a white mask.

Preparing for his expedition, each day Luiz Gustavo imagined the Prophet's glorious asceticism on the island a bit better.

Surrounded by a desert of pewter colored water, equipped with a simple tent, a portable stove, and provisions for several months, when the 83er wasn't reading he would stretch out in the snow, listen to the wind, or meditate before the unchanging horizon and equanimous life of the local fauna. Landing on the island, however, the helicopter charted by the Brazilian struck panic in the ranks of penguins. There was a crush, and several were injured. No human was on that inky rock, and Luiz Gustavo, at a loss, felt crushed like never before by his own stupidity.

That excursion cured him of any romantic notions. Back in São Paulo, he sat in his office to reflect. He could no longer follow his desires or outside rumors.

The Prophet, he reasoned, had chosen to reside in a place that fulfilled several criteria for security.

There should be no reason to look for him there. This excluded places that he'd already visited, those that he may have, even just once, mentioned he would like to visit, and finally the destinations that, like the island Luiz Gustavo visited, the peak of Mount Everest, or the northern-most city in the world, charmed minds such as his own that were smitten with elegant solutions but lacked common sense. No chance finding him on Desolación Island, in Farway, or at Solitude Mountain Resort either. If his goal was never to be found, he had every reason to avoid puns, symbols, and eccentricities.

He would also need to limit travel to avoid identity checks and spare himself the uncertainties related to arriving in new places, where he would not have the protections he normally possessed in everyday life. But he probably also needed a large city's varying entertainment options in order to endure this forced sedentariness. Plus, a large city would increase his chances of going unnoticed.

Luiz Gustavo set the floor at 1,000,000 inhabitants, which, from Odessa to Shanghai, still left him 346 options. So he bet: 1) Raphael had fled France where his risk of being recognized was the highest, and 2) he had moved to a country where he understood the language to blend in with the crowd more easily. That said, he only spoke English. This reduced the list to around twenty cities, from which he removed London, New York, and Chicago (Raphael had already stayed in the cities for more than a week), as well as Dublin and Sydney (he had told Sonja Bachmann he would like to visit them).

There remained slightly over fifteen cities following this line of reasoning, whose flaws were numerous, but still it did restrict the investigation to places where the Prophet had a real chance of being found. Seventeen teams of three investigators were hired and secretly dispatched to Adelaide, Birmingham, Calgary, Dallas, Johannesburg, Houston, Cape Town, Los Angeles, Melbourne, Philadelphia, Phoenix, Pretoria, Vancouver, San Antonio, San Diego, Toronto, and, after some hesitation, Montreal, which Luiz Gustavo hardly believed a viable option, but at this stage, for only a few thousand euros more, he felt it a bit stupid to eliminate without having inspected it.

To the detectives he employed, the Brazilian scion had imposed one critical rule: once they had catalogued the French, Belgians, Swiss, and Quebecois between the ages of twenty and sixty who had been residing in the city for less than six months, their investigation was over. He would do the rest. Because if he was doing all this, he asserted, it was for the thrill of the hunt, in which, in the end, would remain only hunter and his quarry.

Nearly every city offered potential Prophets. In the first three Luiz Gustavo visited, Calgary, Cape Town, and Birmingham, the investigation was fruitless. Then, at the end of September, two months after Raphael's disappearance, the young Brazilian visited Los Angeles. No fewer than 11 French speakers had been located who might correspond to the man he was seeking. He had deliberately sketched an extremely vague profile. A 48-year-old lawyer from Martinique who landed at the airport with his wife and three children and was working relentlessly since his arrival for an energy management company, for example, had remained on the list of suspects, despite evidence that indicated his name should be removed. Luiz Gustavo believed the Prophet capable of all types of subterfuge.

A certain Bastien Rémy claimed to have arrived in Los Angeles from Paris in June, but his name did not appear on any flight manifest going to California during that time period. An investigation of passenger lists extended to the past year yielded nothing either.

And even if a quick check on the internet showed five Facebook accounts open under the name Bastien Rémy, none seemed to correspond to the individual the investigators hired by Luiz Gustavo had indicated: a thirty-something man with a shaggy beard and full head of hair, who claimed he was a French actor dreaming of Hollywood but who had never attended a casting call.

Suspicion became certainty when Luiz Gustavo was able to study the man on the terrace of a bar where he was sipping an iced coffee while paging through the *L.A. Times*. His long bushy hair, beard, and coppery tone made him nearly unrecognizable. The back of his wrist was now decorated with a mandala tattoo, which, for a moment, gave Luiz Gustavo pause, along with the red tank top in a breathable fabric, oversized shorts, and old tennis shoes he was wearing. Although for the past two months in his mind the Brazilian had variously situated the Prophet in such disparate places as a misty jungle, the depths of a Turkish prison, an islet lost in a sea of ice, and then in one or another of the seventeen cities where he thought he would find him, Luiz Gustavo always pictured him in the dark, fitted clothing of an elegant Parisian.

He followed him in a supermarket and then to a video store where the Prophet rented several old Hollywood movies. The following morning the Brazilian was in the bus that dropped the 83er off in front of the scorched grass of Griffith Park, where, after some stretching, he ran for an hour. Luiz Gustavo was finally tasting the joy he'd been anticipating: he now knew what everyone else did not. He was elated that at any time he could peer into the Prophet's cards like a sharp.

The same day, as the superhero left with a towel around his neck and a beach bag under his arm, Luiz Gustavo used his skeleton key and entered his home for the first time. It was a one-bedroom just off Hollywood Boulevard in a two-story complex. Raphael's neighbors were an old, dying smoker on a ventilator and a large, overweight Hispanic family. The 83er had sublet the apartment from a couple who had gone to Europe for several months, so Luiz Gustavo couldn't determine which decor elements were the Prophet's: hanging above a couch, a washed out painting of a view of Florence; attached by magnets to the refrigerator door, the photograph of a newborn and a red and blue children's drawing; in the bedroom on a bookshelf next to the bed, a well-thumbed copy of the novel *The Victim* and an essay on survival techniques in nature, whose grainy-textured green buckram binding Luiz Gustavo enjoyed feeling beneath his fingers.

While he lingered in front of a reproduction of an industrial landscape painted by Charles Sheeler, someone lightly knocked twice on the front door. Luiz Gustavo, terror stricken, heard a key slide into the lock, the door open, a "Bastien?" uttered in a low voice by a woman with an American accent, then a few steps, water from the faucet splashing in the kitchen sink, silence, a few more steps, and then the front door clicking shut. He rushed to the living room and, through the slats of the blinds, caught a glimpse of a tall, blond woman walking away. On the kitchen table was a note she'd scribbled down: WOULD 10 P.M. BE OKAY? followed by the name RENEE.

Today she is a strikingly and intimidatingly beautiful thirty-two-year-old woman with a husky voice and broad shoulders. She welcomed me to her villa in the hills of Westlake Village, where she's lived since a cable channel started showing a police drama for which she wrote five or six episodes. The years and success must not have greatly changed the Renee Fletcher that Raphael knew. On her tattooed body she wears a tank top emblazoned with a heavy metal band, skintight jeans, and round-toe cowboy boots. She still smokes heavily, and her lips leave bright red marks on her wine glass.

At the time when Renee met Bastien, she was writing the beginnings of novels and trying to place a screenplay with an agent. She spent the end of her teen years modeling and then too quickly married a wealthy fifty year old, who, two months after the wedding, decided to buy them a ranch in Oregon, an isolated property at the end of a gravel road, which they would stock with horses, pigs, and children, and from which she decided she would escape on the first night. While waiting for the divorce, she came back and lived with her sister, two streets over from the apartment where Bastien was living. Her husband had also returned to Los Angeles, begging her to give them more time, and threatening to put a bullet through his head if she wouldn't change her mind. She had to change her number. He worried her. To avoid a scene Bastien and Renee would see each other mostly at his house, after dark, in the utmost secrecy.

Nothing about the Frenchman's behavior shocked her. She found him to be serious, but in her mind all French were somewhat like that. He didn't work much, never drove, and didn't have a cell phone, which in Southern California easily came across as a lifestyle choice that shouldn't be discussed. She'd believed she could tell that Bastien had come less to find success in the film industry than to change his life. While they sipped ice-cold beer on the front balcony of the apartment, he would say things like, "You gotta make the most of everything right away." Then they'd go make love in the unmade bed.

She'd met Bastien shortly after he arrived in the area at a neighborhood resale shop where he worked every afternoon. It was a large warehouse filled with desks from the 1950s, brass lamps, beds, leather shoes, vintage postcards, and movie post-ers. There was nothing like it—a cigarette case or a figurine set with abalone between its hands—for imagining the story of its owner or the curious way the items made their way here, and soon you're excited to buy, for not that much either, an old eccentric Argentinian's favorite accessory or the souvenir of a lost love found on a farm in Nebraska that was about to be razed. She liked it quite a bit.

I don't think I would be exaggerating to say he was in love. First off because he'd always had, as far as he could remember, a beloved to occupy his thoughts, his daydreams, his plans to declare his intentions and run away together if she said yes. And even if he later recognized that he was wrong, that he liked the idea of loving and the feverish state the idea put him in more than the person who elicited those feelings, he still would let himself be swept away by a new crush.

Luiz Gustavo is also convinced that for Raphael this

relationship was much more than something to pass the time. One day at the beach, after watching Renee walk toward the waves, the 83er leaned over the t-shirt she'd left behind and breathed in deeply. A few hours later, as the moon was rising and the beach was emptying, they billed and cooed, exchanging sweet nothings, noting that life was beautiful, all the more so since they'd met. At one point she started humming a pioneer song her grandmother had taught her. The lovers slowly strode back to Renee's car, shoulder to shoulder, and she continued to sing. Her low voice drifted off in the night air, and the sea breeze blew the words to Luiz Gustavo, who was walking behind them.

He decided to keep the discovery to himself. He told the investigators working for him that Bastien Rémy was not the man they were looking for. And, to keep up the charade, he made a few of the planned trips—Dallas, Vancouver, Toronto—before announcing that he was pulling the plug, that his method included too many question marks, and that they'd never find anyone this way.

At least once a month Luiz Gustavo would go back to Los Angeles alone. It was his guilty pleasure. He felt like he had the Prophet under his thumb and was observing him in this city he would never leave, like an animal held prisoner in a cage. The thought that the captive was happy lessened his nascent remorse, however.

"We never made the slightest plans," explains Renee Fletcher. "We didn't talk about the future. And he couldn't've asked me more than three questions about what I'd done before." They ate a great deal, having discovered they both had huge appetites as well as a love for the taco joints in Boyle Heights and on Figueroa. They watched old movies and slept until hunger woke them, around 10 or 11 in the morning.

On fall evenings, the streets still warm, they'd lean against the balcony railing and watch kids play in their yards in front of porches. Winter came, and they holed up inside the apartment, cranking up the radiators, and lounging in the living room, naked for the most part. When a delivery person would come with food, they'd barely put on any clothes to open the door and pay.

In his journal, which has very few entries from this era, Raphael sporadically notes: "The inside of Renee's arm." "Renee's dragon tattoo (ugly)." "Her fine hair strewn across her face when she sleeps in the morning." She shrugs her shoulders with an embarrassed laugh when I mention these few notes. They spent time looking at each other, she replies softly. Raphael started it. People don't pay enough attention, he used to say. Every day he wanted to concentrate on one part of Renee's body. And she started doing the same: Raphael's flat stomach, his cock, his foot. It was like meditation exercises. And they were filled with wonder.

In the apartment building across the street where he rented a furnished flat to observe them, Luiz Gustavo soon grew bored. Happy people don't make gripping characters. And in his mind he was hatching a new plan. Now that he'd found one, he started to imagine he could hunt down other fugitives, discover where they were hiding, the stories they'd invented, and never tell anyone a word, of course, because a missing person ceases to be one the day they're unmasked.

He'd heard of a German banker hidden in the Indonesian Archipelago. Then of a French jihadist, named "Grand Ali," living clandestinely somewhere in England. These would be his new prey. Raphael, thought Luis Gustavo, was the first object in his unique collection: ghosts only he could see.

XXIV

Two WEEKS AFTER the blunder in Ménilmontant, Gregory went to his oldest daughter's grade school. He had been summoned. Lucille had bitten a classmate for the third time.

The school's director must not have liked the French superheroes very much. As soon as he walked in the door Gregory could sense it, he related, through a certain stiffness in the director's bearing and his darting, indecisive eyes that avoided making contact with his own. The Captain forced himself to remain calm and courteous, even when the man spoke to him of *sociopathy*. It wasn't definite, he explained, several elements, however, lead one to make that diagnosis. Lucille had formed no bonds with her classmates. Although she always understood what was expected, it was obvious she didn't listen to instructions. On several occasions she had exhibited a penchant for cruelty. She never felt any remorse. This was most noticeable in the malicious smiles she flashed when other students showed signs of distress. And then there was this series of bitings.

Gregory nodded, his head burning and hair glued to his forehead in the stickiness of the overheated office. He closed his eyes and concentrated on his breathing, remembering the advice of a therapist he'd started to see.

The parents of his daughter's latest victim, continued the

director, were very nice people. They absolutely didn't want word of this to get out. Given the difficulties that Lucille's parents were going through, they were very conscious about avoiding this. But they were expecting the parents to do something. Had to follow up on the issue.

No, thought Gregory, the director didn't like the 83ers, and he enjoyed humiliating him without appearing to.

The Captain wanted to tell the director he was exaggerating. A run-of-the-mill incident was being given a significance it didn't deserve. Right then and there he should have gotten angry, but he lacked conviction. Maybe this evil man, who seemed to have figured out this seven-year-old child's true nature, which she kept shielded behind good manners and a well-behaved, almost absent appearance, was right after all.

At the slightest vexation, Lucille would sink into fit of rage from which only exhaustion offered an escape. She'd recently become obsessed with fixing her hair, and a hundred times a day Gregory caught her brushing invisible stands of hair off her forehead. In order to leave the apartment she followed a strict ritual that required her to walk backward out the door and rebutton her coat several times. Friends and family assured the Captain it was the separation that was upsetting Lucille. It would all pass. But he, on the other hand, believed her problems went deeper.

From a very early age his daughter had displayed a proclivity for order that delighted guests and made her parents proud. At three she could spend an hour folding her clothes on the coffee table. She lined up her crayons and colored without ever going outside the lines. But at approximately the same age, they had to return a new set of chintz curtains they had installed in the living room without telling her, which she threatened to tear down. Anything unexpected was unbearable. If her father walked to school to pick her up instead of driving like normal, she would lie on the ground and scream, refusing to move, and he could make out on her face, while not daring to push her and quietly ordering her to get up, a smile of victory, strangely sad and frozen. When he heard people talk about the unconditional love their children inspired in them, Gregory envied this seemingly obvious fact. He saw Lucille as some indecipherable alien creature, and he was not upset that his separation from Jeanne kept him away from her half the time.

The night after being summoned, dead drunk, his mind probably muddled by an incorrect dosage of his antianxiety medicine, the Captain stooped to badmouthing monogamy outside the opening night of a bridal show, which he went to without exactly knowing why. He quoted Beaumarchais from memory, whom he'd studied for his baccalaureate exams in high school: "Oh, woman, woman, woman, weak and deceitful creature!" A witness's telephone recorded nearly the entire tirade, which at times the uncomfortable and condescending laughter of the bystanders crowding around him drowned out.

The regrettable video of the wooly-tongued 83er, which, as expected, made it around the world in a couple of minutes, garnered, as expected, unanimous condemnation from the Élysée to the Vatican, including those who manufactured equipment he used, the charitable organizations he represented, and the celebrities who never missed an occasion to flaunt their virtue on Twitter. Thérèse and Saïd distanced themselves from him, too. Virginie, however, was an exception. It was all too easy, she asserted, to judge Gregory in that state. She herself was dealing with an intense form of depression and refused to condemn a man who was obviously not in his right mind.

When he came across the video the following day, apparently

Gregory was neither surprised nor shattered. Virginie confirmed that he felt a strange relief to have gotten to this point, as if something inside him was delighted by this disastrous turn of events. His lip was purple and swollen from some punch, but he didn't know who had thrown it. He remembered hugging a woman who licked his ear in a restroom, but he couldn't say if it really happened or if he just dreamed it. He was unable to recall what he'd drunk or ingested over the past twenty-four hours. Around him, his advisors' faces, their telephone conversations, hushed like at a deceased person's home, up to and including the bleak appearance of objects themselves, which one might have said had been tarnished by a layer of grey powder: everything bore witness to a world that had been destroyed. Ultimately, it resembled the idea he had of his own state. But in good stories, he knew, the main guy falls very far and then climbs back up again. Soon, everything would sort itself out.

To advise him on the Ménilmontant scandal, Shivaji Rai, an Anglo-Indian strategic communications expert, was recommended. This forty-five-year-old polyglot, with a colossal build and impeccably cinched Italian wool suits, had successfully gone from managing the image of sports stars implicated in sex scandals to public relations for a petroleum group embroiled by an oil spill that was contaminating seals. From their very first meeting Rai was categorical: no statement would be enough to end the crisis. Gregory needed to appear on the nightly news as soon as possible. Words must elude him. Emotion must choke him up. Tears must be shed.

Gregory balked at that idea. But the situation didn't really leave him much choice. He had struck an innocent person in plain daylight. A wonderful young woman who had instinctively pulled back the stroller, which Benaddane was ready

to mow down in pursuit of the reckless driver, was in serious
condition after the actor's scooter crashed headlong into her—
and even though Gregory could not be held directly responsible for her injuries, all of the witnesses confirmed that his
actions definitely made the vehicle veer toward her. Finally,
since his unfortunate tirade at the bridal show, people regarded
the Captain as a macho alcoholic, a loser, a real asshole. "So,
you're really going to need to have a really good cry," Shivaji
Rai reportedly said. "A crying asshole, that's at least a start."

Opinion polls revealed that the undertaking was rather successful. He didn't mention overwork or any other extenuating
circumstances. He avoided saying the word "error," which was
too weak, and without blinking assumed responsibility for a
"mistake," which he deemed "very grave." He didn't offer his
apologies, but asked the French, as this was more humble, to
forgive him. He didn't say, "I take responsibility," which ran
the risk of appearing arrogant. Instead he mumbled: "I can't
look at myself in the mirror."

For those like me who remembered his first appearance on
television after 1/19, there was something startling in seeing
him wearing the same suit and a nearly identical tie, across the
table from the same newscaster, but this time with red eyes
and looking peaked—after negotiations with the news editor,
Shivaji Rai had reached an agreement that his client would not
be made up. Gregory hadn't cried since his mother's death. He
didn't think he could. But Rai, just before going live, repeatedly asked him how he felt, if he was going to hold up, if he
needed a tissue, plus his way of rubbing Gregory's arm, of
gazing up at him with his round eyes shining in commisera-
tion, eventually filled the Captain with emotion, making him
overwrought. When the moment came, he cried.

However, skeptics had been out in the streets starting the

day after the blunder in Ménilmontant. It would soon be two years since the 83ers had first appeared. Taking stock of the situation, it was disastrous:

- Jean-Baptiste—Killed in action
- Thérèse—Handicapped
- Virginie—Half crazy, in a rest home
- Mickaël—Also crazy, neutralized
- Raphaël—Vanished
- Saïd—Suing the French government
- Gregory—Ultraviolent

From the jail cells where they awaited trials, those who had dealt with the 83ers finally got a sympathetic ear. Their accounts mentioned brutal arrests, humiliations, gratuitous violence, an occasional damaged inner ear, sleeping issues, and trauma. Sure, they were bad guys, but now that there were doubts about the Captain, they had rights, too. People demanded a bright light be shone on the French superheroes' transgressions and on the complacency at the highest levels that supported them. People wanted a model democracy. They called for a referendum. Each day the number of protesters increased. High schoolers skipped class. In some neighborhoods several cars were burned. Riot police were stationed at intersections. Only the Prophet, naturally, escaped criticism.

So Gregory panicked. He felt he'd gotten the shaft. With this mishap he was going to pay for the others' mistakes, for Mickaël's insanity, for Saïd's cynicism. He would never be forgiven for anything. "They hate us," he said. And it was possible, he thought more and more frequently, that the world's screwed up. That people who are deserving, such as himself, are never rewarded. There's no justice.

He looked on the internet for everything he could find

about the Prophet. He combed through pages of news, images, and discussion groups. Every time he came across some muckraking—and it existed, in spite of everything—Gregory would gloat. But most of the time, after each new click, he gritted his teeth. It was nothing but a long series of celebrations, inane remembrances, and puff pieces.

When the affair between Jeanne and Raphael was making headlines, to the wounds of the cuckold's lower self-esteem was applied the salve of a comforting thought: at least the Prophet's popularity would decline. And people would sympathize with him. He was a victim, and those two were conspirators. In France, the public is scathing with homewreckers. But not this time. It seemed as if scandals slid right off the Prophet. The criticisms focused on Jeanne, and her silence was not likely to change that.

On two separate occasions, for an interview granted to the website *Absolute!* and one on TV, Gregory aired his grievances with the Prophet. This was not the betrayed husband who was speaking, he began, but the friend whom the 83er had betrayed. He told of their mutual affection, and the birth of a rare friendship at a moment when, their lives turned upside-down, they were learning to be wary of everyone. However, Gregory remembered he'd been bothered on several occasions by the ease with which Raphael unscrupulously lied. "It was non-stop dodging," he explained. "It was nearly a behavioral disorder."

On television, one of the hosts insinuated that the only reason he agreed to appear now was to damage the Prophet. Gregory protested. He knew everything they owed him, but the hero had other facets as well. They couldn't just be ignored. Raphael was manipulative, hypocritical, and fiercely egotistical. Following up on those words, the host asked the Captain if he believed his former friend, when confronting Mickaël, might have put himself in danger so we'd admire him, so we'd idolize him. Wasn't he just trying to subjugate the masses, too? Gregory fell for the trap, answering that this idea couldn't be completely discarded. Now, condescending smirks surrounded him. The cuckold's bitterness had no limit.

Even his advisors found it difficult to follow him when the Captain, returning once again to the subject, found a new reason to denigrate the Prophet's accomplishments. What will the history books say a hundred years from now? Before disappearing, a certain Raphael Zabreski saved the world. That's the only thing people will remember.

What about Gregory? Small posters with his face crossed-out and the caption NOT IN OUR NAME; young people gathering behind turned-over cars, arms crossed on their chests, the new rallying symbol for all those who wanted a world without supermen. In the fall of Year II, they were in the majority, according to polls. Georges Perec's brief novel, *A Man Asleep*, stood as their Bible, and a song by an obscure group, which was remade by two American teenagers on YouTube, became their anthem:

> *Let me go*
> *I don't wanna be your hero*
> *I don't wanna be a big man*
> *Just wanna fight with everyone else*

Faced with an ever-increasing number of hostile demonstrations, Shivaji Rai showed no sign of concern. It's just the people in the streets, he would say. They'll wear out. No, what worried him were the two injured parties that were being set against Gregory. Karim Benaddane, the actor, was incredibly likable, funny even when anger overcame him, and possessed an unshakable, witty demeanor every time he appeared before the cameras to denounce the lawmen who thought themselves above the law. "The worst," he explained to the newspaper *Libération*, "is that if I'd been some regular old Arab, we never would've heard about this. 'Cause he's slugged plenty of guys with fugly faces like mine before he got me." The young woman in the hospital, Alice Letellier, had a dark, pretty complexion and large, bright eyes. She had an 83 tattoo on her forearm, and declared that she was "extremely disappointed" in the Captain. She was said to be very calm, generous, and soon to be married. She was a pharmacist's assistant and supervised cultural outings with epileptic children during her spare time. Shivaji Rai grimaced. They were the perfect victims.

A week after the blunder, at the height of the skeptical questioning, Gregory holed up in a large apartment on the Boulevard Gouvion-Saint-Cyr in the seventeenth arrondissement, which the Interior Minister had put at his disposal. Here, he discovered one of those places people stay while passing through—VIPs under police protection, foreign officials on mission, or government workers looking for a place to stay in town and who got a set of keys from a colleague. Next to the limescale-coated sink, on shelves, or among the mismatched dishes were enigmatic objects left from other lives—an ashtray from an international forensic science conference in Jaca or an engraved bronze Louis XVI candlestick, underneath which chewing gum had been stuck.

In his isolation, Gregory wanted to examine himself with brutal frankness. Jeanne had cheated on him, but he had his faults. He now admitted that it's a two-way street. Was he too demanding? Was it possible that he'd smothered his wife trying to find perfection everywhere? Had he bored her by repeating the higher principles that guided his actions too many times? (For he did love, once they'd made their way back to the living room couch after the kids had been put to bed, to tell her what he'd done that day so as to draw some moral conclusions and pontificate a bit; he did recognize this.) He would ask Jeanne for clarification, even if it would be painful to hear. And he would go even farther. He was probably harrowed by false ideas on love, relationships, and what we are entitled to expect from existence. Yes, illusions that had supported him for years in a hazy, uncomplicated world needed to be dispelled.

On the brink of this great stocktaking, one photograph held his attention. On the beach in Courseulles, he and Jeanne and the two girls were together in the spring sun, blond and smiling in yellow windbreakers, squinting to look at the lens despite the blinding sunshine. Now these smiles seemed suspicious to him. Had their life always been as blessed as he and Jeanne told people? Before their separation, even before his wife's affair with Raphael, they had hardly ever made love anymore. They lived in fear of Lucille's tantrums. They hadn't wanted to examine anything, no, that could refute bit by bit their enchanted tale. Sometimes, when they were together, even after several days apart, they had nothing to say to one another. When out to dinner in a restaurant they would ask each other polite questions, like acquaintances.

But soon Gregory wondered if, under the influence of bitterness, he hadn't fallen to the other extreme, wanting to tarnish and wipe out everything. Something in him rose up against the harshness of his mood, such that, through an unexpected effect that rallied him to the opposite opinion, he reveled in the contemplation of that era, happy in spite of everything.

He reread the text messages Jeanne had sent him before their separation. They pertained to delays she might have, hesitations about the dinner she was thinking of making, nights she wished him were good, trips she hoped were safe. And Gregory believed he could perceive, still attached to these brief messages, the days they were written. Those days may not have all been calm or perfect, but they floated in a halo of even light, one of a world where everything had its place, a world of known dimensions, governed by natural laws that none could abolish. They knew who they were. They trusted each other. They loved each other.

Shivaji Rai returned after a few days. An ex-cop he'd hired had excellent news. Karim Benaddane's girlfriend was the daughter of a Corsican gangster who'd been shot down by a rival crew. The building she lived in, actually the one Benaddane was leaving the morning of the incident, was owned by one of her father's friends, a shady businessman who was letting her stay for free. The investigator also suspected cocaine usage. This information definitely brought up some questions.

Alice Letellier's situation was even more promising. Bipolar issues had tainted her high school years. She was still popping pills using forged prescriptions for Xanax and Vicodin. She'd been bombarding her neighbor, whom she complained was too noisy, with offensive emails, and he dropped off a logbook, complaining of harassment. "Another few days and you'll be clear," Rai reportedly guaranteed Gregory.

Like others, I am inclined to believe that the 83er's sense of morality must have bristled at the stated plan. But they probably presented the usual counterarguments. Benaddane paraded around everywhere with his busted-up face, and he for one did not refrain from dragging Gregory's name through the mud.

They wouldn't be spreading rumors, but using established facts
to embarrass both him and the woman. By pushing them to
avoid reporters and their questions, they would simply make
them stop talking.

The method was obvious, as several reporters noted, and
Gregory thought he was lost for good. But it is true that Karim
Benaddane and Alice Letellier didn't talk much after that. It
probably took little more than a week for the matter to reach
a semi-somnolent state, where news lingers before slumping
into oblivion. Yet, as Shivaji Rai had predicted, other scandals
slowly annexed the headlines. We learned that a young legislator, known for his conscientiousness and who was seen as a
future minister, had gotten mixed up in insurance fraud, while
on the contested construction site of a power plant a police
officer had killed a militant ecologist. Ménilmontant faded
from people's minds.

The President had denied in person rumors that Gregory's
contract would soon be broken and that he, along with all the
83ers, would be banned from exercising their powers. As proof
that he was now in their complete confidence, Gregory left his
refuge for operations abroad. Between missions, he enjoyed
frequenting exclusive airport lounges and luxury hotel rooms.
He felt the softness of the English carpets under his feet and
savored the meals that chefs had prepared for him. All the priv-
ileges of a successful life seemed to be served on these trays, and
with the bouquet of a world-class Bordeaux radiating across his
palate, long wafts of comfort rose through his head. He would
listen to relaxing works by Thelonious Monk or Fauré on his
playlists. In Yokohama, where an earthquake had called him,
after he had, thanks to his infallible ear, detected and rescued
three people still alive under the rubble, a sensible looking
young government minister whispered to him that she liked

him most of all. Sadly, waving their tiny flags, young school children cried as he flew off back home.

In France, the appetite for controversy ended up pushing the Ménilmontant scandal, which had taken on a complex and repulsive direction, into obscurity. Those who were still following this nearly month-old story had just learned that Alice Letellier had signed an apparently lucrative book contract. She was more likable before, when she was merely a volunteer turned victim, fighting to keep the use of her hand. Karim Benaddane was now criticized for making too big a deal out of it. He'd been tactless when he declared that beatings were like cocktails for the 83ers, always free. Virginie and Saïd protested through their lawyers.

In spite of everything, Gregory was surprised. Karim Benaddane and Alice Letellier's past mistakes by no means erased his misunderstanding of the situation nor his unfortunate actions. During their final meeting, just before he took the train back to London, Shivaji Rai shrugged his shoulders. He had worried about how long it would take, he explained, but he never doubted that the Captain would be absolved in the end. Ultimately, France is a caste society. People like Gregory are safe from everything. And then, what would the French have left if their 83ers were taken away? Had he even thought about that?

When he saw his two daughters again, Gregory did not face the dreaded Lucille, vicious and uncontrollable, whose visits he'd ended up pushing off, citing made-up hinderances at the last minute. She still followed obscure rituals, could be difficult, and demanded attention, but not any more or less than many kids her age. Instead of hurling her toys against the wall or repeating in a fractious voice that he wasn't her father, she pouted, of course, and protested, but he was able to turn her attention elsewhere without too much trouble. The director at Lucille's school, that bastard, had nearly managed to convince him his daughter was crazy. And, awash with remorse, Gregory felt he loved her even more now that he'd almost condemned her, distanced himself from her, and ultimately lost her. As for his second daughter, Marianne, she was a wonderful baby, calm and plump, who slept twelve hours a night and didn't expect anything from life, it seemed, except building blocks and some hard bread for teething. In the morning when she took her bottle, Gregory squeezed up against her, eyes closed, his nose pressed against her warm, round cheek. At times like those, everything seemed easy. Things were looking up.

He had photos taken with his daughters on the living room couch, all three wearing gray sweaters with sailor collars, smiling with toothy grins, their faces bright as if illuminated by the happiness of being together.

Finally, a renewed sense of enthusiasm surrounded the Captain when people learned that he and Virginie had started seeing one another. While his first wife had a bad reputation, once again damaged by photographs showing her in the arms of a younger lawyer (people now remembered: Jeanne was the one who'd screwed everything up, who had leaped into the Prophet's arms. She was that kind of vile, insatiable woman.), Virginie, on the other hand, had started to elicit sympathy.

The day a journalist and a photographer were admitted to the rest home in Saint-Germain-en-Laye where she'd been staying for the past two weeks, she had succeeded in showing a chink in her armor. The young woman with a reputation for being difficult, curt, always in a rush, appeared in a wrinkled white blouse that highlighted her pale complexion. The reporter later said that the 83er often had the gaze of someone lost. In the published interview Virginie revealed that she had

lost more or less everything since 1/19. Her marriage had shattered when her powers were revealed. Her daughter wouldn't
speak to her anymore. When she wasn't on a mission, the
relentlessness of the paparazzi confined her to the solitude
of luxury hotels, cars with tinted windows, and islands for
wealthy socialites—she never felt as alone as when at their
parties. Readers didn't necessarily know that during her youth
she had watched her mother fight and lose her battle with Lou
Gehrig's disease. They also learned that, shortly after his death,
she had Jean-Baptiste's name tattooed on her upper shoulder.
And, most of all, they assessed to what point her special ability,
that speed of execution that people envied, had turned into an
accursed gift. In a reedy voice she attempted to explain what
living mired in the slowness of the world, in this kind of waiting that never ends, was like. Because you absolutely did need
to give others time to act, react, finish their sentences—the
drawing out of every sentence, which, after the conjugated verb,
was elongated with complements and precisions, was torture
to her. It seemed like stumbling over some invisible surface
one hundred times an hour. "It's kind of like when a web page
takes a while to load," she said. "Like if all around you there
were these web pages loading and the status bar is half full."
She was overcome by crying fits. She pulled her hair. She lost
consciousness and would wake up two hours later at the foot
of her bed or shower. She was cursed, but exemplary. For she
would continue, despite the ills from which she suffered, to
work. Never would she shirk her duty. Readers discovered a
good person.

So it happened that in the beginning of November two
83ers—battle worn but still attractive, heroic but resigned
to the mundanity of everyday life—grew close to each other.
Although Gregory would hardly comment about this relationship, and perhaps he was not deeply in love with Virginie,

the scandalmongers who never saw their relationship as anything but a publicity stunt, were almost definitely wrong. They
avoided playing at the royal couple. They didn't parade around
at philanthropic galas, nor at celebrity weddings, nor in the
President's private box when the French national soccer team
played. And the photograph in which they are flying hand-in-
hand above Mont Blanc was in fact stolen. They by no means
wanted that photograph published.

"Virginie really mattered for Gregory. If only because she
proved to him that something else was possible after Jeanne,"
confirms Benoît Jourdan, one of his advisors. "Plus they had
loads of stuff in common. The desire to act, a form of moral
rectitude. Regret, too, regret for the lives they'd had before."

It's true that Virginie could at times become impatient
when Gregory recounted his day, with his habit of always
starting with a few general considerations. He could grimace
when gazing upon all the medications she'd swallow and the
zombie-like states during which, limp and dazed, she seemed
ten years older. But nothing terrible, both of them thought
to themselves. These days, they didn't believe in soulmates
anymore.

They would read novels by Daniel Pennac and John Irving
aloud to each other, which they'd already read when they were
twenty but wanted to rediscover again. They'd get away for a
weekend in a luxury chalet on the shore of the Saint Laurence.
They loved hearing the squeaking of their snow boots in the
white, snow-covered countryside. They listened to Cat Stevens
and Leonard Cohen albums on repeat. Being by his side, she
was almost cured of her addiction to speed. He gained the
conviction that one can get over anything.

All was well now. He was resurfacing.

XXV

Shortly after being wounded, Thérèse dreamed of a new book. The first two novels she had published in the mid-2010s had never really sold until after 1/19, when, out of curiosity, tens of thousands of people had wanted to page through them. They were difficult, mannered books that her readers generally deemed too slow. Critics were divided. Some lauded the arrival of a new talent while others were of the opinion that she was gazing at herself writing.

When she mentioned her desire to return to literature now that she had the time, her agent suggested she compile her memoirs as a superhero. Not something sensationalist, he backpedaled. But he didn't defend himself well. Plus, that's not what she wanted to do, at least not exactly. The agent insisted, she didn't take it well, and they had a falling out.

She gathered preparatory notes during her convalescence, which she started at a rehabilitation facility for elite athletes on the Côte Landaise. She hated the place and the life that people lived there: the crazy hopes of the injured she ran into regularly, the smell of perspiration, the din of bodies on the machines, the technical jargon of the care providers. It was only at the end of the day in the calm of the swimming pool, pushing herself through long walking sessions, that she forgot where she was and what, because of a stray bullet, her body now looked like.

"You look at the scar," she later shared on a radio show. "You look at your leg every morning. And you look at other people's legs on the street. You and them, it's like two different realities. You can line them up, but they don't exactly coincide. You're no longer really there, at least not in the same way. Some people can live with that. Others forget. And then there's all those like me who can't really do one or the other."

Thérèse had finished her first two books almost in spite of herself, by virtue of sitting at her worktable and struggling each day for four or five hours at a stretch against the temptation to scroll through Facebook or consult Wikipedia entries convincing herself that reading them was indispensable for what she was working on at the time. She wanted to be a writer more than anything, but when the time came to write the fortitude and the desire slipped away, and she, who was so industrious and so methodical with everything, suddenly found herself stricken with an irrepressible need to procrastinate.

A Half-Second of Eternity was published by Grammont in February of Year III. It was the story of a former superhero (even though this word never appears) who spends a weekend at the sea with a son who has grown up without him. To make it through she hunkered down in a large apartment in Font-Romeu, a ski resort village in the Catalan Pyrenees. She stayed there by herself after letting her last remaining assistant go, a twenty-two-year-old kid who always said yes and mindlessly flattered her. During the three months of the summer she stayed there, Thérèse only left the apartment to buy food and force herself to walk for fifteen or twenty minutes, leaning on a cane, which still embarrassed her. In a corner of the living room were a stationary bike and a monitor for watching exercises an army trainer had devised for her. But ever since she

knew that no matter what she did her right leg would always
have a limp, physical therapy was no longer a priority.

The internet didn't work well, which was a blessing. For
eight hours a day she wrote. Thanks to her hypermnesia, she
felt like she had access to a treasure trove of precise words and
lived emotions from long ago, overheard sentences and small
eloquent gestures, whose veracity brought to her characters
the substance they'd been lacking in her first two books. This
time a barrier had been broken down, and her style managed
to have air and inspiration, becoming more sweeping and agile.
While normally she was guarded, too thoughtful to reveal her
feelings without circumspection, she dared to state it straight
out: this would be her best novel. Perhaps this war wound had
been necessary for her to realize that her special power made
her a writer, a real one, and she imagined that people would
soon read: "Wounded in her body and soul by the tragedy in
Northern Niger, Thérèse Lambert chose the novel as the refuge
where she would learn to live again. The result is magnificent."
Or, even better: "There's only one superpower—literature."

The first review was bad and even rather cruel. It was from
the pen of Olivier Caillebois, a showy, young critic who never
missed an opportunity to rail against dubious successes in a
tone that was both brilliant and full of spite. Thérèse's second novel had already borne the brunt of his causticity. She
knew what to expect when reading his article, yet several of the
broadsides he launched must have mortified her nonetheless,
notably when Caillebois blasted a sentence from the very first
page that she herself, it appears, regretted:

> The soft, spongy dawn was pierced with ladles of past
> light that limped on the low clouds like the groping
> paintbrush of a lighthouse.

"In Lambert's novel," Caillebois sniggered, "the over-accumulation of metaphors gives birth to a fantastical world: light limps—just like, as everyone knows, certain paintbrushes . . . especially when they are gripped by lighthouses."

Thérèse wasn't sure about the overall merit of her books, but she did take pride in their style, which required her to be extremely inventive, hours of revisions and checking in dictionaries, grammar texts, and copy editors' or linguists' blogs. She could disparage an author's entire corpus, even one she had passionately loved, if she detected on just one of their pages a careless mistake or lack of taste. It was thus that Julien Gracq and Claude Simon had been banned from her personal library. After having decreed that there's nothing more clumsy than an adverb ending in -ly, she could also malign her contemporaries who overused it. She was comforted when she was finally able to spot in Flaubert, whose mastery was discouraging at times, some howlers (the poor guy had written, "The blades of grass stand erect like a coward's cowlick," she liked to remember). Her jealousy and her doubts abated before her conviction that there was no such thing as a genius.

There was hardly anything after Caillebois's article—a favorable review in *Le Quotidien du médecin*, ten innocuous lines in the Brussels newspaper *Le Soir*. In bookstores her novel had been removed from the top of display tables. Her new agent sought to console her: nothing sold anymore, except graphic novels and smutty tell-alls by former celebrities. The 83ers' falling popularity since Gregory's indecorousness also helped explain this slow launch. Thérèse, on the other hand, was already blaming herself for her lack of discipline, certain convoluted sentences, and an excessive modesty that thinned out her characters.

Fortunately, Françoise Cartier promised a review. Thérèse

still remembered the article that the critic from *Le Monde* had dedicated to *A White Calm*, her second novel. Cartier praised the novel's musical qualities, the precision of its shading, and the voluptuousness of its phrasing. One evening the 83er recognized her at the theater, but didn't dare approach. Françoise Cartier was an elegant woman with abundant, curly hair. Red lipstick, which she liked on the intense side, accentuated the wrinkles and starkness of her face. She must not be easily impressed, thought Thérèse. And yet she'd liked Thérèse's second novel. Since then, the 83er always made a point to read her reviews and admire her judgments, which, for the most part, were merciless.

Apparently, even though Françoise Cartier was loath to let her opinions leak out before publication, she was going to defend *A Half-Second of Eternity*. Marie, the publicist, had sensed it over the phone, and Thérèse felt herself quivering so strongly in relief at this news that tears came to her eyes. If the merits of her novel had not escaped the most demanding minds, that almost made everything better. The article might not be enough to reinvigorate sales of the book, but anything could still happen, her editor assured her. A good review, that's at least something. It can be the spark that sets things off. Lots of booksellers read *Le Monde*.

The day the article was scheduled to appear, in order to keep her impatience at bay while waiting for the paper, which was never available on Parisian newsstands before 1:00 P.M., Thérèse took her father to visit the old Royal Menagerie in the Jardin des Plantes. In the hope of livening up their visit, Thérèse had gathered details on the Arabian oryx, the red panda, the snow leopard, and even Przewalski's horse (whose name came from a Polish explorer who discovered them not far

from the Gobi Desert, and this taxonomic rarity—Thérèse had
planned on pointing this out to her father—gave the curious
impression that in seeing them, Przewalski became the creator
or owner of each member of the species).

In front of the enclosures, her father, a former history
teacher who had appreciated guided visits in the past, did
not react to his daughter's very complete presentations except
for some inattentive head movements. Two years previously a
stroke had dried up his conversation and placed a sullen looking mask across his face. Now and then, he would puff out his
cheeks and exhale loudly, as if he were exasperated. Thérèse
had learned to mourn the passing of her first father and not
to blame the second for the repeated incidents of unseemly
behavior.

In the sweltering heat of the Vivarium they observed a croc-
odile, a hydrosaurus, and some snakes, all motionless, disappointing like actors on a stage who refuse to play their parts,
unless, on the contrary, one should be astounded by their
stasis, seeming to proclaim that they were completely from
another world, more persistent and full than our own. Thérèse
hesitated between these two impressions.

She would later tell me that while observing them she
recalled the reptile costume that Jean-Baptiste had briefly
worn about for three months after 1/19. He even joked about
it himself, afterward. A total disaster, from the shiny rubber
look of the exterior to the perspiration issues the outfit caused
him. Wearing it was a sweat bath. After two or three hours the
itching in his elbows and knees was insufferable. And when he
took off this costume a persistent odor of old onions lingered
on his skin. The worst, he confessed, was that he just couldn't
throw it away.

Outside the orangutans, while Thérèse was reciting

information she gleaned the previous evening (the latest studies to ascertain the apes' intelligence had fascinated her), her
father pulled on her arm. He wanted to leave. Thérèse noticed
that it was just after 1:00 P.M.. Her phone would soon ring.
She had no idea how long the review in *Le Monde* would be. It
mustn't be too short. A short rave or blurb in the breakout box
of another article would only disappoint her, that she knew.
Generally, Françoise Cartier was given at least half a page, if
not an entire page to champion or rip to shreds the book of
her choice. But she wrote brief reviews, too. It had to be a full
page, not a brief review.

Her father had stopped in front of a balding camel that had
seen better days. "What about that?" he asked. Thérèse, who
had researched the oddest specimens in the zoo, had nothing
to say. Her father, looking fixedly, seemed captivated by the
animal, which, driven by some kind of mutual interest, was
now staring back intensely, its misaligned jaws chewing who
knows what kind of fodder in an expression of casual and nearly
seductive showboating. When her father eventually puffed out
his cheeks and exhaled through his teeth, as if he'd finally come
to realize the mediocrity of the camel's performance, Thérèse
approved with a curt laugh. She then led him toward the exit.
It was about 1:15. Why hadn't the publicist called her?

Before leaving her father asked for a drink at the snack bar.
He wanted a Coke. Since his stroke he claimed he needed
sugar, and Thérèse watched him take advantage of the pity he
inspired to gorge himself on sodas, pastries, candy, and milk-
shakes. She had him sit at a picnic table and walked away to
call Marie. Too bad if she'd promised herself that very morning she wouldn't bother her publicist or beg anyone for info
about the article. The call went directly to the young woman's
voicemail—maybe still in a meeting. Thérèse, after the beep,

said a few nervous words, which she tried to keep short while making fun of her nervousness.

From where she was she could see her father sitting alone at the picnic table, his back straight, his eyes downcast. The can of Coke was knocked over on the table. Puddles of brown liquid were dripping on his beige pants. Thérèse wanted to turn around and leave him there. He lifted his head and looked around. He was searching for her.

"Houston, we have a problem," he said, smiling sheepishly when she came back.

They were walking toward the Austerlitz station. Thérèse looked at the brown circle on her father's pants with embarrassment. But he didn't pay it any attention. He was holding her arm tightly. He was being affectionate now. So what difference does it make, she told herself.

At the newspaper stand she rushed to the stack of the day's edition of *Le Monde*, which had just been delivered. Even before paying she paged through the book review section. A good half page was dedicated to her book. But she blanched when she saw the title. "Has Literature Become a Competition in Obscure Words?" asked Françoise Cartier, who opened the review enumerating a few of the adjectives culled from Thérèse's third book, "reechy," "mazarine," or even "tremulant." The critic then meditated on the very French obsession of "doing a book," whatever it takes. Politicians, news anchors, directors, and now superheroes, everyone wanted to make their own little mark in the publishing world, as if a novel was going to give you more what? Legitimacy? *Gravitas?* Ultimately, these hacks were all cast from the same mold, she concluded, laborious examples of middle schoolers polishing their essays.

"It's not exactly what we expected," Marie admitted later.

Everything had led them to believe the review would be positive, but there had been no assurances, ever, she defended herself, while Thérèse, looking for someone to blame for her misfortune, turned her consternation toward the young woman.

Back in her apartment, she sat on the floor and watched
night fall on the unfinished scale model of Bayeux, which she
had retrieved after Jean-Baptiste's death. He had no siblings, and
his father was declining in a retirement home. As for Martha
Brookes, the short-lived English fiancée, she hadn't wanted
to keep anything. After her convalescence, Thérèse, with the
help of André, the physical trainer the two of them had shared
before the tragedy, had emptied out her friend's apartment
and had packed a hundred or so books, about the same number of DVDs, some photos, some clothes—almost nothing,
really. She knew that one day, when the pain of mourning had
passed, Jean-Baptiste's last effects would be nothing more than
a pile of mute, lifeless things without purpose. Then she'd get
rid of them. But for now she needed to keep them near her,
especially the model, which she liked to examine, still finding
details—a magician running away, a bouquet of flowers forgotten in a tree, a well-dressed gentleman being accosted by an old
prostitute, a poster announcing the end of the world—absurd,
little scenes her friend had arranged with that subtle humor
that she'd been one of the few to enjoy during his lifetime.

It was then, as a flood of umber shadows advanced across
the wall of her living room, darkening each object, slowly
inundating its outlines, as the day ceded to this noiseless and
endless engulfment, that she laid her literary career to rest.
All of her efforts, she now realized, resulted in books that she
didn't really like, that to her seemed flawed. She had gone
down the wrong path. Thérèse recalls that she then got up and
made something to eat. This decision to give up had not been

painful, she claims. The following days she simply felt, like when looking at a photograph of a person you believed you loved, a slight sadness in recognizing that she could indeed live without writing, she, who had always believed the opposite.

XXVI
"What's the Point of Knowing That?"

VIRGINIE MATHIEU-BRUN: They told me it was the same as PTSD. During the first year it was like I hadn't reacted, actually. Now I believed the opposite: 1/19 saved me from some kind of void. I was truly happy with what happened to me. The first couple months, I remember, life had flavor. But it was like an incubation period. I only felt the pain later. Besides, the first symptoms were the opposite of pain. I remember something really gentle. I used to lose myself in the city. I would walk for an hour or two and couldn't say why I was outside or where I was going. Plus, I'd stumble over words, more and more often. Peoples' names and words, even really simple words, started to escape me. It was very gentle, really. Maybe 'cause I'd never let go like that before. Especially the missing words, it was kind of like I was floating, suspended, and every time a word would finally come back, I felt reassured, but also kind of let down, too, like when you're let down because you didn't push yourself enough, when you latch on to the easiest solution.

After that, things really went downhill. It got ugly. I'd find myself up in the sky somewhere at 3 A.M., flying full out, and air traffic controllers are shitting themselves. In Australia I rented a Bugatti, and it turns out a speed camera radared

me at over 300 kilometers an hour on a straightaway in the
Nullarbor Plain. I was in a daze. I don't remember a thing.
And then I started shooting up at home, epinephrine, amphet-
amines. I would crank up music. I'd scream. I'd lost control.
That's why I agreed to go to a rest home. But that didn't cure
me of anything. I had a ton of relapses after.

And how did Gregory react?
He did what he could, poor guy. I don't know . . . He was
sweet. And that'd make me feel even worse. Times like that, it's
like falling backward into a bottomless pit. You fall faster and
faster. And the kindness of other people, their concern, just
pushes you further down. Okay, maybe in spite of everything,
realizing what he was doing helped me. I don't know. I don't
want to talk bad about him. I want to tell you the opposite,
all the nice stuff. There were times . . . Times when we were
really one with the other, together. When we came together.

What does that mean, specifically?
Specifically, it doesn't mean a thing. 'Cause it wasn't specific,
in fact . . . It's hard to explain . . . You make friends, you meet
them in cafés, supposedly to catch up, and you start a relationship, supposedly because you're attracted to each other,
because you want to make love, because you want to start
a family, but the only real motivation in all that, in fact the
only need people actually have, is to talk about themselves, to
be able to pour out on others all their failures, all the sadness
they shoulder for still being here. And the others with their
own issues, their long faces reflecting back at you like a mirror,
are the last thing you want. You stay with them 'cause there
needs to be somebody around for when you want to get stuff
off your chest.

I didn't feel that with Gregory. The two of us were in about the same place when our relationship started. Our lives were a train wreck. And for him, the fall seemed even bigger. Because he'd held something in his hands that seemed like his idea of happiness: his family, his popularity, that kind of calmness his former life had, when you've got what's sort of the proof your existence is justified—he'd lost all that. But he recognized it. He was naked and didn't hide. Now me, I was in denial, totally. Like everyone else, in the end. 'Cause we all think that's how we're going to save ourselves. By making ourselves believe that nothing's happened. That we didn't get our teeth knocked in. That we're not in that much pain. And then by hoping, too, that things have to get better, that just around the corner something awesome'll be waiting for us. Gregory was done with all that. Once everything fell apart he never tried to lie again. And I admired his courage. Even today I wish people would recognize that about him. He changed like not many people can. He ended up knowing who he was, what he was afraid of, what he needed. He could stand up without all the fairy tales people tell themselves so they can get out of bed in the morning. And he taught me that too, a little. I just wasn't as good of a student as him.

So why didn't it work?
It worked. Just not for very long, that's all. Why should it last a long time? I mean why would that be the measure of a successful relationship?

But you must have an explanation for why the relationship was so . . . short-lived.
I wasn't doin' that great, and Gregory quickly figured out that he wasn't the one who could save me. That if he stayed it was

going to be one of those relationships, there are loads of 'em,
very ugly, where on one side you have the sick person and on
the other side you have the caregiver. But he was such a generous guy . . . so stupid fucking nice . . . He could clearly see
there was no one else but him. He couldn't leave me alone.
It was up to me to free myself. So I told him he needed to
leave. At one point I even did everything I could to make that
happen. I didn't want him to move in with me in this kind of
dreary place that depression constructs around you. One night,
it was around the beginning of Year III, beginning of March,
I trashed a hotel room. I hit him. And I ended up telling him
about Lucille . . .

What do you mean?
I'm the one who told him his daughter was going to die.

But the accepted version of the facts. . .
I'll keep my mouth shut, if you prefer.

Please continue.
We were in that room. I'd just hit him, and then knocked over
the TV, and then thrown everything I could get my hands on
out the window. He was looking at me with his big eyes, in
shock. But I felt like I wasn't getting to him. Not the broken
furniture or the dishes thrown against the wall, not even all
the mean stuff I would yell at him . . . Nothing really got to
him. That was the Gregory I loved and hated at the same time.
Superior, inaccessible. Transparent. So I said the only thing
that could destroy him, which Raphael'd told me: his oldest
daughter was going to die on July 10th.

But do you know how Raphael found out?
He told me that it happened one night, in Courseulles-sur-Mer, at Gregory's second home. He was reading Lucille a bed-time story, like usual. The two of them got along well. But that night Raphael saw a red glow on the upper part of her head, above the left ear.

That wasn't enough to learn the date of Lucille's death.
Raphael's capabilities had progressed, too, apparently. When he saw the glow he saw everything in flashes. The place, the time, the circumstances. He saw everything at once. At least that's what he told me.

How did Gregory react when you told him this?
I don't really know anymore. I was in another daze. I believe he slapped me. But maybe not and I just thought to myself afterward that he should've bashed my face in. 'Cause I immediately regretted having told him that. The following day when I woke up—they'd evacuated me out of the hotel and had transferred me, don't know why really, to a PSIS site [*Protection Services for Important People, a unit within the French National Police*]—I thought that was the worst thing I'd ever done in my entire life.

Why?
Because I believed, and I still believe today, the same thing as Raphael. What's the point of knowing that? It would only ruin the lives of those concerned. When Raphael confided in me it was exactly because he needed to talk to someone to decide what to do. He didn't want to tell Gregory, but he needed to be sure he was making the right decision. And I told him he was right. No hesitation. With my mother, they'd informed

her toward the end of her illness that most likely she had no more than six months to live. Not lying to her, because she should know the truth—that was, I think, the stated reason. You know what? She spent the worst six months of her life. And everyone who loved her, too. Waiting for something you can't change, looking at a not-yet-dead person like a soon-to-be-dead person, what's the point?

Some people say it's better. It lets them prepare. To more fully appreciate the time that's left.
That's bullshit. I don't believe that for one second. It creates dread, that's all it does. Do you have kids?

. . .

You've got kids, I know. I saw them on your Facebook page. Okay, so when you go back home to Santiago, I want you to do this little experiment for me: tell them goodnight imagining that in three months they'll be dead. Then send me a message to let me know if it made you feel good knowing that or if you would've instead preferred seeing them simply as living children, without an expiration date. Then you'll ask yourself this other question: are you going to tell them they're going to die, or not? How far does the right to know go? And to whom?

PART FIVE

XXVII

HE HADN'T BELIEVED it. She was crazy and miserable. He knew that. She liked to hurt other people. It was the only thing she still had left to make her feel connected to them. Nonetheless, one night as he was leaving his daughters' room, whose angelic, sleeping faces triggered a sudden worry in him, the fear of losing them soon, Gregory called Virginie and heard her say that she'd made it all up. Another day, at the end of March, he pushed back his departure for a mission until the last minute and went unannounced to the extended-stay hotel where she'd washed up in Plaine-Saint-Denis. "It was bullshit," she sobbed on both occasions. "I said it to get a reaction out of you. Total bullshit." But the Captain could tell through her inflection that she was lying, and he become sure that the opposite was true.

One other possibility did remain: Raphael could have fabricated a fake revelation, which he imagined would one day be repeated to Lucille's father and would devastate him. Nothing would happen on July 10th. The Prophet simply would have put him through hell for a few months at least. But why inflict such a trial on him? Following the simple reasoning he loved, it was hard for Gregory to imagine that one could devise such a depraved stratagem. And a memory fought against this

hypothesis in his mind. "Several times," a close friend confided, "Raphael had told him he couldn't bear having his power
any more. He knew too much." Up until this point, Gregory
had thought his friend was referring to the life of others in
general and this surfeit of knowledge that his power burdened
him with. Seeing people's future too frequently meant becoming the only witness to their decline, from the sicknesses that
would weaken them to the renouncements by which they
slowly became withered souls. Now Gregory grasped that the
Prophet, in a semi-confession that was so characteristic of his
lack of willpower, was probably talking about Lucille when he
breathed that he knew too much.

In turn, Gregory searched for Raphael. Contacts in French
intelligence confirmed what he feared, any trace of the Prophet
had indeed been lost. He hired a private investigator, a sort
of old-school detective with wrinkled linen jackets and whose
office was buried under drifts of old music magazines. The
man had made a name for himself by finding a young Korean
soloist on the shores of Lake Como who had disappeared two
hours before her concert at the Salle Playel in the arms of a
supposed admirer who was making her sign checks.

In mid-April the detective picked up the scent in a work-
ing-class neighborhood in New Orleans, proposing to expand
his investigation. Unable to wait any longer, and perhaps fearing inflated expenses (the man had a habit of staying in nice
hotels and a taste for drink), Gregory himself flew to Louisiana.
On April 18th of Year III, he scoured the streets of the Irish
Channel incognito, looking for a tall silhouette that he could
pick out anywhere and even ended up, in the middle of the
night, entering the modest looking home of a suspicious
Frenchman.

"My girlfriend and I had had an argument, and I was sleeping alone in my office on a blow-up mattress," Matthieu B. remembers today. "Suddenly I must have sensed something. I open my eyes and there's this dark figure above me. A guy with an American baseball hat and dark glasses, totally buff. I didn't for a second think that guy could be the Captain. I thought it was some friend of my girlfriend, maybe her side guy. I don't know how long he'd been looking at me. He asked me in unaccented French to tell him my name. Then to keep talking to him . . . and that was the hardest part, 'cause I was terrified. But he encouraged me. He just wanted to hear my voice. So, I told him about what I did, my job, my coworkers. And when I didn't know what else to add, he told me I needed to go back to sleep, and he left through the window."

Back in Europe, the Captain placed his trust in intermediaries, middle-aged men with doughy faces and vague job titles, consultants or experts, former diplomats, spooks who tested his patience with their ambiguous smiles and unfinished sentences. But he listened to them because they found it highly unlikely, as he himself believed, that the governments of the Western world had absolutely no idea where the Prophet was. His connections in French intelligence had lied to Gregory. Someone was protecting his former friend. Information was certainly out there. They'd end up getting their hands on it. Gregory paid their fees and implored them to let him know as soon as they had any information.

He had hidden from Lucille the fears that had been troubling him and wanted, he told his entourage, for nothing to change with her, and for her life to remain simple and happy, a child's life. But Lucille, alert and sensitive, must have sensed that people were worried.

Gregory had her undergo a series of medical tests that revealed nothing anomalous. Every two weeks machines verified the condition of her heart and inspected her brain. Blood tests confirmed no major illnesses had affected the child. A bodyguard now escorted her to her classroom door and waited in the hallway until school was over. From dawn to dusk a hushed attentiveness surrounded her. Several times she saw Jeanne crying. She had sleep issues. New fears made her life difficult. She invented an imaginary enemy named Aurélia who persecuted her.

There was never a question of her parents getting back together, even if maybe the Captain had thought about it at least once. "It's true, he must've said it one time. But after a divorce everyone has at least one thought along those lines, a regret, something not quite right. The rest of the time he'd moved on, completely," nuances someone close to him. He hoped at least, given the circumstances, that they'd stand together, they'd take it easy. But Lucille's security imposed too many tweaks, too many restrictions, too many logistical headaches to avoid disagreements, which fanned their discord. Every once in a while Gregory would say to Jeanne, "Look at what we've become" or "Do you hear how we talk to each other?" Jeanne would shrug. Every time she contradicted him it was too easy to give her a pitying look or stare at her in outrage. (Perhaps she also resented him for not being able to get his hands on the Prophet. This is what people who didn't like her say.)

Gregory suffered when Lucille lost her temper and her grumbling or uncontrollable shaking resurfaced. Now that she was in danger, he wanted there only to be delightful weekends and peaceful evenings. He wanted to hold her tight, take her picture, look at her, hear her laugh. When she would scream at her sister, or slam the door to her room, or bury her face in the corner of the living room, it seemed to the Captain that the obscure force he was battling against was winning.

One night at the end of April, as she was going to sleep, she asked him if she was going to die in July. Gregory wanted to know who had told her. Lucille swore it was Aurélia. When he insisted on knowing the name of the *real* person who had told her such a silly thing she burst into tears. So he repeatedly assured her that Aurélia was making stuff up. With a super-hero's daughter, it makes sense that people would take care of her and make sure no one hurt her. "But this won't last long," he whispered. "It's just gonna be like this for a little while."

He kissed his daughters, left their room, went to his sound-proof office, picked up a chair, and threw it against the wall. When a bodyguard came in he picked him up off the ground, choking him. Was he the one who told her? The man swore no. Gregory pushed him away, opened the window, and flew off. The bodyguard recounted that he saw the Captain floating a hundred meters or so above the house, and that, from there, he could hear him screaming.

Three days later Gregory made the situation public. It was straightforward: the Prophet had learned that Lucille, age seven, was going to die on July 10th of Year III. He had dis-appeared without saying a word, neither to the child nor her parents. Lucille's father wanted to save his daughter and begged his former friend to tell him in detail what was threatening her so that, if there were a chance of saving her, they could do everything possible.

Several French, English, Spanish, American, and Brazilian newspapers published the Captain's open letter.

The strategy was clear: implore the Prophet without attack-ing him, putting Lucille and her suffering first. In spite of everything, it was apparently with regret that Gregory accepted to pose with Jeanne and their children for the glossy, *Paris-Match*. "Of course it was over the top," Saïd later opined. "When you're upset or super anxious, ideally you want to stay dignified. But, okay, they must have told him he needed public opinion on his side, that it was the only way to get Zabreski out of his hidey-hole. The tear-jerker with pretty photos, they had to try it. No other choice."

On social media, the possible death of a child, and more-over of a celebrity child, naturally mobilized people. But another reason certainly helped support the *Let Her Live* cam-paign, which shared the Captain's open letter and intensified after photos of Lucille were published. Although there were a few voices who lauded the Prophet's action, whose decision to disappear could be interpreted as the ultimate testimony of his humility, nevertheless a French public opinion poll from February of that year shows that most of the respon-dents expressed some reservations. Certainly his choice should be respected. However, the crime rate, it would appear, was increasing again, and a car bomb recently exploded at the open-air market in Béthune, the first since 1/19. If the Prophet hadn't left, how many tragedies could have been avoided? How many lives saved thanks to his predictions?

It was among his most enthusiastic supporters that the bit-terness was the most acute. They simply missed the Prophet. His fans had been able to resign themselves to the idea that for a period of time their hero would pull back from public life. He'd earned it, but his absence now seemed long, nine months already, and they were losing patience.

Sports stars, billionaires, American singers and actors, and reli-gious dignitaries joined the *Let Her Live* movement, posting selfies with a photo of Lucille in their hands from improbable locations. [*During those years, viral philanthropy campaigns had the best chance of success if they required internet users to accept an amusing challenge. In this instance it was showing Lucille's portrait everywhere. She thus appeared in Red and Tiananmen Squares, in the steppes, on the bow of an oil tanker sailing in the Barents Sea and the deck of an old shipwreck in the dried up Aral Sea, on the summits of Kilimanjaro and Ayers Rock, in a Cardinal's office in the Vatican, at the bottom of a silver mine in Potosí, at the Dumont d'Urville polar station, and even aboard the International Space Station.*]

Despite all these appeals, the Prophet did not appear.

He didn't answer the two emails Gregory had sent him, either. The second, sent on the night of May 10-11, was probably done only at the Captain's initiative, without having any of his advisors read over it. Flashes of anger appear, which his first letter had carefully suppressed:

> Raphael,
> You wish to live in hiding, very well. But it's harder to understand why you won't respond to our messages. I showed you a perfectly secure way to contact me. You have to answer me. I'm not the one asking, the world is. You must tell me what you know. You don't have the right to keep it to yourself. And since I know you, I know you know that, too. You have two months left to change the way the world sees you and the way you see yourself.
> Regards,
> Gregory, with Lucille

The following day the Captain received a message. It

wasn't sent to him by the Prophet but rather by a certain Luiz Gustavo Mora.

The international mobilization had informed the Brazilian of the threat hanging over the child, and for several days he went back and forth. A feeling of guilt prevented him from sleeping. He would laugh nervously all alone. He was going crazy. "It was like being the accomplice to an assassination that supposedly had already taken place, but that could still be prevented," he later explained to me. "Two feelings of guilt in one."

As Raphael was the most prized piece of all of his collections together, he insisted on personally taking the Captain to where the fugitive lived. After a fraught meeting with his advisors, Gregory decided to travel to Los Angeles without support. No one would force his former friend to talk. And it was out of the question, in the Captain's mind, to use illicit methods to obtain his confession.

He flew during the night of May 15th. In Los Angeles he met up with Luiz Gustavo at a car rental agency off of La Cienega.

The two men arrived in front of Raphael's apartment building just before 6:00 P.M. The Captain put his ear to the apartment door—no noise, not even breathing. They knocked just to be sure, but no one answered. So they decided to come back later, when Raphael would be home.

For two hours they lingered over a soda on the terrace of a café. "We talked about sleep," Luiz Gustavo remembers. "He told me that he was sleeping more and more, that it appealed to him more and more. I also asked him what he was planning on doing when he was face to face with the Prophet. He just smiled and told me something along the lines of, 'We'll talk calmly.'"

When they returned at nightfall the apartment windows were dark. This time Gregory insisted on going inside. Luiz Gustavo opened the door with his skeleton key. The apartment was basically the same as when he'd discovered it a few months previously. On the counter of the kitchenette bar lay junk mail, the key to a bike lock, and the number of a Chinese take-out place scribbled on a Post-it. In the bedroom, at the foot of the wardrobe, a pile of clean wrinkled clothes. On the nightstand, a copy of the *L.A. Times* from the day before. Raphael hadn't tried to settle in more than that. A large yucca was drying out by the bay window.

The two intruders waited.

They didn't understand at that moment that, somehow tipped off to their presence, Raphael had already left the city.

XXVIII

To THE DRIVERS who picked him up hitchhiking, he said he was Swiss and wanted to see State Route 1. He must have arrived in San Francisco before May 17th, staying less than a week. His journal implies he didn't have enough money for a hotel and the other street people scared him. He didn't want to fight. He worried about looking like them. A ukulele player by the name of Shane or Shaun talked to him about 9/11 and the conspiracy that made the attacks possible. He wrote to Renee to apologize for leaving without letting her know and to tell her he loved her. Then he headed to a gas station and got on a semi headed north.

In Portland, Oregon, he learned from the homeless people squatting along the river where the shelters were and when they distributed food. A young Indian recommended he get a tent and set up in the forested area of Washington Park. The weather would be turning nice soon, and he would be better alone in the great outdoors than in some dorm with strangers.

He set up camp in the hollow of a cliff behind a thicket of bramble bushes, which could only be accessed by squatting down and passing through a natural tunnel about fifteen meters long. This inconvenient access reassured him. The hideout was located near a stream whose water appeared clean and only thrity-five minutes by foot from the main branch of the Portland Public Library. Invisible among all the misfits who congregated there, he would read biographies of explorers and nap on benches in less popular sections. No one paid him any heed.

It's also at the library, thanks to free computer access, that he returned to the internet. No one verified users' identities. It didn't seem that imprudent. He never made the error of checking his email, but he didn't need to in order to learn of the messages Gregory had sent him. They were everywhere now.

To the offbeat selfies, marches and rallies were now added. There was a countdown until July 10th. Anger was rising. In every language on the planet editorialists and intellectuals, one after another, inveighed against the Prophet. The tearful petition of a young American actress looking directly into the camera had received more than 300,000 likes in one day.

In his journal on May 28th the Prophet recorded a list of words he most frequently read about himself: "Cowardice hypocrisy cruelty shame shameful bad Evil." Then, under some abstract doodling from which the clumsy outline of a large bird emerges, he added: "Everyone certain. Justice is theirs. Don't worry about it."

He was unable to follow this commandment. On the rare instances when he turned to his journal it was to express his anger over the public trial of which he is the target: "Always the same insults. The same hate." "Gregory's new scheme— the Pope!" [*Here he is referring to a comment made in passing by the supreme pontiff during a visit to Zimbabwe, asserting that "we must do everything in our power when children's lives are at stake," which was interpreted as an appeal directed at Zabreski.*]

For food he counted on soup kitchens and expired products that employees gave out behind certain supermarkets.

The several hundred dollars he had in his pocket allowed him to brighten up his everyday existence—a beer every now and again in front of the television screens at a bar, batteries for his flashlight, a pair of heavy, leather shoes unearthed in a used-clothing store to replace his leaky tennis shoes.

Was he afraid of being found out? What did he imagine the rest of his life would be like? For a long time I wanted to believe that he had found in this Oregonian idyll some kind of peace and even fulfillment.

Portland is a pleasant and somewhat sleepy city. It's full of nice people who bike, sort their garbage, and hardly ever raise their voices. Even the rain falls softly there. In this safe harbor, Raphael had reduced his needs to a strict minimum, and now he could read and think. Reasons to rush or worry no longer troubled his mind. With his knit cap pulled down over his head, his long, tattered overcoat, and a book in hand, he had become one of the stately bums that inhabit American cities.

This version of history, my favorite, is not based on any tangible proof. I am one of those people who like to believe, even if this belief is at times tinged with jealousy, that others—dissidents, free spirits—have obtained the blissful state of wisdom that solitude and frugality at a distance from modern life provide. However, it is also completely possible that Raphael felt as miserable as a hunted animal. His journal remains sparse concerning his life in Portland. He was undoubtedly furious that he had been forced out of hiding, that Gregory, that bastard who'd already ruined his life by posting his photo online, appeared in person at his doorstep and expelled him from the anonymous sanctuary he'd managed to build for himself in California. If he loved her as much as he claimed, he must have missed Renee. I doubt he had much desire to associate with the human wrecks who congregated along the Willamette River or those he stood next to waiting in line at charitable organizations. It has never been possible to establish that he made friends in Portland or that he had acquaintances. Those who claim to remember him all describe a lone wolf, hoodie covering his head, avoiding eye contact. Moreover, it is not certain that Raphael went through the ordeal of squatting in the cold water of a stream to bathe or eating low-quality food nearly every day. Cleanliness was important to him. He had never expressed a desire for a life without modern conveniences. So I'll make this shorter than what I had imagined: he was homeless, he took precautions so people couldn't locate him, he had organized his everyday existence so this could continue over the long term, and what he thought of all of it, no one can say.

On June 10th he hitchhiked the hour and a half between Portland and Eugene, the capital of Oregon. He went inside a public library, sat down in front of one of the computers, and at 10:46 A.M. created a new email address from which he sent a message to three French newspapers, as well as his sister Judith and Laurence Granec, who had been Raphael's publicist before his disappearance:

> Two years ago I was struck by an illness of unknown origin. As a result, the future of some people became visible to me.
>
> I now refuse to use this power, which I consider to be a source of unfairness and misfortune.
>
> Since I am unable to help everyone, I refuse to help some people but not others. There is no selection criteria that seem valid to me.
>
> Since some of the events I foresee are impossible to prevent, I refuse to make those who cannot escape

them lose hope prematurely.

I also refuse to keep this awful information to myself and live in the neverending pain of knowing what others are yet to learn.

I will never again use my power.

Act as if the Prophet no longer existed.

I hope you understand.

If not, go fuck yourselves.

Raphael Zabreski.

It was easy for Gregory, in the response he sent almost immediately, to point out the inconsistencies in Raphael's declaration:

Dear Raphael, or rather, Dear Prophet,

We read your message to mankind. Your scruples do you honor. But some aspects of your letter are surprising. Please allow us to make a few remarks and ask you a few questions:

1. "Act as if the Prophet no longer existed," you command at the end of your message.

This, however, proves you're still living, which, we must admit, we are happy and relieved to see finally confirmed. It is true that for many years we lived years without foresight. Just as we lived for millennia without the wheel, without electricity, without the internet. Now that this capacity exists, thanks to which you have saved numerous lives, you wish us to act as if it doesn't exist? You're hurtling us into a fictional world.

2. Should we stop acting on the grounds that we can't do everything? Should police work, for example, be suspended since, in spite of their efforts, crimes still

take place every day? Is the fact that you cannot help everyone a valid reason to help no one?

3. You mention selection criteria. Are Lucille's young age and the bonds of affection that link you to her and to us not enough? We all wish to help our fellow man, whomever it may be. But what's so outrageous about looking after those who are closest first? With saving children's lives first? (You're looking for criteria. Here you go.)

Time is of the essence. With July 10th looming, we're doing all we can, employing every resource, to make Lucille's life safe. Any information you have would be most welcome.

We hope you understand.

Warm regards,

Gregory and Lucille

"To me this response was completely asinine," François Scherwiller maintains. "'Message to mankind,' I remember being against that. It was unnecessarily hurtful. Like the rest. The textual analysis, the rhetorical questions—it could only rub him the wrong way."

According to Scherwiller, the Captain himself did not seem terribly at ease with this response, which several of his advisors had dictated to him. It was easy to see through the ploy: they wanted to pass Raphael off as heartless, a close friend suddenly stricken by indifference, while it was widely known to the public that he and the Captain had been on bad terms for ages. In all likelihood Gregory was the one who had divulged Zabreski's name and photos as revenge for Raphael's affair with his wife. Before learning that his eldest daughter was going to die, he hadn't refrained from sullying the Prophet's name in public, either. Some commentators remembered this quite clearly. In online forums it was the last point of Gregory's message that caused the greatest debates: protecting those who are closest first—was that so obviously justifiable?

It is unknown if Raphael returned to Portland afterward. He could not have ignored the fact that by creating an email address on a computer in Eugene he had just given an idea of his whereabouts. Perhaps he was already regretting it. He shouldn't have answered. He had no need to justify himself. Now searches would be launched in Oregon and the surrounding states. He would be found.

He purchased a train ticket, or he hopped a freight train, or he hitchhiked, or he flew at night at a very low altitude. Regardless, he headed east.

This wasn't a good idea. The interior of the country is sparsely populated. A foreigner, alone, without a car or a job, has no chance passing unnoticed in the small rural towns where he'd need to stop from time to time to eat, shower, or sleep. Later, he was reported in Idaho, Wyoming, and then more to the north in Montana. Alerted of these appearances through social media, fans, busybodies, wack jobs, and headline chasers got it into their heads to find him.

Somewhere along the line Raphael decided to sleep during the day and travel at night. He would find a deserted riverbank or abandoned barn to lie down. He would buy food from convenience stores during the middle of the night, his face obscured by his hoodie. But that wasn't enough to safeguard his flight. From time to time he noticed suspicious individuals around him, characters who were poor actors. He was being followed. American intelligence, he thought. He was tempted to move on to an abandoned farm not far from the Canadian

border. Through the window you could still see dishes in the
drying rack. In the tall grass several generations of cars were
rusting. I visited houses like this when I retraced the Prophet's
journey; they're peaceful ruins.

A man who washes cars in Kincaid, Saskatchewan (Canada),
claims he spent about ten minutes with the fugitive. I met the
man, and his account seemed credible to me. At lunchtime one
day, looking for some shade to eat in, DeWayne Rogers sat down
on the loading dock of an empty warehouse. He'd already taken
a bite of his sandwich when he noticed, a dozen or so meters
away, a man who was sleeping "in a weird position, squatting
down." Rogers thought he must be a junkie who had just gotten off a freight train. He was getting ready to finish his lunch
elsewhere when the man stood up and walked toward him.
According to Rogers, the Prophet—if it was indeed him—
asked if he could borrow his phone. He wanted to check the
internet. Rogers, who himself admitted he's wary by nature,
noticed that the man spoke with a foreign accent ("I thought
he was English") and was surprised by how well he spoke. He
didn't dare refuse. Raphael walked a dozen or so steps away
and stood there for a few minutes, without moving, mutter-
ing to himself, as the sun beat down. When he handed back
the phone "you could tell he'd gotten bad news," DeWayne
Rogers stated. The unknown man seemed agitated. He mumbled good-bye and started walking determinedly toward the
other side of the warehouse.

Rogers, himself a stranger in these parts (he was an
American from Atlanta who had recently arrived in the area),
was familiar enough with Kincaid's minimal geography to
know that there was nothing in that direction, nothing but a
kind of Saskatchewanian steppe, a vaguely charming landscape
for newcomers if they give in to the exhilaration of immense

horizons, then more and more distressing as the eye habituates
to the scene—for one must accept the fact that over hundreds
of thousands of square kilometers nature daubed the same
patterns and repeated the same combinations, like an abstract
painter who had run out of ideas.

DeWayne Rogers wanted to let the stranger know he
was going the wrong way and called out to him. But no one
answered. Then he went around the corner of the building.
The man had disappeared.

Without hesitation Rogers admits that the next thing
he did was check the phone he'd lent him. The headlines of
the *New York Times* was the last page consulted. It had just
been announced that one of the last 83ers still in action, the
Captain, had taken members of the Prophet's family hostage.

XXIX
"Life After the End"

SAÏD MECHBAL: I still remember my new agent's face. He was backstage, what, like ten meters or so from me. The magician, I totally forgot his name—he wasn't really a magician anyway, he did a couple tricks, but he always seemed like some warm-up act to me—he turns toward me, very theatrical-like, and in English he says something like, "You see that big Arab behind me?" and the joke's that I'm supposed to disappear on the spot. Except nothing happens. And Nick [*Horovitz*], my agent, opens his eyes really wide, I mean I didn't think you could have your eyes open like that. They were like saucers. That's the only time in my life I saw someone almost faint because I stayed visible.

Were there any warning signs?
None. Much as I had a sense that Micka was gonna blow a gasket, like I told you before, this time I saw nothing coming. Just the month before I'd won my lawsuit. [*After a tough judiciary battle, Saïd had his contract with the French state nullified and obtained the right to exercise his abilities in the professional setting of his choice.*] I finally felt free. I'd always dreamed of the States, and Horovitz seemed like the right person to start

something there. The idea, before trying to land movie roles, was to work on my acting and make some money doing small, custom Las Vegas-style shows.

The side-show freak bit . . .
Nah, that didn't bother me. Anyway, that's what we were already. I know Virginie and Thérèse said some mean things about me at the time, but if people want to pay eighty or one hundred bucks to "touch the invisible man" and then take a photo in my arms, personally, that bothers my conscience less than helping the G8 powers maintain control over their new colonies. I'm not going to tell you I was thrilled to do this, either. We'd perform at these galas for the super-rich or charity dinners, and the show itself wasn't in very good taste. I looked at it all like an apprenticeship. The malfunction bit wasn't part of the show. But I've always had a great sense of timing with nasty surprises.

At the time your mishap remained a secret.
'Cause no one knew what was happening. 'Cause I did what I do best, my cheesy Saïd bit. I raised my arms, I started yelling . . . It was a fancy event organized by Samsung, and the only thing that came to mind was for me to yell stuff about Chinese workers who are dying making our cell phones—I don't know anything about it, and it never stopped me from having a phone, but I really needed to find something to make it seem like I was refusing, like a new scandal for Number Seven. And then I remember Nick's following me down the hallway of the hotel, foaming at the mouth. I swear it's true. There was spit bubbling at the edges of his lips. He was holding a fire extinguisher, swearing he was going to bash my brains in. I kept yelling that I'd had enough, that I was done with bullshit like that. Then I noticed I could still levitate. I jumped out

the window. Adios, American career. I flew to the skyscraper across the street, then to another, and finally I flew south at full speed all the way to the Gulf of Mexico. I sat down on a beach. And I cried. I cried like a baby.

You thought it was the end?
Worse than that: life after the end. I'd thought about death a lot. Even though we might be supermen, there are situations when you feel like you might not make it. Once in Syria, it was intense, very, very intense. But our powers diminishing, us losing them, that's something I never thought about anymore. The first days after 1/19, yeah, when it was still like a new suit, that was kind of on my mind, sure. I'd say to myself: "This ain't possible. It's gotta end at some point." But then it's normal, you get used to it, you change, you forget. So that night feeling like everything might disappear, that everything was going to be taken away, was really terrifying.

Did you talk to anyone about it?
To Virginie. And then to a bunch of quacks I consulted, too. But that was later, when it got out to the press. Virginie described basically the same symptoms—mild dizziness, occasional headaches, and especially the feeling that she was doing everything slower. She thought it was related to her depression and maybe the meds they'd given her. It was hard for her to concentrate. Each time she used her powers she'd feel totally wiped out, so it didn't seem illogical to think it could all be related. But when I told her I had the same shit—I couldn't always disappear, and I had to concentrate, and activating my powers for just a couple minutes gave me migraines—she understood what was happening to us. We'd started to get weaker. Our powers wouldn't last forever.

You refused to accept that.
Totally. In any case, I could never stand acceptance, all these
philosophies of acceptance they drum into you now. It's like
people who are mortally ill: however much you tell 'em they're
doomed, they're still looking for some way out. They want to
believe. They cling to something, even if it makes no sense.
And us, the 83ers, we didn't have to search too hard, everyone came to us proposing their services. I did every kind of
crap imaginable. Swallowing shit, lying down on these sort of
experimental machines that stimulate the brain. Ridiculous.
In the end I was even almost taken down by an Australian
newspaper's sting operation.

You've never given your version of what happened . . .
Because at the time I wasn't very proud of the fact that I almost
got fucked over. It doesn't bother me to talk about it now. I
don't give a rat's ass.

It was a classic setup, but very well done. You meet a very
pretty girl. She's from Perth or Melbourne. You spend the
night with her. Like everyone else back then, she's heard of
your issues. [*The website Mediapart's exclusive investigation,
posted online on June 17th of Year III, had revealed that the
French superheroes were growing weaker.*] She mentions this
friend of a friend she has who might have a solution—but she's
a pro, right, she knows how to weave this into the conversation
and even make it seem like bringing up the subject was your
idea. You meet the guy at a hotel near the Champs-Élysées in
complete secrecy. He's a neurosurgeon with an Arab-sounding
name and, since they're good at their job, you find a bunch of
fake references on the internet that make you think he really
exists. He talks to you about a more or less secret procedure,
something they can try to boost your powers back up. But he's

got a favor to ask in exchange. He wants to know if you know of a sure way of getting a weapon past security at CDG. He figures, since you're able to make yourself invisible, it must not be too hard.

How did you realize it was a setup?
On my way home I'm thinking about what the guy asked for again, and it doesn't make sense. He can't be sure I'll say yes. If he's really putting together an operation that totally smells like a terrorist attack, that implies months of prep, a huge investment, and he's not going to risk all that on a deal with some guy like me who can still fuck it all up. So I head back to the hotel. I turn invisible—this time it decided to work—and I luck into finding the two of them in the lobby paying for the room. They were independent journalists associated with Rise Up Australia, the anti-Muslim political party, who were trying to set me up. I don't even know anymore if they were taken to court.

Did this misadventure put an end to your efforts? Did it incite you to be more reasonable?
No. I told myself I was going to stay away from anything illegal, that was for sure. But that still left tons of things to check out. I moved on to the so-called softly-softly approach. I started psychologizing it. You can always find lots of people to tell you it's all inside your head, and so naturally what's happening to you is partially your fault. The problem's with you, your way of doing things, your lack of willpower, crap like that. And there you go, you're on a very slippery slope.

How did you get yourself out of that?
I was with my good friends, the Russians, at a private clinic.

We'd get up at 5:00 A.M. We'd eat these disgusting, greenish soups, made from local roots. They were starving us there. Then, we'd meditate on these foam mats. I don't know the name of the movement anymore, I can't remember who turned me on to it. This sort of guru was named Arkady So-and-So, and he looked like an old Russian writer from the 1970s with a beard and smoked glasses.

One morning I get text a from Gregory, which I still have, actually. [*He shows it to me. It reads: "Are you that unhappy?"*] That pissed me off to no end. I told him to go to hell. But actually it . . . [*He chokes up. He lets several seconds pass before continuing.*] I never understood what motivated him to send me that message. And I totally knew he didn't write it to piss me off. In fact, it was the opposite. He was worried about me. He'd held on to all of his kindness, the bastard. But kindness like that, in its pure state, it's insufferable. It crushes you. [*He clears his throat.*] I left the clinic that same night, and I stopped whining.

Would you say that Gregory and his message helped you move on?
That's not how I'd explain it, no. But if that's how you want to portray it, go ahead, say that, write that. Okay, next topic.

In reality, the decline is slower than initially reported.
Yeah, it's true that at first people were saying all kinds of things. Me, too, actually. I thought I would lose everything at once. With invisibility, if it's not a sure thing, from an operational standpoint, it's only a minor advantage. There's not one single mission you're going to be able to mount banking on that power. In fact, in my current contracts it's clearly stipulated that the client cannot count on it. I'm still the Invisible Man, but the new version has some bugs . . . Sometimes it works,

sometimes it doesn't. And no one's ever been able to explain to me in a convincing manner why it's screwy. But it's true that in terms of the rest—endurance, speed, and even combat techniques—I've still got good days ahead of me. So my appointment book is full. I've got work. I make a good living. Got no right to complain.

The fear has passed?
More or less. I tell myself it's like getting old. I'm starting to get white hairs in my beard. In any case, it's been scientifically proven you start to decline at thirty-five. To deteriorate. And so I'm an aging superhero. There are still times when I can't stand it, like when I run into guys at the airport or in hotel lobbies who make little jokes about my health concerns. I want to throw 'em through the wall. 'Cause I know they're right. The rest of the time it's fine. I accept it now.

XXX

GREGORY WAS WALKING on the only paved street of this godforsaken place way out in the middle of nowhere, New Mexico, where dust yellowed everything. The inhabitants had retired to their homes, like in a western just before the final showdown. In the distance, an engine was running, perhaps of a car getting ready to leave; he feared it might be the Prophet's. Once again he would elude him. Heart pounding, Gregory hurried. He was almost running, but always too slowly, like in a dream when your legs wear out from trying to cut through nearly solid air. He reached a cafeteria clad in white sheet metal, sizzling in the noonday sun. It must be stifling in there. Then suddenly he saw him, sitting inside, the only customer in the large, old-timey dining room with Naugahyde booths. There were several partially eaten dishes in front of him, and Raphael was biting into a chicken thigh with a gluttonous zeal that even he seemed to disapprove of, judging from his knit brow. He chewed, grimacing, and his eyes grew wider each time his jaws neared the meat, as though this movement were beyond his will. Gregory stayed there a moment like he was concerned, ashamed, and outraged even about this shame of discovering his former friend in this situation. And finally he would wake up.

He spoke very little about growing weaker. More affected than the others, he had problems flying. At times he couldn't take off. He freely admitted that he experienced some "dysfunction" at times. The sexual innuendo, which made some people smirk, left him, on the other hand, expressionless. He also added that what had happened to him was neither good nor bad, "like just about everything when you think about it."

The website PurePeople revealed that he had been suffering from hearing issues for at least three months. At night phantom sounds droned in his ears, which he described to several specialists he consulted as a storm rumbling in the distance. A numbness around his temples along with a dull aching sensation in his neck bothered him almost daily. When he was in the city, jackhammers, horns, and the illegally modified exhaust pipes of scooters screamed in his eardrums. When he wore hearing protection earmuffs, however, the irritation lessened. As for the rest, even though his abilities measured lower, he did not seem concerned. There were only a few days until July 10th, and his entire attention was occupied with Lucille's fate. Across the shattered nation, Gregory was once again the hero that nearly everyone loved. However, despite general sentiment, some people dared to criticize: his personal situation was heartbreaking, absolutely, but the Captain hadn't participated in any mission for three months, yet taxpayers continued to pay his salary, which still and all was quite high.

Furthermore, on July 5th the newspaper *Le Parisien* broke the story on Gregory's secret trip to Los Angeles, which, based on incorrect information, it claimed was paid for by the French Republic. That same day, the 83er, out of breath and upset, entered the newspaper office, grabbed the editor-in-chief by the collar, lifted him off the ground, and shook him. He was convinced that Raphael or the people protecting him were leading this new attack. The editor, a level-headed man who, moreover, would not press charges, tried desperately to deny any intention of deliberately doing harm, they just cared about keeping the public informed, when the phone rang in the office. A shrill screech pierced Gregory's ears, and he loosened his grip.

Several hours later he would recount that at that moment it was like he was outside his own body. The editor, sitting on the floor, face red, was silently tucking his shirt back in his pants. Through the glass wall the Captain could make out the feet, backs, and heads of reporters hiding behind their desks or crawling toward an emergency exit. He wanted to leave this suffocating office then and there. But the glass door, which he had slammed too forcefully when he entered the editor's office, was jammed shut. As he struggled with the recalcitrant doorknob, he caught a glimpse of himself in a distant mirror.

The following day, July 6th, four days before Lucille's announced death, he put a plan into action that he'd been developing for approximately the last week.

Just before 1:00 P.M. he called one of his contacts at the Ministry of the Interior and informed him that he was holding Raphael Zabreski's mother, sister, brother-in-law, and niece hostage. He was holed up in the Yvelines area west of Paris on a farm and had booby-trapped the immediate surrounding area. If Raphael did not appear within twenty-four hours of this phone call, he would kill the prisoners.

History was repeating itself. That's the impression people had, and perhaps he had, too. A superhero had lost his mind. He was holding innocent people hostage in an isolated house, causing a police force to be deployed, while a crowd, vast this time, squeezed around the guarded perimeter to show their support for the maniac.

It had been pouring for the last three days in northern France. In the fields surrounding the farm puddles grew larger; ponds formed. As a nearby river was threatening to overflow its banks, security measures were cited to force the protesters back. But they condemned the move on social media and called on their fellow citizens to join them. An immense traffic jam was predicted at the exit for Saint-Germain-en-Laye.

The local Prefect, who wanted neither a riot nor a flood, called for the situation to be brought to an end as quickly as possible. Several assault teams had taken position around the farm. The soil was so saturated with water that people were mired at every step. Legs sunk in with sucking noises, and some officers were stuck in their restive boots, unable to lift their feet.

Around 5:00 P.M. the Captain released Raphael's brother-in-law and niece. "I could tell he was hesitating," Carlos Renaudin, one of the negotiators who spoke with him over the course of the day, recounts. The bombs that the 83er claimed to have placed around the house were nothing but crude decoys. The Captain had requested that his two daughters join him, then retracted the demand twenty minutes later. As for the remaining hostages, at times he promised not to hurt them, then, his anger returning, claimed that he would kill them if Zabreski didn't come.

Behind the police vehicles various scenarios were examined. This time, superhero or not, a well-run assault would be successful. But public opinion seemed divided. There'd been too many failures. People didn't want to hear about the 83ers anymore. Moreover, the Prime Minister announced an immediate tightening of legislation. [*Under the guise of better managing the superheroes' activities, their powers would become, for all intents and purposes, illegal.*] Nevertheless, in the eyes of a good part of the population, Gregory was still Lucille's father.

This was a desperate act. And who wouldn't have been drawn, in such circumstances, to the same extremes as he was? For those French, the person responsible for this ongoing drama was Raphael Zabreski.

The email that the Prophet sent to various news organizations was made public around 3:00 A.M. The following day British police reportedly determined that he had connected from a cybercafé in Warlingham, in the suburbs of London, but no charges had been filed and there was no plan to apprehend him.

The message most frequently found on social media read as follows:

> I was greatly distressed to learn of the extremely dan-
> gerous situation my loved ones are in. Even if I must
> suffer, I will not give in to a man who chose terror as a
> means of satisfying his wishes. Lucille will die on July
> 10th. No one will change that.
>   RZ

On websites such as *Le Monde*, however, the last two sentences were not part of the published message. Today, its authenticity continues to be debated. Several sources confirm that the email they received did not include any reference to Lucille. But if these sentences had been added at some point, then who is the author? Perhaps a practical joker at some publication. Someone with a taste for the sensational. A fan who found this overly laconic message lacking. Another hypothesis cannot be completely discounted: Raphael sent a first version of the email, then a second version that he had edited, either removing or adding the pronouncement about the child.

It was this extended version that circulated the most, in any case. It heightened the tension around the hostage situation. Gregory would eventually discover for himself, either by television or phone, Raphael's words. The worst was expected. A strike team was ready to move in, but the incessant rain prompted caution, regardless of the situation. There was a risk of getting stuck outside the farm. They couldn't count on a sudden attack. In fact, it would probably be a hard slog. Carlos Renaudin and one of his colleagues persuaded the military brass to wait a bit more. And around 11:00 A.M, just as they had hoped, the Captain agreed to release the last two hostages.

The men who laid siege to the farm found the superhero in an armchair, his eyes lowered. He grunted when hands went around his arms and he was ordered to get up.

With the threat of flooding and all the protesters rushing to the area to support the Captain, the roads were no longer safe. A helicopter took him. The rising Seine River made people fear major disruptions in the capital, and there was talk of transferring him to Marseille. The Paris police chief, however, refused to give up such a prestigious suspect. The Captain was remanded in custody at 36 Quai des Orfèvres, in the police buildings next to the Palais de Justice.

His lawyers were waiting for him there. But even with them he remained silent. He only asked for one thing—to see his daughters.

It hadn't stopped raining outside. Suddenly the Seine swelled. The waters were now licking the arches of the Pont-au-Change Bridge, which had to be closed to traffic like all of Paris's bridges. The sky was so dark that it seemed as if night had already fallen. Wind blew over trees in parks. As a precautionary measure, hospitals were evacuated, while in many neighborhoods the power was out.

The Captain's first hearing was scheduled in one of those improbably small, closet-like offices which made 36 Quai des Orfèvres famous—maids' quarters converted into police offices with dilapidated computers, childhood decorations, and leatherette couches for napping. However, while waiting for the commander who was to lead the interrogation, the Captain stood up, broke the chain of his handcuffs in one movement, and approached the dormer window. He was going to see his daughters.

Two police officers tried to stop him, but he knocked the first one out and broke the second one's arm in a quick, firm motion. Since he was not carrying a weapon, and since it was the Captain—even if no one present ever admitted that his status intimidated them—not a single shot was fired. He was only escaping, after all. That doesn't give you the right to shoot.

He easily ripped the bars off the dormer, stood on a metal cabinet, and launched himself into the void. His free-falling body would regain altitude in a flash. Two witnesses attest they saw him flap his arms to fly.

But his power didn't work, and this time he fell.

It is said he had the time to murmur a few words to the random people gathered around him. He spoke of Lucille, whom he loved, or of the Prophet, whom he hated, or of Jeanne, or of a voice he heard. The autopsy results indicate, however, that his jaw was broken. That he would have been able to utter even a single word seems improbable today.

He did not die instantly, but several minutes later on the firefighters' rescue boat, which was whisking him away through the flooded city.

XXXI

WIND AND THUNDER besieged the northern coast of France. Some foolhardy people went missing, swept away by giant waves. Inside the country rivers overflowed their banks. The Bay of the Somme was again underwater. On highways throughout the country, cars slid, jamming into one another. People were now talking about the storm of the century.

In Paris, water entered the Cour Carrée at the Louvre and submerged the Trocadéro like the great flood of 1910. People had underestimated the threat. In the case of flooding the plan was for four-meter high mobile partitions to be erected around the main subway stations; two thousand transit workers would wall up the subway entrances to protect the underground areas. They were smart plans, but ambitious. They were based on a level of coordination and a speed of execution that was basically out of reach in a city that little by little was sinking into chaos.

This chaos was not violent, as some legends continue to make people believe. There was no looting or widespread panic. The Parisians I interviewed remember the storm as an astonishing moment, heightened by secret excitement. The telephone lines were saturated. Stuck at home or in their offices, finding refuge under covered bus stops or in the stairwells of unknown apartment buildings for some, they were shocked to see how quickly the familiar surroundings around them gave way to a new world.

Through windows they discerned, slowly swept away in oily water, cars floating like oversized children's toys, debris, trash, and these sort of shiny large tires, which people eventually figured out were drowned bodies.

Even though flooding on such a massive scale was bound to occur one day or another, many wished to see this as a sign of destiny. When they heard on the radio what was first presented as the Captain's suicide, some thought that a funereal atmosphere was necessary for the death of such a man. Others believed that, from his deep slumber, Mickaël was warning them of his return, which would be biblical in its violence. "I was one of them," admits Virginie. "The decrease in the amount of light, especially. Nighttime in the middle of the day. That gave it a kind of end-of-times feel. It was so unusual you couldn't not think that it portended something even bigger."

During the first hours of the catastrophe, she'd felt the need to leave her bed, where she'd been vegetating for the last three days, to join the overwhelmed aid workers. Since the hostage situation the previous evening, superheroes in theory were forbidden to use their powers, but faced with such an urgent situation, no state official was thinking about invoking the ministerial decree.

She carried men on her back across a flooded boulevard and then stopped a drifting car with a mother and her children trapped inside. In one leap she jumped to the roof of a newspaper kiosk pulling with her a young woman just as a wrecked bus was about to hit her. Even though her speed and power had diminished, she gave it her all. For her, being applauded in the middle of Paris was like returning to the exultation of her first days. Headphones covering her ears (a song by Herman Düne played very loudly on repeat so she'd have the courage to continue), she watched the survivors' mouths move and tears of gratitude flow. This day should never end.

She was catching her breath in a first-aid station when she heard someone report the Captain's death in a low voice. Even though the radio was broadcasting the news, she still refused to believe it. And even a bit later, when it was said that the Prophet had just reappeared in the middle of Paris, she didn't take any heed. The most extraordinary rumors were circulating that day. "Plus I'd already written my end to the story: Gregory would survive us all, and Raphael would never return."

But he had decided once and for all to be done with the Captain. The more days went by, the more he gave in to his anger. It had taken over everything, his sleep, reading, meditation exercises, even the faces of those he crossed along his journey, faces with malevolent looks, as if hatching murder plots. He himself felt monstrous, disfigured by the rage of knowing that this man, on the other side of the planet, was turning the masses against him, persuading them that he was a scumbag and almost a murderer. He brooded. And with this obsession he figured out he was slowly dying. Gregory was making him crazy. Gregory was killing him.

When Raphael learned Gregory was holding his family hostage, he was overcome with hate. He flew to London where he rested for a few hours and sent a message stating that he would never give in. One might believe, reading his refusal to give in to the blackmail, that he would not intervene. But that was only a strategy. He'd had enough of the dithering that had paralyzed him his entire life, enough of that cowardliness disguised as reason that was whispering to him that Gregory was expecting exactly this, for him rush there, and this was ordering him to run away, to disappear.

He took off again. As he was nearing the farm he discovered that the kidnapping had been thwarted. But that wasn't enough. It's either him or me, he said to himself. Even any thought of Gregory had to be eliminated. Then everything would be fine. Yes, everything would have fallen into place. He would once again be the missing person, the beloved, the man who peacefully read books chosen randomly at a library in Oregon. He flew as fast as possible and reached Paris at the exact moment when, in the corridors of 36 Quai des Orfèvres, the Captain was taken out of his cell and was being escorted, handcuffed, to his first hearing.

Maybe. But in that case why didn't the Prophet go directly to the police station? Why did he instead rush headlong into the Solferino subway station, which was inundated by bubbling flood waters?

He was a good man. He had ended up regretting his silence, and he was going to meet Gregory brimming with peaceful intentions. He was going to tell him what he had seen in Lucille's future. This would not change anything with the little girl's future. On July 10th, just before noon, her heart would stop beating. Jeanne, who would be holding her hand in the safe room they'd planned to spend this dreaded day in, would let out a long, horrified scream. And the doctors questioned on television a few hours later would explain that in some cases, not quite as rare as one might think, death strikes without people being able to detect the slightest weakness. In some cases the victim dies, and that's all there is to it. But the Prophet had finally understood that in this world, principles, however just they may be, should never take precedence over human suffering. He would talk.

He would not harm anyone when he arrived at Quai des Orfèvres. He would be granted permission to speak several minutes with Gregory. But, on his way there, as he was about to cross the Seine, he suddenly realized that law-abiding citizens were trapped by rising waters in the Solferino station. He had granted himself the right to remain silent on what he knew about all forthcoming deaths, not to turn his back on lives threatened a few meters away from him. This is possible.

He entered the subway station, heard the cries of Justine Conticello and Lassana Kanté, and swam with all his might toward them. The water had almost reached the ceiling where they—she, a young dancer, he, a security guard—were trapped. He chose Justine first, whose face appeared to have a deathly pallor already. He told her to hold her breath. He carried her beneath the water. He emerged just in front of the station steps, looked for a safe place to leave her, flew to the balcony of an apartment in a building across the street, and asked the people living there to take good care of her. Then he went back to the station to save Lassana.

He had never left Paris. Everything I wrote about his stay in America would then be false. Those who bore witness lied, and the proof that people like me brandish is obviously fabricated. A slew of convincing reasons can explain why he continued to live in hiding here. It's even, and by far, the most probable scenario.

He loved strolling incognito in this city where everything reminded him that he was a hero of the nation. At newspaper kiosks, magazine headlines perpetuated the Prophet's legend. A theater troupe was presenting his early years. The 83er's disappearance had frozen his facial features forever. They were those of a good man, perpetually good, as elemental as water in a glacier.

Oh, the pleasure of overhearing—near a fountain in the Palais-Royal, on a subway platform, in line at a movie theater in Montparnasse—a conversation about him! Everything that reminded him of his achievement unburdened him, for a time at least, of the fatigue of being what he was: complicated, fickle, hardly more than a man, in the end. In the stories making the rounds about him, he proved to be straightforward and up to the task.

When the waters of the Seine started to rise, he knew the moment for his return had come. All superheroes return to work. There's no end, just occasional breaks. In his lair (which was, according to different versions, a hotel room near the Porte de Clichy, a mechanical room in the depths of the Châtelet subway station, or Jeanne's apartment, whom he'd won back), he pulled out a suitcase, which had been stored on top of a wardrobe, and removed his white mask. Spread out across his knees, face empty and mouth puckered, the mask seemed to be sulking. "I'm here," said Raphael. He slipped on the mask. The power was out, and he examined his profile in the shadowy reflection of a mirror hanging on the front door.

Outside, the humid air and wind from the storm made him shiver. He hadn't used his abilities in several months, and, flying just a few meters above the waterline, he heard himself roar with laughter.

Near the Solferino station, individuals were waving their arms. Several people were trapped inside. People had heard them. They were going to drown. The Prophet dived into the black water, which was streaked with gasoline. He was afraid of not getting out of there either, but he didn't really have a choice.

He was to die that night. One night in the mirror he glimpsed a reddish glow around his neck. He only hesitated a few seconds. He put his thumb and index finger on the area. He learned he was going to drown. And since he felt hopeless, since he'd been hunted out of his American paradise, since he felt like his life was slipping through his fingers, since it was already too late at 37, since he no longer felt anything, even when he put his hand near flame, he headed toward his own death without looking back.

Or perhaps: since he'd become inflexible, since he believed that man's greatest virtue is faithfulness to his principles, and since, all too infrequently, he'd had the opportunity to display this, he made up his mind to do nothing to impede the course of events. He decided that, quite to the contrary, it was absolutely necessary to go forward and die without saying a word, because that's what was written, because there's no other ending than the one you've been dealt.

He did not die that day. His body was never found. The timeline was hinky. Justine Conticello's account was not reliable. The official reports contained inconsistencies.

He'd grabbed the only chance he had to leave this story for good. With perhaps some collusion, he did his utmost to stage his own death. And now? He was free for the first time in his life. He was walking north along the roads of Saskatchewan. He was sleeping in the shade of trees on a tiny island in the Marquesas. He had returned to his life in Paris among the shadows. He was no longer anyone, and he was happy.

PART SIX

(Endings)

XXXII

RELOCATED THREE TIMES by the police, the encampment is currently situated two kilometers from the exterior wall. It looks like a temporary city, an orderly, and, it appears, well-financed shanty town—there's talk of English and Argentinian donors—where people of twenty-three nationalities live together. Tents and shelters line numbered streets. In a small valley, taut strings delineate the plots that will soon be allocated to new arrivals. "It's like a Far West outpost," jokes an old man guiding me around. Reported to be a bit more than 2,000, Mickaël's supporters are gathered in the commune of Saint-Christol, as close as possible to the 83er who is maintained in a prolonged coma on a military base now called the Koenig Zone after having been, under a different name, one of the French nuclear weapons depots for four decades.

The community of Mickaëliens have set up an elementary school, a library, and even, just recently, a militia. When asked about possible places of worship, the inhabitants respond that all religions are welcome. The guided tour does not allow me to see any of the altars dedicated to Mickaël, which some observers have said are scattered throughout the encampment. And the 83er's portrait is not attached inside the tents, nor on the electric poles, nor on the rear windshields of cars, as I had read.

Had everything been tucked away before I arrived?

"We're nothing but a bunch of idolaters," Cecilia Gester, the spokesperson of the camp, says ironically. [*She objects to the title of leader, which the press has bestowed upon her, and after our interview will send me two text messages to ensure that I do not use that "misleading" term.*]

Gester arrived here five months after Mickaël's neutralization. There were only a couple dozen people here when the produce truck dropped her off. Contrary to those who felt lighting candles and offering up prayers in the hope of hastening the 83er's awakening was enough, for her it was necessary to raise funds in order to organize a legal counteroffensive. Today, "believers" are tolerated on the grounds of the encampment, but they are expressly requested to avoid all public demonstrations. Of the *Lightness Pact*, which they were still loudly hyping a year ago (much to the delight of reporters who were more than eager to film these zealots' wackiness with their fitness sessions or their dietetic workshops), there's not the slightest trace. If Gester is a cult leader, as she is frequently accused of being, it's a strangely secular one—no priests, no chapel, no liturgy.

When she discusses the battle in the courts, however, Gester is invigorated with an evangelical fervor. She seems convinced that the judges will deliver Mickaël from this sentence that is a death penalty in everything but name. "In the end, reason always prevails," she asserts. I am of the opposite opinion. You may have sensed that reading this book. It seems to me that always and everywhere satisfying the most pressing desires ends up interfering with any plans and betraying any long-term projects. In our shared history I only see cataclysms we weren't able to avoid, injustices continually perpetuated, truths denied with a fool's aplomb. But Gester brushes off such talk. As a

joke, I apologize for being nothing but a heathen. She asks if
I'm blind or pretending to be, and adds that I want to act like
what I didn't understand doesn't exist. It's a form of belief, she
concludes. A lazy and convenient belief.

Gester was afraid during the Twenty-Seven Days. Mickaël
did not fascinate her, she swears, nor any of the 83ers. [*She
has frequently stated that after 1/19 she ran a skeptics' movie
club that would organize "Antihero" nights with Woody Allen
films.*] But when she learned how Mickaël had been tricked
by the Prophet, when she saw how this treachery was unani-
mously celebrated, her mind was "opened." The tyrant could
be arrested, put on trial, and jailed if it were proven that he
deserved it, but we didn't have the right to sentence him to
eternal sleep. It's as simple as that: a democracy dies each time
it abandons its founding principles, and the Awakening, in the
Mickaëliens' eyes, is nothing but the re-establishment of the
rule of law. "We're not doing it for him, but for us," people
said to me several times during my visit.

A Spanish journalist is finishing an interview with Gester
when I meet her in the large tent that serves as the encampment's computer center.

"If you could have, would you have killed Hitler?" asks the
journalist.

"Certainly not," Gester responds.

"Even if he was going to kill you?"

"Certainly not," she repeats.

Annoyed, the journalist puts her recording equipment
away. I cannot say if it's the content of Gester's answer that
upsets her, or the feeling that this answer does not contain all
of Gester's thoughts.

A young man named Paul Demarcy lived in the encampment

for a little while. At the time the Mickaëliens considered him their finest prize. This officer from a respected family, who was one of the men tasked with supervising the 83er's sleep in the Koenig Zone, left the army a year ago and publicly expressed his support for the Awakening. He is currently renting a studio apartment about twenty kilometers from the military base. Without stating it directly, he discloses his loneliness in this tiny town where he knows no one, but he can't imagine moving. It's difficult for him, he explains, to distance himself from Mickaël. He went to Paris to speak with the media on two separate occasions and couldn't bear it.

He hasn't had any contact with the encampment for just over six months. Cecilia Gester's not telling the whole truth, he contends. "Of course they want to see Mickaël get down to work. And me, too. We're all nostalgic, but for something that didn't happen. We want the next episode. The next part of the story, regardless of the price." It is this hypocrisy that supposedly led Demarcy to distance himself. People at the encampment, for their part, avoid speaking of him. "He's rebuilding his life. It takes time," Gester will simply tell me.

When I meet him, he starts recounting his experience in the Koenig Zone of his own accord. Actually, he didn't see much. The room where Mickaël sleeps is a dark, large round hangar. Maybe a thirty-meter radius, Demarcy estimates. The 83er is lying down in the center in a kind of open sarcophagus surrounded by various pieces of diagnostic equipment and cameras. There must be a room someplace where the filmed images are displayed on control monitors, a room with a close-up of the sleeper where the slightest twitch on his face cannot go unnoticed by those who monitor him, but Demarcy never had access to it. Men like him walk in pairs through the corridor that surrounds the room. They've been ordered never to stop and are not supposed to turn their heads toward the sleeper. Those who disobey only catch a glimpse of the profile of Mickaël's frozen face, a blurry spot in the darkness, and, from time to time, doctors or senior officers bent over his body in consultation.

Demarcy told that one night, suffocating under the silent rage that Mickaël's situation had engendered in him, he slipped into the room and walked up to the sarcophagus. At first he was disconcerted by the rumbling of a generator that maintained the hangar at a constant temperature. He hadn't imagined, from the soundproof corridor where he had dreamed of this intrusion, that Mickaël could sleep in the din of an engine room.

Demarcy was now about two meters from the 83er. And he noticed that his dry face, veined with red streaks, the source of which was unknown to him, was frozen in an expression of terror and pain. This finally convinced him the punishment should end.

Two months after the first interviews, he once again made headlines, revealing that he'd never had access to the room.

Concerning his retraction, he told me what he had explained to others: it was to satisfy his interviewers' curiosity and also because he was convinced of Mickaël's suffering, that Demarcy made it all up. However, such an effraction was unrealistic. "Can you imagine if the first soldier to come along could open the door and enter the holy of holies?" Demarcy details the access protocol: must be in possession of a code that is changed every two hours, biometric identification, unlocking initiated by central command. But a good number of the 83er's defenders refuse to believe these explications. For them, Paul Demarcy was intimidated, or bought, and his retraction is fabricated. For them, Mickaël's face is precisely like the one Demarcy says he invented.

XXXIII

"Everything was way easier for us." People are quick to forget, the leader of the 96ers is in the habit of saying. With the first group of French superheroes, he remembers, it was an utter shock. "On the other hand, when it suddenly happened to us, we knew what was happening. And our fellow citizens did, too." The context wasn't the same either: "When they appeared, we were still in the middle of a crisis. France doubted itself, we hadn't yet returned to being the great power we are today." Given these conditions, Gabriel Teysserand believes there were too many expectations and not enough patience.

The day his publicists were finally able to find a time slot for our meeting, his lumberjack shirt, its sleeves rolled up over his biceps, and his twisting tattoos, which coil over his forearms and neck, make you forget the well-bred young man from a good family and university student in management he was not so long ago.

When I ask him his opinion on the 83ers' exploits and overall track record, Teysserand is harsh. According to him, his forebears had the means to succeed. "But with powers like ours, if you don't take care of unity and leadership issues, you're going to run smack into a wall."

In order to clearly indicate their differences, Teysserand

enjoys, I can sense it, enumerating measures taken from the very beginning of the 96ers: passing a charter setting a strict obligation of professional restraint and confidentiality, the election of a leader for three years who serves as the group's only spokesperson and who provides operations command ("but can be removed, if conditions require," Teysserand insists), and finally the famous annual contract, which establishes a guiding principle for the superheroes' actions. "It's sad to say, but all the mistakes they made really helped us out. We wouldn't have done any better if we'd been first."

He gives me a tour of the 96ers' HQ, situated on a large avenue that leads out toward La Défense to the west of Paris. At the far end of the *situation room* where a long rosewood table sits, Teysserand pauses before the group's official portrait, a black and white Richard Avedon-style photograph taken five months after their appearance, in December of Year V. He laughs: "That might be the day we argued the most in our lives." The 96ers' faces are relaxed and smiling, however. "Ibrahima got up on the wrong side of the bed. The Kid thought the hairstylist had totally messed up, and Geoffroy didn't want to be at the edge of the frame . . ." Their group is made of a lot of big egos, Teysserand recognizes, and sometimes tensions surface. But what on multiple occasions he calls their "project" always ends up defusing the situation.

"Without a roadmap," he opines, "we would have imploded," smiling at the memory of the Captain's somewhat empty speeches and his repeated references to a capital-G Good, yet no one ever exactly understood what fell under that umbrella. "The 83ers were scattered. For us, it's jihad, jihad, jihad. We don't do humanitarian stuff. It's obvious we don't please everybody, but at least we're being upfront about it." Socially conservative, economically liberal, having chosen the war on international terrorism as the primary focus of their actions, the 96ers were able to win people over, Teysserand deduces, because they've always stayed true to their mission.

"This kind of integrity needed to be supported by a new generation." Young people accustomed to communicating via the internet, they quickly surrounded themselves with a battalion of web masters and watchdogs tasked with transmitting the 96ers' messages and defending their e-reputations. Totaling around fifty, they work in an open office space on the third floor. I notice a basketball hoop attached to a pillar, caricatures from *Charlie Hebdo* tacked here and there, and muted monitors broadcasting Eurosport, yet the atmosphere appears studious. On the back wall a quotation from Walter Benjamin is printed in silver letters: EACH EPOCH DREAMS THE ONE TO FOLLOW.

[*Later, back in my hotel room, I will discover that the attribution of this quotation is in fact questionable. At the time, I merely ask Teysserand if he's already read Walter Benjamin. He shrugs his shoulders and gives me a hard look for a moment without saying anything. Someone must have mentioned to him that I had frequently defended the Captain's memory in my articles, and he must be worried that I met him with the sole intention of disparaging the second generation of French superheroes. This I cannot deny, and please excuse me if this chapter suffers from it: their dazzling success leaves a bad taste in my mouth.*]

Alright, "each epoch dreams the one to follow." To remain faithful to the spirit of the place one might want to add, "and definitely not the previous one." According to Teysserand, "the 35- to 45-year-old generation [*implying the 83ers*] grew up with mass unemployment, AIDS, a lot of fear, and not a lot to find comfort in. Ultimately, it's really just a bunch of lost people who lack ideological consistency. I can get away with saying that because they themselves recognize it."

Walking me back to my car, parked in an underground lot where several vehicles emblazoned with the 96ers' blue lion are parked, Teysserand recalls the Parisian municipal elections that the Captain participated in. At the time Teysserand was part of a student group that campaigned for him. "He came to the university to see us. I don't really remember what he talked about. It was probably a little nebulous. But he believed in it himself. And that made you want to believe." During the final weeks jeering by activists on the extreme right had turned into altercations. But Teysserand hoped to the very end that the Captain's ticket would qualify for the second round of elections. He'd even purchased a bottle of champagne with his meager savings. When the results were announced he and one of his friends walked to the Seine to throw the bottle off a bridge. They needed, he explains, to do something melo-dramatic. "But the bottle of champagne landed in the water without a sound. That really disappointed us," he adds with a smile. Then, as he's shaking my hand good-bye: "We would've been better off drinking it."

XXXIV
"Perfect People"

SAÏD MECHBAL: Did he do the generations bit? That's Teysserand's thing. I don't know why. It must make him feel better, having these kind of cubbyholes you can categorize people in by ten- or fifteen-year chunks. Sure, I grew up with the comedy troupe Les Inconnus, Mitterrand, and then rap, Captain Tsubasa, and all-night telethons on TV. And there were millions of us watching the same crap on TV. But sorry, this generations idea doesn't really mean much to me. I grew up poor in a country of rich people, brown in a country of Whites. That makes a huge difference, right? From guys like Marville or Zabreski, I mean. Okay, so maybe we were the same age, but we definitely didn't have the same life.

Have you met Gabriel Teysserand before?
I saw him one time at the very beginning, two or three months after the 96ers appeared. Not because I wanted to 'cause since my lawsuit against the French government I'd absolutely no desire to meet a good little servant of the Republic. But we ran into each other backstage at a TV show.

Speaking of which, what were you doing there?

I liked the host. That was around the time when I started being attracted to everybody: men, older women, ugly people in the street . . . It was my pansexual period. I wanted to take everyone in my arms. And at the same point, every time, I'd start blubbering. There I was, buck naked in bed with these strangers, and I'm crying like a baby. Worst thing is, it was good for me, crazy good.

The host called me by my first name, like we were friends. He'd say my name at the end of every sentence, "That would be awesome, Saïd," "You're quite right there, Saïd," and he had this cute way of touching my arm . . . I dunno, it was sweet the way he acted with me. I wanted him to like me. I wanted to take him to a fancy hotel for the weekend and have him all to myself. So I thought I could just go back on his show and clown around. He'd like it, and then we'd probably go have dinner somewhere together. I was thinking I'd say a couple terrible things about my autocratic friend Shevchuk, but then one of the commentators changed the subject and started asking me about jihadist terrorist attacks and why "we moderate Muslims" weren't more engaged. And so right there I get on my high horse and I'm like super serious. You should never talk seriously, at least not when you're hitting on a young TV host. So when I said, just to be a smartass, that we had the right to be immoderate Muslims, that there was no law against it in the Republic, I could see right away he didn't like that, and he got all red telling me I was acting like an apologist for terrorism. They started telling me that, that it was obvious what I was saying, that immoderate meant extremist, and we all started screaming at each other. Right, so I was kind of riled up when I left the set, but more sad, 'cause I told myself I wasn't going to see my cute TV host anymore. And lo and behold I run into Teysserand, who was in makeup, and I'm sure he didn't miss a bit of my appearance on the show since there're monitors all over the place backstage.

Do you remember what you said to each other?
He said that he was awed, that it was an honor for him to be able to shake my hand. He even used the word "moved," I believe. A total load of crap . . . And I don't know, with his humble smile you could tell he was gloating, the little shit. The shame and ugliness of others, that's what gets people off. He'd just seen me make a fool of myself. He was going to go on next and show you that the new generation was the exact opposite of Saïd: good people, nice guys, who aren't into half-assed provocation, who have statesmanship. So I think that must have been the ultimate personal pleasure for him—just before walking on set, seeing my dripping face, kissing the ring, and doing his little princely false modesty bit.

Afterward did you follow the 96ers' exploits?
I didn't miss a thing. They were preening so much. I wanted to see 'em screw up. That's all I was waitin' for. *Schadenfreude*, as the Germans say: getting pleasure from the misfortune of others. There's no word in French for that, which is weird, since it's kind of our national pastime, right? I bought the special issues, I watched the 24-hour news channels, I created alerts on the internet to get all the news. It became like an addiction. Rather painful, I have to say, 'cause their successes rubbed everything we'd messed up in our faces. And when you saw them, especially Gabriel and Geoffroy, it seemed so easy. They seemed so sure about their reality, you know what I mean? When they've got their press conference to say that human rights are nice and all, but when confronting the barbarity of terrorists some *adjustments* have to be made, they say it with such assurance it's like it's an obvious fact. They knew

how to make themselves obvious facts. Now that's the ultimate political art. On the other hand, except for the Captain, we dithered. Our questions, our scruples, everything was fuzzy with us. For me, I felt like I kind of started liking 96ers for that. And then after six months, when the first question marks started to appear, when we slowly got back to what we know how to do best in France—spit on people and, if possible, kick 'em while they're down—I think I liked them even a bit more.

It didn't make you happy to see them struggle?
Not really. Not as much as I thought it would, in any case. When there was Ibrahima's first scandal [*he was accused of sexual harassment by one of his assistants in February of Year VI*], I just thought history repeats itself. And that was devastating to me. 'Cause I think, like everybody in fact, that I wanted to hear an extraordinary story. The day he was naturalized, the account *Le Monde* had on their website gave me goosebumps. Me. The story of this little guy from Mali who grew up here but who was never accepted, and he's recognized, finally . . . and he's so modest, staring at his shoes. It was sublime. Then there's the 96ers' policy statement, the moral lessons they're teaching all of us, that assurance they had setting the bar very, very high . . . Even if we didn't think the same way at all, I wanted them to exist, these perfect people. So, when Ibrahima came and made a public apology, and there were people there, even among the reporters, who were ready to boo him off, I don't know, I felt sad for a reason that went beyond his situation. Sad to be pulled back to reality. Gotta be an animal, maybe a dolphin or a bird, to do something truly pure in the world. We muck everything up.

It's been said on occasion that the remaining 83ers could join the 96ers. Precisely to offer their experience.

No, that'll never happen.

And might we see a headline about the 83ers reuniting?
There's very little chance, honestly. I don't think so.

But you yourself stated, which was surprising, that you were in favor.
Yeah, but it's not up to me, even if I seem to be the one who was always kind of stirring shit up. Let me tell you, it's even a bit sadder than that: even if the three of us could agree on trying to do something together, I'm not sure we could manage it.

Why?
There're too many ghosts with us . . . I'm sure you know we got together for the anniversary of Jean-Baptiste's death. It was nice. Not the ceremony itself, which was awful, with the Prime Minister and the overblown, pompous production. Jean-Baptiste would definitely have hated that. But with the three of us there was this kind of tenderness, the tenderness of those who have experienced something extraordinary together. And I told the gals the three of us still had things left to do. The ones who are left, we may not be the most flamboyant, but we've still got a good deal of strength and know-how. But Thérèse is off in Jean-Baptiste land with her film project. And Virginie, what she told us, and she's absolutely right, is that before we start anything up again, we'd need to talk, set things straight, tell each other face to face anything negative we have to say, things that have weighed on us. Except I don't think anyone will have the energy to do that.

So, that's the end?
Not really, since we're not there yet. But it's ending, yes.

XXXV

"Something To Live For"

VIRGINIE MATHIEU-BRUN: When they found me, I'd been stabbed with a knife 20 times or so. I was very weak from all the blood I'd lost, and they said I was delirious, but I'm not sure that's true.

When you were committed, many of your admirers talked of a plot. The statements you made when you were released leave room for doubt. What's your take on this incident now?
Conspirators didn't gather around a table and then say: "Alright, today we're going to lock up Virginie." I might have believed that at one time, but that's not how it happened. I was put in a psychiatric hospital because I'd become a danger to myself. It's obvious. The surveillance footage from the parking lot, nobody tampered with it, even though you can always find conspiracy theorists to tell you the opposite. 'Cause there's nothing more exciting than denying reality. It's like a magic power. For me, the minute the video shows there's no one else in the parking lot, that it's just me stabbing myself 20 times, I shut my trap, I tell myself I've become some sad, crazy lady, and they're absolutely right to commit me. Afterward, did hostility toward the 83ers play a role? Maybe around the

edges. There are some people who got satisfaction out of seeing me where I was. The doc who was caring for me, for example, now I'm sure he did everything he could so I'd end up there. He'll tell you the opposite if you go see him. Martin Bronner. But I for one never believed his big, pity-filled eyes or his soft, smarmy voice. I think he enjoyed watching me cry. And then sending me off with the other nut jobs, and you got to realize I'd become a zombie with all the meds they were giving me. I'm sure that got him off, too.

Did you always stay hopeful during your hospitalization?
No, why? Because I got out, you think I necessarily fought, that I never let go? That it's a question of willpower? I had no hope. I thought I was totally screwed. Like some broken-down machine—good for the trash heap. And the meds they give you, you feel like they're going to finish you off. You can't salivate any more. You can't enunciate. So you talk louder to try to make yourself understood. And because you're talking too loud, they tell you to calm down, and eventually that makes your blood boil. So they put you in isolation, where everyone can see you through the glass door all alone with your slop-pail and bed that's attached to the floor, and there's just a nurse who comes 'round once a day to slip you two Largactils and a Haldol, and you know that the more you knock on the door, the longer you'll stay. That's where it all ends, in there.

And yet you got out.
Yes. But I don't really have an explanation. I just think we're all more resistant than we believe. And so something grabs on. We want to live. It's genetic. It happens in spite of ourselves. What's hard is letting go. It's welcoming death. We don't want to die even if we know it would save us from all life's

disappointments. I thought I was screwed, but I was wrong.
The meds, the rest, the strength to survive, that's been inside
us since the dawn of time: this is what got me back on my
feet. Not my willpower.

And how do you feel now?
Not great, but not terrible either. I'm back on my feet, like
I said. I know who I am after all these years, that's one small
victory. I know I need meds, at the right dosage. Some manage
to live without, but not me, and I have no problem admitting
that. I also know I need to be alone frequently, because staying
with me isn't good for people. Staying a long time, I mean. I
can be very difficult at times. I'm much more balanced than
before, but it still happens. Since the last time we spoke I had
another breakdown, for example. And in those situations I'm
violent, I get very angry, I say horrible things. That's why, even
if I fought against it, it's good that Julien has custody of my
daughter. I really believe that. She doesn't need to see me like
that. She knows I've gone away now and then. There must be
people who tell her her mom's crazy. But she's never seen me
in that state. That makes a big difference for me.

[*She will also say that she had to change everything in order to
come back and live in her apartment: the gray Habitat sofa was
replaced by a chaise longue covered in red suedette. The personal
photos and children's drawings attached to the refrigerator door
were thrown out, as were the dishes, the paperback books, and the
sheets in which all too frequently she lay prostrate. She had the
walls of a sunny bathroom with southern exposure knocked down
to have a kitchenette installed, which she rarely uses—since her
divorce she doesn't cook—but she likes to look at it, she explains.
On ceramic tile nearly translucent birds fly off toward the window,*

and picture-perfect fruit (shiny apples, clementines, mangos) are
heaped on a large, Japanese-style stoneware platter, next to three
or four food-themed coffee table books, which have probably never
been opened. All the walls in the apartment are white and bare
except for one in the living room on which hangs a reproduction of
a face painted by Michelangelo in the Sistine Chapel: the Delphic
Sibyl whose turned head and open mouth allow a hint of disquiet
to slip into the monastic decor. When I ask her why she didn't
prefer to move, she just shrugs.]

Do you work a lot?
No, not a lot. I spend time at the gym, I work at the track with
my trainer, I sleep at least ten hours a night, plus I try to read
more than before. A novel every two weeks at least. Mostly
American mysteries, some Scandinavian ones, too. Supervising
the 96ers only takes about a third of my time.

Can you explain what this surveillance entails? You hear a lot of
different things.
So just the word "surveillance" bugs me a bit, because everything I do is with the blessing of the 96ers. It was even their
idea that their operations be checked by someone. They suggested there should be more regulations, more transparency. So
they needed someone to be in charge of that, and that someone is me. I don't go everywhere, 'cause I don't have the time,
and in some situations the discretion necessary for the mission prevents me from being present. But whenever possible I
accompany one or several 96ers into the theater of operations,
and I simply make sure they act in accordance with the law. I
observe. I write a report. Sometimes, but not all that often, in
the heat of the action I need to remind them of certain rules.
Concerning suspects' rights, for example.

That must put you in an uncomfortable position at times, no?
Not really. First off, because I'm not really in a position to
participate in operations anymore myself, too fragile mentally,
and, anyhow, my special power has greatly diminished. Today
I can only run the 100 meters in 9.3 seconds. And that, even
that's on days I really give it my all. It's still really good, but it's
almost back to human levels. So I need to move on to something else. There's no frustration there. Then, with the 96ers,
we've got a good working relationship. They know that if I'm
there it's to guarantee they did things by the rules. It keeps
them above suspicion.

*Saïd says you're being exploited. You don't have the means to per-
form this surveillance completely, and lots of things get past you.*
Saïd says what he wants. More than anything, he's sad, right?
You went and interviewed him recently. You surely noticed he's
very bitter. If I were in his place I would be, too. Of the three
of us left, he's the one who lost the most.

He says he's free. He in fact sees himself as having succeeded.
I don't believe that's true. And since he's clear-headed, I'm
pretty sure he doesn't think that. Saïd's problem is that he
wanted to be on the outside as long as there was an inside. He
liked being the rebel of the group, but he needed the group.
And now that the 83ers have ended, obviously he misses it.
He's the most nostalgic of the three of us. When we celebrated
the anniversary of Jean-Baptiste's death, he was bawling, he
was inconsolable, and I believe it was sincere. But it's not just
Jean-Baptiste's absence that made him cry. It's especially the
fact that everything happened so fast, that it's all over, and
that there were so many missed opportunities. For him even
more than for the others. 'Cause we at least took the time to

be together. We tried. I clearly remember one night at HQ, it must have been just before the first summer, we were having drinks at the conference table, and he preferred to sit outside on the patio by himself with his laptop and headphones, and I watched him through the patio door, and I thought one day he'd regret it, these times he could have spent with us. They were not these extraordinary moments, but that's exactly the thing. You had to live them to not regret them. And now Saïd's caught in this trap. He talks about what we could have done. About Jean-Baptiste who was so pure. About the others, too. He imagines a life he didn't really live and which certainly never existed.

Do you yourself have any regrets?
Not really, no. You know, me, I've got my own story. Gregory used to say that the fairy tales had to stop. But he was strong. He'd found the courage to live without telling himself stories. No illusions. Not me. I need my meds, and I need my own little story. And what do I tell myself? That everything that happened to me, there was nothing to be done about it. That I was unbalanced. That I'd started to spin out of control well before 1/19. That when everything happened to me, I played my role as a good little soldier, I repressed stuff, and that I became a ticking time bomb. That it was bound to blow up in my face one day or another. And if I ended up in the psych ward, it's because I'd been lying to myself for too long. It's because I'd become completely fake. A fictional character. And I've also got explanations to help me understand how I got out of there. I told you—I actually didn't have the strength to die. My body refused. I had to live. I make myself believe I still had something to live for. And *this* is it, right here, right now. Inspecting the other superheroes' work. Feeling others look at

me who think they're mistaken. That, in fact, Virginie, she's better than they thought. That at least people can trust me. Feel that I'm getting by pretty well. Better than a lot of people my age. Better than Saïd, better than Thérèse. Not too bad a story, is it? The fall, the redemption. It's undeniably too simple. It's undeniably not 100% accurate, but what difference does it make? As long as it helps me live, to accept this life, it's not very important knowing if stories are real or fake.

XXXVI

FILMING IS ENTERING its eighth week. A humid, spring green forest is the location for the day's shooting. Seated behind the monitor, Thérèse Lambert watches take after take of Jean-Baptiste Fontane conversing softly with a French intelligence officer. Wearing tracksuits, their new running shoes squishing in the mud (Jean-Baptiste was running in the woods when the other man, who was also jogging, appeared), they both seem like two dads out for a run who got lost in an adventure movie. The smiles of several technicians punctuate the end of each take, but Jérémie Renier, the actor playing Jean-Baptiste, twists his mouth and still appears dissatisfied. Even though the team is already an hour behind the shooting schedule, they grant him another take. "He's looking for something more fragile. He's right," Thérèse notes. After closely following the writing of the script, she is now observing the shooting as a consultant.

The resemblance between Jean-Baptiste and Jérémie Renier is far from obvious, but Thérèse swats away any concern before it can be stated. "Might as well stop making the film right now if we're going to play at guardians of the temple." She's well aware that *People Like Us* (*Des gens comme nous* in French) has stirred controversy from the word go and that some moviegoers will not miss the opportunity to point out inaccuracies.

She herself reacted negatively when it was announced that a film about her friend was in pre-production. She didn't accept to join in the adventure until after a meeting was requested by the two producers who launched the project, the American John Wasserman and the Frenchman Antoine Baeyens, who came off as "two schoolboys asking someone to correct their homework." "She committed when she felt the movie was going to happen no matter what," confirmed Wasserman in an email. The best way to defend Jean-Baptiste's memory, the 83er surmised, was to oversee the project from the inside.

After getting her hackles up over every invention in the script, Thérèse ended up accepting that some shortcuts and approximations were necessary, given budget limitations and the film's length. It's not a big deal. The most important in her eyes is to remain uncompromising on "the truth behind the facts."

Aren't there more troubling constraints associated with a production of this magnitude: casting famous actors, stunning special effects, action scenes magnified to epic proportions as superhero movies require? For every answer Thérèse smiles like she used to smile at me in Santiago when I knew her as a student, looking like she's distancing herself far from you. You can't tell if the look shows her discomfort when faced with the aptness of the question you're posing, or the complete opposite—her amusement when faced with another example of your stupidity. (Later she will burst out laughing when I ask her about her working relationship with Émilie Dejean, the actress who portrays her. "Before filming started I didn't even know what she looked like." When I express surprise that she didn't want to meet her, Thérèse once again graces me with a dreamy smile.)

Even though she won't comment on this subject either, *People Like Us* probably came at the right moment in her life. People close to her say that Thérèse had been brooding over the same memories since Jean-Baptiste's death as well as the failure of her third novel. She was obsessed with the day of July 5, 1992. That afternoon during the traffic jam something or someone had contaminated her. She didn't feel she had the strength to wage a battle, basically on her own, to compel the authorities to tell the truth. But she knew that someday someone—on a computer, at the bottom of a secret safe—would probably find a brief document in which the alarmed writer would report on a scientific experiment that went wrong or perhaps, why not, on an event that would implicate visitors from another planet.

This incident, whatever it was, had sealed her fate and cursed her for life. Nothing she had to endure now would have happened without it. People made her recognize that she had experienced some extraordinary moments since 1/19, that she still had wonderful things to live for, but every morning she herself only saw a bony figure in her full-length mirror, a handicapped woman with a waxy face and graying hair whom people occasionally loved, no question, but that love was unfairly inflated by her celebrity and the pity she inspired.

She inspected every detail of that July day in search of a clue. The headaches that this research inflicted left her, at times for up to three days, nauseated and too weak to leave her bed. As the date was distant, it had been difficult to glean certain details. For days on end her power would run up against the same end of a sentence that trailed off into silence, the same minute that faded away, the same unfinished head movement that prevented her from seeing what she had seen before—seeing again something that, perhaps, would explain everything. Through sheer obstinacy, however, the puzzle pieces had been reassembled. She was in possession of the complete scene of the traffic jam.

But then a feeling of failure crushed her: in everything she saw and heard meanings that escaped her, probably forever. The gas station attendant announced that there was a huge traffic jam just before Valence. If they were going to be stuck, might as well wait it out at the next rest stop, where there'd be shade. Had he said that in an attempt to save the young girl from the destiny that awaited her? Was it plausible that the man's nylon jacket was immaculate and that one could still make out an ironed crease on the sleeves? And what object was he hiding in the bulge she noticed on his chest?

And the man who had stared at her just after 2:00 P.M., a beanpole with bushy eyebrows and a cardboardy complexion cramped in the front seat of a black Renault 5, what was he doing here alone amongst this pile up of cars packed with luggage and children?

To get away from these ruminations, she let some people talk her into giving speeches at self-help and motivational conferences. Now that idleness was a risk, being a speaker didn't displease her. She liked that someone waited for her when she got off the train, that they wanted to know if she liked her hotel room, and that people applauded at the end of her talk. I'm not sure she really believed what she said (her talks had titles like "Reconciling Yourself with Yourself" or "All Imperfect: Reflections on What We're Really Missing"), but that's not why people attended. Audience questions were almost always about the 83ers and Jean-Baptiste in particular. He was the one they liked the best. He was the one who hadn't betrayed anything. He was the one who died too soon. Thérèse had truly known him. Her memory was famous for being infallible. Plus she was good at speaking about him.

In the middle of her presentations she had noticed signs of impatience in the audience, which, after three or four conferences, stopped offending her. They had listened to her. Some had even compelled themselves to take notes politely. And when the moment came to evoke Jean-Baptiste, everyone smiled at her. She would say she was happy he'd become so popular after his death, even though these memories and words of admiration would have personally bothered him immensely. Then she'd make them smile or cry with her well-phrased anecdotes in which he appeared as the clumsy lover, a superhero Woody Allen, a wise man without doctrine, and, at the moment of his death, a simple and courageous soldier.

People would have accused her of being jealous or simply bitter if she had told them that Jean-Baptiste rarely admitted his mistakes, that he worried about everything, and that he could be condescending at times, even a bit snobbish. People wouldn't have understood if she had revealed, other than to sully his reputation, how cowardly he was, not like she was in the theater of operations, but in life. People seemed too complicated to him, and their problems were too heart-rending. He was cowardly when he asked to leave on a mission, only so that he could cancel a trip to see his father whose early symptoms of Parkinson's disease depressed him. He was cowardly every time someone solicited his serious opinion and he avoided answering with a witty comment. He was cowardly when Thérèse decided to write and say she loved him and he didn't respond, acting as if he never got the message—persuading himself, most likely, that she herself must have immediately regretted sending it and that the best thing was to never mention it again.

The day after my visit to the set, a car drives us to Normandy where Thérèse is meeting a group of middle school students.

It's a long-standing commitment, which she assures me she will enjoy. Sitting next to her in the back seat, I make use of the time in the car to ask her what she plans to do after the film wraps. She says she could do with some sun and relaxation. Some people told her about Baja, California, where everything seems simpler. She could easily see herself spending six months there, at the beach, reading a bit, doing nothing. But what's most likely, she adds, is there will be other requests related to Jean-Baptiste, and she'll answer them.

Of the middle schoolers listening to her, assembled in the school library, at least half are too young to remember 1/19. Thérèse talks about her physical therapy, the difficulty of accepting the limitations her handicap imposes, but also about the wisdom one acquires by accepting them (that's her niche).

Twenty minutes later, after the applause, the microphone is passed among the students. The first question is about Jean-Baptiste. A timid boy would like to know what happened to the model of Bayeux. This unexpected question causes his classmates to snigger. A teacher, in an effort to squelch it, suggests moving on to another question, but Thérèse wants to answer. She whispers that to her knowledge the model was never finished. Then, briefly, while a studious young woman formulates the next question, she looks at me, and I lower my eyes.

She will not tell them what she confided to me the previous evening: just a few weeks ago the model filled two-thirds of a spare room in her home. After Jean-Baptiste's death, which she refused to accept, she had made it her duty to continue working in his stead. He definitely would have liked that. But she found no pleasure in constructing and decorating the small cardboard buildings. As for the figurines to populate the neighborhood, which she tracked down on Amazon, they seemed fake to her once she arranged them in the streets, like the model was slowly filling not with pedestrians, cyclists, children, police officers and street sweepers, lovers, old ladies on the steps of an apartment building, delivery people and artisans, or readers on park benches, but with actors participating in a simulation, frozen with their overly colorful costumes in poses that even they did not believe. She particularly regretted having placed, on the sidewalk of an avenue, a group of six travelers straight out of the 1950s—their small suitcases in hand, the men, one of which was wearing an apple green double-breasted jacket, in hats, the women with permed hair and royal blue suits (maybe stewardesses)—that looked like an acting troupe miming *The American Way of Life.* Thérèse decided to remove them after a few days. They left six dark ocelli on the base, like miniature pools of blood, she thought. At that moment she noticed that smears of rust-colored stains had appeared on one side of the model. The glue that Jean-Baptiste had used turned brown as it dried. One morning she called the number for bulky item pick-ups. They hauled the model away the following day.

Another student asks Thérèse if her hypermnesia still works. Like the other 83ers' powers, she responds, it has eventually lessened. Some memories, especially the oldest ones, have become inaccessible to her once again. Others are becoming less precise. Does that make her sad? Thérèse shrugs. "A bit, inevitably," she whispers.

Her memory is now like a museum overtaken by disorder and neglect, in which, night after night, looters would not be satisfied with randomly purloining a few new objects, but would also toss away the keys to several doors and do their utmost to mix collections together, vandalize displays, and scratch out all useful information from exhibit labels. She remembers less and less about July 5, 1992. A conversation with her father, which even two months ago she could recite word for word, has faded away completely. The face of the gas station attendant who advised them not to get back on the highway has disappeared, replaced by a vaporous oval. Every time she revisits the scene, something is missing or in a different place, has lost its shape or its outline. Soon there will be nothing left, nothing from that July day, or from 1992, or from the preceding or following years except a few silent images, a few names, a few ideas about sentences that were more or less uttered, the vague remnants of a past just as uncertain and incomplete as our own. Soon 1/19 itself will be affected by this flickering that precedes forgetting. When she no longer remembers anything, when the museum is nothing but a ruin, it will seem that this entire story was no more hers than anyone else's. And Thérèse confessed to me that, more and more frequently, when faced with this ongoing disaster, she feels a sense of appeasement.

CPSIA information can be obtained
at www.ICGtesting.com
Printed in the USA
JSHW030502160223
37826JS00002B/2